TURNCOAT

by

David R Ewens

Grosvenor House
Publishing Limited

This book is published by
Grosvenor House Publishing Ltd
Link House
140 The Broadway, Tolworth, Surrey, KT6 7HT.
www.grosvenorhousepublishing.co.uk

A CIP record for this book
is available from the British Library

ISBN 978-1-83975-698-6

About the Author

David R Ewens worked for many years in the English further and adult education sector. He lives and writes in Kent.

Also by David R Ewens in the 'Frank Sterling' series

The Flanders Case
Under the Radar
Rotten
Fifth Column
The Golden Spurs

Acknowledgements and disclaimers

This is a work of fiction. Names, characters, businesses, places, events, locales and incidents are either the products of the author's imagination or used in a fictitious manner. Any resemblance to actual persons, living or dead, or actual events, is purely coincidental.

Indeed, readers in the Canterbury area thinking that they recognise certain characters, or fictitious places among the real ones, will be sadly deluded. Characters in particular are fusions, adaptations and figments of a febrile mind. No one real appears in this book.

Thank you to my partner Ruth Gould for her unstinting support, advice, critiquing and willingness to listen to me drone on about the difficulties and challenges of writing, even during lockdowns.

Thank you to my reviewers for their hard, uncomplaining work and welcome comments and insights: Maggie Fieldhouse, Terry Monaghan, Carl Parsons, Peter Taylor-Gooby and Eleanor Waller. Special additional thanks to Terry Monaghan for tutorials, including practicals, about beer. I forgive my reviewers the contradictory opinions and feedback that made revisions so challenging. Thank you to my editor Joanna

Booth for her diligence and wisdom in addition to the editing. Thank you to Indie-Go for the cover design and artwork, and to my publishers Grosvenor House. As always, any faults with the novel are the responsibility of all these contributors, whereas of course any available accolades should accrue to me.

Chapter 1

The two young men were in high spirits as they walked along the river path. Things had turned around after the precarious first few months of their time in England. The jobs, at the Sainsbury's up ahead, and the flat, along the Sturry Road, were making all the difference. They jostled and sparred, feinted, weaved and ducked in a kind of play-fight as the supermarket and the early shift loomed closer. They'd hit it off straight away the first week in the warehouse, and English was their common language.

'A quick smoke before we start?' said the taller of the men. 'Usual place?'

They moved off the path to a subsidiary one and down the gradient to the river. It was a comfortable regular habit to stand on the jetty and enjoy the quiet early summer morning with a cigarette before the early shift.

'Bloody hell,' said the short, wiry man, as they rounded the corner. (An English girl he was sweet on in the shop had been teaching him expletives.) The body splayed out on the bench was clearly dead, his head a gory and battered mess of hair, bone and oozing brain matter.

The short man had spent a couple of years on a poultry and pig farm in his native Transylvania. He had generally lived his life at the sharp end, and was used to blood and guts, farming accidents and unsightly death. His friend was a towny from Krakow from a family of teachers, whose only contact with blood had been childhood scrapes and grazes, and whose only experience of death his grandmother in her casket, respectfully prepared by the undertakers.

While the towny lurched aside to vomit, his friend approached the body to check for life even though he already knew there would be none. Check briskly completed, and English-style emergency training fresh in his mind, he dialled 999 to summon the emergency services. Then he went over to his pale and shaken friend, lighting up cigarettes for both of them. They were new to Sainsbury's, and wanted to make a good impression for punctuality and hard work, but after the shock of the discovery began to wear off, they agreed that finding a dead body was a good enough excuse to be late clocking in.

*

Banal. That's what Detective Chief Inspector Andy Nolan, dragged from his bed, was thinking at 7 am on Thursday, June 10. He looked down on the figure sprawled across the bench next to the turbid Stour, at this time of year more a large stream than the river that usually flowed in spidery veins through Canterbury. He wasn't sure why banality was on his mind. The bashed-in skull was gruesome enough, but he'd seen so much violent death, whether premeditated or not, perhaps it wasn't so surprising. The causeway onto the new estate that had sprung up behind the river had been closed because of emergency repairs. He'd had to park in Sainsbury's car park on the other side of the river, cross one of the pedestrian bridges, duck through the gloomy graffiti-spattered underpass of the inner ring road, and make his way down. That had surely contributed to his feeling. The tag *Dimzy*, letters large and lavishly delineated, had been prominent in blue and white on the water-dappled concrete. A Canterbury anarcho-syndicalist had also made his, or her, presence felt with the distinctive 'A' sign, its lines spilling out of the black circle encompassing it.

The victim, his face handsome and unlined, was a few metres along the river path beyond the underpass. Scene-of-crime technicians in white coveralls were already setting up a crime-scene tent, rustling around taking photos and putting little flags in the area on and around the jetty. Little swirls of mist still hovered around the water as the sun began to make its presence felt. Nolan ran his hand over the lower half of his face, and his bristles rasped. The body was in plain sight on the jetty itself, but gawpers, even on the second floor of nearby houses and flats, would have had difficulty in seeing through the foliage. The other side of the river was a deserted industrial area, locked up and waiting to be re-let. His number two, Detective Sergeant Murphy, appeared noiselessly next to him.

'So, Bill, what have we got?' said Nolan

Murphy flicked open his notebook. 'A couple of blokes – Eastern Europeans – walking along from the flats down near Barton Mill, found him on the way to their early shift at Sainsbury's and phoned it in just before 6 a.m. They didn't see him from the path because you have to cut through the bushes and down to get to the bench and the jetty. They stopped for a quick smoke, and knew about the place because they occasionally do a bit of fishing here. We've got all their details, and I had one of the uniforms walk them to work, just to be sure there were no wrinkles in their story. Our victim is well and truly dead, and was, they say, when they found him. No ID yet. No CCTV around here. No mobile or wallet, which suggests that maybe robbery was the motive. We don't know how long he's been there. Pathologist is on her way. It looks as though he was struck from behind. Possibly he fell and banged his head, but surely unlikely.' Murphy raised his eyes and looked directly into Nolan's. 'I'd say, guv, a pony to a pound, that we're at the beginning of a murder enquiry.'

Nolan puffed out his cheeks and let the air drift out from his mouth. He thought about The Murder Book – official title *Murder Investigation Manual, 2nd Edition (2019)* – on a shelf in his office; how he'd hardly see his children for a week or two; the blepharitis that afflicted his eyes when sleep was scarce; the rubbishy, bolted-down food that would upset his stomach, especially the prawn mayonnaise sandwiches that were often all the canteen had left; and the execrable late-night coffee from the machine in the hallway when all the civilians had gone home. None came close to dampening the frisson that coursed right through his body from his knees upward. The adrenaline flow had started, and would doubtless recur at key junctures in the investigation. He looked down at the body, focusing on the victim rather than the crime and the opportunities it would give him. The man couldn't have been much more than thirty. A pitifully short life, and an abrupt, painful ending. In death, he needed justice.

'Agreed, Bill. Let's get cracking. You know the drill, but let me rattle some things off, and then you can come in with anything I might have missed out.'

Murphy nodded, his pale blue Irish eyes sparkling. Energy and excitement radiated from him.

'Phone back to the nick and have them set up the Major Incident Room. It's going to be all hands on deck here in Canterbury, but we'll need the OK from County about staffing. That will be ongoing. Who is this bloke?' muttered Nolan, virtually to himself, diverted from his organisational tasks.

He didn't flinch as he looked down again, this time more closely, at the battered head. The face was intact, though muck from somewhere had made dirty striations on one cheek. There was no discernible expression on the features – not surprise, not fear, not horror – perhaps because he had been attacked from behind. Nolan didn't need to moderate his first impression. In death, as he would have been in life, the man was good-looking, his features regular, his nose straight and his teeth even and well kept. Despite the damage, and milkiness of the lifeless eyes, Nolan could see that they were deep blue. The mouth could have been a flautist's if it had been a touch less wide, and the skin was smooth and unblemished, with the vestiges of a tan. At just under six feet, the body Nolan surveyed was slim and well-proportioned, with evidence of gym membership or at least regular exercise.

Like Nolan, Murphy lived in Canterbury as well as being based in the police station there. 'His face is familiar. I don't know him, and I'm sure I wouldn't have moved in the same circles, but he's local. I'm thinking that I may have seen a photo or something in the local paper.'

'You're right,' said Nolan. 'I can't put my finger on it either, but when we've got a decent photo to circulate, I reckon we'll identify him pretty quickly. Meanwhile, as well as the investigations room, get uniforms to canvass the estate back there – people with their kids in the playground, and especially those in the houses and flats that overlook the river. What about CCTV? The river path has lamp-posts, but just looking around I can't see anything.'

'I'll check, but we'll need to establish time of death first, guv, won't we?'

'Of course, but we can do the preliminary stuff.'

There was a commotion behind them, beyond the crime scene tape. A woman's cut-glass voice drifted over. 'Yes, I am the new pathologist,' it said to a uniformed police sergeant called Peterson whose grey sideburns suggested grizzled experience.

Nolan and Murphy watched as he examined her credentials at the end of a lanyard. 'Thank you, Ma'am,' said the sergeant, making a note on his clipboard. 'We have to check. You've no idea what shenanigans we get in situations like these.'

The small woman nodded, ducked under the tape that the sergeant held up, and approached Nolan, Murphy, and the corpse.

'Anthea Tilson, pathologist.' The woman offered her hand.

'Dr Tilson, Detective Chief Inspector Andrew Nolan, Detective Sergeant William Murphy,' said Nolan in matching clipped tones as he and the woman shook. 'You've made a timely arrival. We're hoping that–'

'—I'll tell you precisely when this happened, whether it was an accident or not, and if not, who did it and what with, after my preliminary examination.'

Nolan looked hard. Was that a tiny smile playing around those red lips? He chanced it. 'Well, not "who", because DS Murphy and I would be out of a job, but the rest of it would be handy.'

Murphy frowned, not the quickest on the uptake. Tilson laughed. Different pathologists, in Nolan's experience, had different ways of dealing with the gruesome aspects of their job. This approach was... unusual.

'Time of death, no matter how approximate at this stage, will be helpful. We're more able to be patient about the other stuff.'

Tilson nodded and approached the body, squeezing and slapping on plastic gloves as she put her battered leather bag down. She began a low-level humming as she went about her work on the body, rummaging in her bag for instruments and paraphernalia, and then returning to the task.

Nolan and Murphy exchanged glances. Nolan thought of snooker players going for a 147 maximum – 'in the zone'.

Tilson looked up after a few minutes. 'Given all the circumstances – time of year, temperature overnight, location of the body on the bench, usual development pattern of rigor mortis, blah, blah, blah, and taking into account that this is strictly a preliminary examination, I'd say that time of death' – she paused to look at her watch – 'was around 10 o'clock last night, give or take an hour each way.'

'Dark, then,' said Murphy, 'within most of that time frame.'

'Yes, Sergeant, dark.'

'Thank you, Dr Tilson,' said Nolan. 'We'll let you get on and get on ourselves. We'll meet again in due course.' He cocked his head slightly and he and Murphy withdrew to beyond the crime-scene tape.

Chapter 2

Frank Sterling, private investigator, tapped his forefinger restlessly on the bar top and looked into the dregs of his pint of Red Top. 'Private investigator' these days meant him doing virtually anything for a decent daily rate, including stuff of dubious legality. The combination of residual froth and brown liquid of the beer was redolent of the muddy water at Sandley quay after heavy rain and a high tide. The smooth bitter used to be his favourite tipple, and still was, he supposed, except that things were going so badly that nothing gave him much pleasure these days. He shifted on the barstool, left hand clasped around the glass, shoulders hunched.

He hadn't sat in the snug doing the *Times* crossword with Angela Wilson, his friend the Sandley librarian, for a week. Her romance with the Kent Police's Assistant Chief Constable, Panjit Mamujee, was going from strength to strength, and occasionally Sterling could hear wedding bells, whereas his rekindled affair with his childhood sweetheart, Stacey Stuppington, had flared and petered out like all the rest of them. He reflected morosely on her final, bitter words as she had closed her front door that last time, tears tracking down her sad face: 'You've pushed me away, Frank. Again.'

He looked at his watch, shaking his head, shaking off the memory. 10.15 pm. Time to go home, given the current situation. He tipped the glass back and edged off the stool. There was a moment of unsteadiness as his feet found the floor. Three pints. He couldn't even hold his drink anymore. Mike Strange, landlord of the Cinq Ports Arms, former member of the security services, strode over from the other end of the bar.

'Finished for the night, Frank?'

'Yep. Busy day tomorrow,' lied Sterling.

Mike looked down at the beer mat. 'I don't like to mention it, Frank, but …'

'I know, I know.' Sterling bristled. 'The slate. It's getting high, I expect. You'll get your money. I just need a bit of a turn-around.'

Mike Strange's wife, Becky (also once in the security services), magically appeared. 'Mike's not talking about the slate, Frank.' She paused. 'You don't look too good. We're getting concerned.'

Sterling dragged his hand over the dark stubble shading his jaw. Shaving had become irregular, every three days. He'd stopped using the bathroom scales as he'd noticed the beer gut around his midriff. He was in a semi-permanent state of sluggishness. 'Well, thank you so much for your concern. I immensely appreciate it. If only I'd had the same level when you spooks were mixing me up in that terrorist escapade down to Dungeness with old Mohamed Husain. Tell me where along the coast I didn't almost cop it.'

'Ex-spooks, Frank. You know we've long left that behind. And we were sorry. We said so. We sorted it out. We made it up to you. I thought we had anyway,' said Becky hotly.

Mike put his hand on her forearm.

'Yeah, well. Maybe you didn't. I'm off home. Now that it's not about the money.' Sterling launched his parting shot and made for the door, walking with measured deliberation and an extra-straight back. Just as he crossed the threshold into the balmy June night, his progress was undermined by an unsteady lurch and trip. *Fuck 'em*, he thought, as he stumbled on. *Fuck everyone. And everything*. It was Frank Sterling against the world, and he'd make sure he'd win. The defiance stayed with him as he ducked into Holy Ghost Alley, hemmed in on both sides by high cottage walls, and then the passageway with its mysterious timbered roof and damp, mossy scent. He broke out into St Peter's Street and then criss-crossed the town centre until he was almost home.

The key was in the door when he heard a familiar tinkling laugh from across the Cattle Market car park. Angela. And if Angela was there and in a happy mood, Mamujee couldn't be far away. Sterling scowled at his front door.

'Frank,' Angela trilled.

The key would not go into the lock, but he didn't turn around and kept up his fumbling. Maybe there was still a chance to get indoors and pretend he hadn't heard.

'Frank,' called Angela again. More loudly.

Sterling turned slowly around. In the rapidly fading light, Angela's skin made it hard to make out her silhouette. Mamujee, the son of Ugandan Asian refugees, was hardly more visible. As they came closer, however, their features magically materialised.

'I thought you'd gone deaf. We've just been over to the Marlowe in Canterbury,' said Angela. '*A Midsummer*

Night's Dream. Perfect for this lovely evening. Have you got time for a nightcap?'

'I'm knackered,' fibbed Sterling. *Drunk*, *more like. Pissed off.*

'Come on, Frank. Join us. Help us round things off.'

Mamujee nodded encouragingly, a tentative smile playing across his delicate, intelligent features. With the smile, his neat, dark moustache straightened upwards. Sterling, an ex-police officer who could never get on in a hierarchy, and who had left the service before a final incident got him kicked out, always regarded Mamujee with suspicion. He was a suit after all, and suits could never be trusted, especially not by the rank and file. The feeling was reciprocated, but Angela held things together, lover of one, best friend to the other.

'No, Angie, I'm knackered.' Finally, the key went into the lock and Sterling got the door open.

Angela's face fell. Her hands twisted around the straps of her handbag. This wasn't the laconic, slyly humorous, maverick character who did the crossword with her, enticed her into research for his cases and sometimes even got her directly involved. Her mouth hardened imperceptibly. 'Suit yourself. Come on, Panjit. He' (she deepened her voice, Garboesque) 'vants to be... alone...'

Sterling slipped inside and leant with his back against the front door, breathing out heavily. He knew lots of people. Many considered him a friend. But Mike and Becky Strange and Angela Wilson were closer than anyone. And within a mere ten minutes, he'd just got on the wrong side of all three. Unnecessarily. But the way he felt now, he struggled to care.

He'd have a nightcap, but by himself. He felt a wave of irrational resentment against Angela, not for the hint of mockery outside, but for the schooling in self-awareness. He'd never been reflective. As a plod, he'd always plunged into any situation. As a PI, that had worked too. Act first, think later. But Angela, in the snug of the Cinq Ports Arms, had added extra dimensions to his thinking. Psychologically, he now knew, his reaction to difficulty was defiance in a hostile world, and allegedly not all that helpful. That knowledge took the edge off wallowing in the pleasure of it. Maybe a slug of whisky would help emotion overwhelm logic.

He moved from the kitchen to the living room sofa. The little terraced house facing the Cattle Market car park was perfect for him, but he'd missed a couple of months of mortgage payments and the bills were piling up. He'd have to start thinking about a regular job. The political situation meant there would always be jobs down at Dover docks in Customs – doing the mirrors under the lorries, rummaging around car boots for contraband, shift work, paperwork, regularity, boredom – everything he hated. He drained his drink and trudged upstairs. Tomorrow might be better, but he wasn't holding his breath.

*

Sterling's office was just above Sandley Library, up some rickety uncarpeted stairs, which he negotiated as quietly as possible so as not to provoke the god of hangovers and to avoid Angela. It wasn't just because of his boorish behaviour the night before that he was keeping out of her way. He was behind in the rent to the County Council, and since she managed that aspect of the Council's business, often with a laxity that she didn't apply to any other item on her job description, he needed to keep her onside while, for the moment, at arm's length.

Although the stairs and the small landing were shabby, the door to Sterling's office was not. He marvelled at its oaken solidity almost every time he put the key in the lock. The previous incarnation had been a thin, fragile affair, hopelessly smashed and mangled in the dangerous climax of a previous case.

Now that last night's drink had stopped talking, he was realising that his situation was precarious. At some point, he'd have to go down and make his peace with Angela. And with Mike and Becky. He might even have to *apologise. Not yet, though*, whispered his angry pride. He hated the thought of being beholden to other people. And anyway, those three got as much from him as the other way around. They were thrill junkies, and his activities occasionally provided those thrills.

He sat back in the office chair behind the window and looked around his office. It could do with refreshing. The prints on the walls, of Kentish oast houses and rivers, were looking old-fashioned. The sofa was getting threadbare. Only the computer on his desk could still qualify as a late model. He turned it on, aware of the patina of dust on the keyboard that probably also rested on every other surface of the room. He needed to get a grip. On the other hand, what was the point? He didn't have a single ongoing case, and the last one had been so sordid – a messy affair and divorce, and appalling behaviour all around – that the miasma still seemed to cling to him.

He logged in to his website – Sterling Private Investigations – and opened the contact page, more in hope than expectation. On the last three visits, all he'd had were messages from every corner of the world about ways to increase site traffic – in exchange for cash, of course, usually requested in dollars. Those and offers of exotic sex from even more obscure corners. There was a new smattering of both types, but among the dross, it looked as if there might be a genuine message from a real human being. He clicked and waited a beat.

'Dear Mr Sterling,

I note from your website the scope of work that you are prepared to undertake. I have a rather delicate problem I'd like you to investigate for me.

Can you contact me for a time for you to visit me? We can discuss the issue thoroughly, go through the options, establish what your fees are, and hopefully move things on from there.

With thanks in advance.

Yours sincerely,

June Selsdon'

Underneath the main body of the message was a mobile number and an address in Whitstable.

Sterling leaned back and rocked in his chair. The fees. He was glad they'd been mentioned. Often, they were the last element of a case that clients wanted to talk about. The e-mail's tone was formal, but that was to be expected. The style was easy and professional, and belonged to someone with a decent education. It had been sent at 11.12 the night before. Beyond that, there was nothing but speculation. He looked at his watch – 10 am – and reached for the mobile in his jacket pocket, keying in the numbers at the bottom of the message.

'June Selsdon,' said a calm, mature, well-modulated voice.

'Ms Selsdon,' said Sterling, 'I'm Frank Sterling, the private investigator you e-mailed last night.' As he spoke, he noticed in himself the strangest feeling. Butterflies lurched in his stomach, but it was impossible to identify the emotion. He tried to set it aside and concentrate on listening.

'Ah, Mr Sterling, thank you for getting back to me. I e-mailed because it was urgent from my point of view, but too late to telephone last night. The matter is too sensitive to speak about over the phone. I have some time today if you are free yourself. I've established that you are based in Sandley. That isn't too far away from me. Would you like to come over, say, this afternoon? About two o'clock? That is, of course, if you haven't got any pressing cases diverting you.'

'Nothing I can't pigeonhole for a little while.' (Translation: *nothing at all*). 'I'm intrigued. I'll see you at 2 pm.'

'Well, *I* think it's interesting. Worrying too. Goodbye for now, Mr Sterling.'

The butterflies were subsiding, but Sterling was no closer to identifying their source. Was it because he might be at the start of another case? That didn't normally happen. It had little to do with his policeman's gut, either. Stirrings in that occurred in the middle of a case, when his brain started making connections in synaptic crackles and everything fell into place. It was natural to think of popping downstairs for Angela's advice, but of course, he'd fallen out with her and she might mention the outstanding rent on his office.

It reinforced his need to do some bridge-building, but for the moment, his pride still held sway.

Sterling didn't have a car. The way the business was going it was an extra expense he couldn't afford, and if he needed one there was a car hire place in the town or he had a pal he could borrow from. But he knew local bus and train timetables off by heart. It was two bus rides to Whitstable via Canterbury and there was a bus to Canterbury in ten minutes from the Guildhall. He closed the office, glided down the stairs, avoiding all the well-known creaks, and slipped into Market Street. Avoiding Angela seemed sneaky, but for the moment he had other preoccupations.

He nodded to two of the regulars he knew as he reached the top floor of the bus. The young girl, elaborately tattooed above her chest, rambling roses and fiery dragons, and along her arms down to the very tips of her fingers, was off for her shift at Primark in Canterbury. The silver-haired German ex-market gardener sat towards the front, ramrod-straight as usual, looking out towards the art deco cinema.

At Canterbury, there was a 'Triangle' bus to Whitstable already in the bay, so Sterling just transferred. Now a substantial proportion of the passengers were students off up to the university, and English became the minority language. He sat at the top again, amid the cacophony of Spanish and Japanese and Italian, and phones pinging and trilling, glad for once to be out of Sandley and starting a little adventure, a paying adventure, he fervently hoped.

After the university, the bus became local, English, and rural again, until it started the long steep dip into

Whitstable, with sea stretching out in the bright summer sunshine.

Sterling fancied he could see the Maunsell Forts of Red Sands off the coast, anti-aircraft gunnery stations in the Second World War. They had been one of his father's madcap enthusiasms, in which he, Frank, was always involved to one extent or another. Sterling couldn't remember his father's plans in relation to this project, or the others. There had been so many, interest in them flaring up and fizzling out like Bonfire Night Catherine wheels. All he knew was that he'd been a sullen, reluctant teenage presence on the boat to see the forts close up, and had got soaked, refusing to wear the uncool waterproof poncho supplied by the charter boat.

The bus crawled through Whitstable's narrow, congested, cacophonous high street, with its boutiques, artisanal bakeries, pubs, gin palaces and coffee shops jostling for business, before emerging into the comparatively open road next to the harbour towards Tankerton and Herne Bay. He pressed the bell as soon as he saw the squat, grey, corrugated block housing Whitstable Indoor Bowls. This is where Google Maps told him to get off.

Just after two o'clock, Sterling approached the front door of June Selsdon's terraced house in Clare Road, noting the dead shrubs in the twin pots on the pathway, the chipped Victorian chequered tiles in front of the steps, and the faded green paint on the door itself. Cobwebs hung from the alcove, but the marble bell button, with PRESS prominently in the centre and clearly an original feature, still worked as the sound trilled through the house. He was just about to press again when a shadow loomed in front of the pane of stained glass depicting a nautical scene of wherries and barges, odds on connected with Whitstable. Instinctively, he ran fingers through his hair and took a deep breath. He needed a case, and not just any old two days in-and-out affair – a protracted, generously-paying case.

Chapter 3

Events were moving quickly. DCI Nolan had phoned Assistant Chief Constable Mamujee as he'd left the crime scene, requesting a murder team and matching resources. Fair play to Mamujee, he was responsive and crisp in his decision-making. After a few sharp and focused questions, he'd authorised exactly what Nolan required. As the body was on Nolan's patch, there was no quibble about confirming him as the senior investigating officer, and Bill Murphy was an obvious choice as his deputy.

There was a rap on the door, and the Detective Sergeant's lived-in face appeared between door and jamb. 'I've assembled the preliminary team, sir. We're ready for the first briefing.'

'Golden hour,' murmured Nolan.

'Exactly, guv. If we're lucky we'll at least get a promising lead or two, perhaps more, while everything is fresh, as it were. Although there's no CCTV at or close to the scene, it's coming from Sainsbury's and from the student village area at the other end of the path. The canvass of the Stonebridge Road estate and walkers along the river path has started. All within the assumed time of murder parameters.'

'Good. Thanks, Bill. Come in and close the door for a second, will you?'

The sergeant gave a quick backwards glance and slipped inside. He cocked his head.

'We were relatively lucky with the crime scene, if that's the right word,' said Nolan. 'Peterson is an experienced copper, and he was the first responder. There was no more disturbance than there might have been given the circumstances. The civilians who found the body got out of there sharpish, and let us know sharpish too. Peterson has established to our satisfaction, for the moment, that they didn't lift cash, cards, or anything else. Checking them out further will have to be one of our 'to dos' though...'

Murphy waited.

'I don't think we're going to get much from the scene, Bill. From an assailant's point of view, it's perfect – dry so as not to leave boot prints, remote enough for the time of day, time enough to remove the victim's identification. There's no sign of a murder weapon yet. What is the pathologist going to tell us about the killing that we don't already basically know? What I'm getting around to is... Well, my gut is telling me that there isn't really going to be a golden hour, an early breakthrough, however energetic we are at this stage. This is no straightforward murder.'

'Not just your gut, guv. I reckon it's going to be difficult and complicated too.'

'Exactly. So, are you up for it? Ready to clear your diary, say goodbye to your sleep and loved ones for a couple of weeks, or even longer? Ready, in other words, for the long haul?'

'Count on it, sir. In fact, I called the missus as soon as word came in.'

'Good. Let's get cracking then.'

The buzz ceased as Nolan and Murphy entered the newly designated Major Incident Room – the clicking of keys on computers, the low drone of conversation, the susurrations of the office. Movement ceased too, as heads looked up or around or across. Nolan noted with approval the large whiteboard with a photo of the deceased man prominent in the middle. He was used to addressing large teams and meetings of every description, but this was the easiest sort. No one was bored; no one was wishing to be somewhere else; no one was resentful of a disrupted schedule. This was murder. It trumped everything. The DCI silently scanned the sea of expectant faces, at this stage around twenty of them, making brief eye contact with each. Everyone had to be on board from the very beginning.

'First off, this is a murder case. That's why we're here. You know me, DCI Nolan. I know you and you all know each other, so that's the introductions. Others may join the team later who we don't know. They'll be introduced at each appropriate briefing. Thank you to DS Murphy for getting us to this point, assembling you, the team, and getting the squad room switched into service as a dedicated investigations room. Thanks to him for the initial investigatory work – arranging to get CCTV and organising the canvassing. I'm the senior investigating officer. He's the Deputy SIO. Over there,' Nolan nodded towards a small, alert-looking young woman to his front and left, 'is Sophie Stephens. She's our office manager.'

'I'm going to give you a full update about what we have so far. Questions and queries at the end unless it's really important.' He smiled a small smile – 'I don't want to lose my flow' – and was rewarded with a titter that rippled through the room. 'Early this morning, we were notified of a body on the river path about halfway between Sainsbury's supermarket and the student village down parallel to the Sturry Road. The victim's skull was bashed in from behind around 10 pm last night' – Nolan indicated towards the photo on the whiteboard – 'it was a man, mid-thirties maybe, in good shape. No identification on the body, so we're yet to know who he is. Seems familiar somehow though. Apart from the victim, there was no danger at the scene, which, thanks to Sergeant Peterson, is relatively well preserved. The pathologist has examined the body and it's probably been removed now. Forensics are at the scene. We'll hear more from them about evidence, whatever they come up with, in due course. We haven't any suspects yet. The men who discovered the body seem kosher, but that's being followed up.' Nolan paused for a moment. 'To be honest, I'm not sure we're going to get much from the scene.

'What kind of murder is this? Bill and I haven't had time to speculate. It could be a domestic – a sexual rival, or even a current or former partner. There's no wallet or money, so possibly robbery. Gang stuff, unlikely. Confrontation, revenge or jealousy, racial violence, a serial killer, maybe also unlikely… Even some motive we don't yet know about. You know the variations as well as me. At this stage and until we know more, we rule nothing definitively in and nothing out. The fact that I'm talking about a crime committed in an open space using a blunt instrument, and the attack coming from behind, will give us some focus going forward.'

'We need to look at what we can and can't do at this stage – our fast-track actions if you like. Sadly for us, we can't instigate victim enquiries since we haven't identified him. We can identify and have identified intelligence opportunities – the CCTV and the canvassing, from which we might come up with witnesses and even suspects. There will be more from the crime scene and post-mortem. We might come up with motives from all this. As for the other stuff – the phone records, the computer information, diaries, lifestyle information – all that – well, we'll have to wait till we have more to go on.'

'Bill and I will be setting our strategy and on that basis allocating tasks for you in the next hour or so. In the meantime, I shouldn't need to remind you – but I will – that there is to be no leaking to the press or gossip outside this team. Anything or anyone that compromises our investigation will be squashed pronto. Press contact will be via our press officer and me. I've got every confidence in every one of you. As a team, we'll crack this.'

The questions came in a torrent, and from all parts of the room. Had there been any recent missing person reports in the Canterbury area that fitted the victim's profile? What about the murder weapon? Had it been found? The river path was a known area for drinking and loitering among the marginal groups of the city – was alcohol involved? Was there any sense of control or (the opposite) frenzy in the murder? Did Sergeant Peterson do sketches of the scene in his notebook? How many routes in and out from the scene are there? Are there records of all initial responses and communications, and recordings of telephone messages? Is the team going to use HOLMES or a paper system for material coming into the Incident Room? What about a press release?

Nolan handled the barrage briskly. To queries about the murder and the circumstances, his most frequent response was 'We don't know yet – that will emerge as we move further into the investigation.' To queries about the steps taken or to be taken post-murder, he said that they had been lucky that the first responder was competent and that they'd be getting good data. To other technical questions, he simply told his team members that they'd know the answers soon enough.

'I'm going to wrap things up now. Your questions have been useful and will help us get a good focus. Right, time to sort out who is going to do what in this crucial early part of the investigation.'

He gave his instructions succinctly. Specific allocations – about the CCTV and canvassing, incident analysis, press liaison, missing persons research and a panoply of other tasks – ensured that heads stayed bent to notepads as people scribbled. Nolan could feel the enthusiasm and adrenaline coursing through the room.

'Remember,' he said, 'this is not just a body but a person – a young man – who has lost his life too early. Whatever the circumstances, and whatever emerges, we shouldn't lose sight of that fact.'

He intended the last sentence to be a final flourish and a rallying call, but out of the corner of his eye, he saw Sophie Stephens pause suddenly and look up. 'What, Sophie?'

'I've just realised... I know who our victim is.'

Now everyone looked up. There seemed to be a collective holding of breath.

Nolan waited.

'Yes, I'm sure of it.' She pointed at the photo on the whiteboard. 'That is Jack Hankinson. Conservative Party Councillor Jack Hankinson, late of Canterbury City Council.'

Chapter 4

'Mr Sterling. Exactly on time,' said the woman he assumed was June Selsdon, as the door opened. 'Please, come in. We'll go through to the kitchen area at the back if that's OK. We'll be perfectly comfortable at the table, and you'll have a surface for your notebook. It will ease my arthritis a little as well.'

Sterling followed the woman down the hallway, past an open plan living room-cum-library and into a light conservatory-style extension. He noted June Selsdon's trim figure and air of energy and purpose, but also the stick that assisted a rickety walk. He calculated that she was in her late fifties or early sixties. She motioned him to sit at the table, and took up station opposite, steepling her hands and giving Sterling a curious, intense appraisal. A small shadow of pain creased the otherwise smooth forehead with parallel lines between and just above the eyebrows. Sterling struggled to decide if it was sudden joint pain or whether he was being measured up and had already been found wanting.

He noted, in a more fleeting and, he hoped, less obtrusive assessment of his own, that Ms Selsdon must have been a beauty, no doubt about that, and still was, despite the encroachments of age. Her perfectly round face suited the large glasses with their multi-coloured, speckled frames. The lenses magnified her eyes slightly and did not disguise their distinctive shade of grey-blue. A light, summery navy-blue cardigan covered a white blouse of which only a rounded, delicately embroidered, predominantly white collar was visible. A mid-length tartan skirt, light-blue tights and Ugg boots completed the ensemble. Her hair was thick, wavy and grey, of almost identical texture as Sterling's own. *My hair will be as grey as that when I get to my late 50s like her*, he thought ruefully, *if I've still got it.* He was thirty-eight now, and there were plenty of grey strands already.

'A drink, Mr Sterling, before we start? Tea, coffee?'

'Tea, please. Builder's. No sugar.'

Ms Selsdon smiled as she went over to the kettle. 'Was it an easy drive over from Sandley?' she said as she looked over her shoulder.

'I expect the bus drivers are used to it.'

Ms Selsdon smiled again, but this time turned away. 'A sense of humour, clearly, like ...' She tailed off with a mutter, preoccupied. 'I had some biscuits somewhere.' There was rattling.

Soon they were ready to start. Sterling sipped his tea. 'Perfect,' he said. 'So, Ms Selsdon, you have a job for me.'

'Yes, but not a very straightforward one. I expect you're used to straightforward instructions.'

Sterling reflected. 'Yes, that's true. Wives, or husbands, want to know about the fidelity or otherwise of their spouses. Insurance companies want to know if particular claims are scams or not - recently there was a local spate of prangs resulting in whiplash injuries that the circumstances did not support, shall we say? I had a missing person case not that long ago, involving a wheelchair user, actually. There was a bank robbery, a kidnapping… But although the original briefs are usually simple, they rarely stay like that in my experience. Anyway, you've not got me over here to talk about this stuff.'

'On the contrary, Mr Sterling, it's very interesting, but it's also confirming my instincts. You are the right person for the job I have in mind. Those experiences, and your reputation, will be very helpful.'

'My reputation? That sounds ominous.'

'Well, you've been in the newspapers a few times, and Google throws up a lot about you. Surely, you'd think less of me if I hadn't done some research of my own.'

Sterling nodded and spread his hands on the table, notebook and pen at the ready.

'Getting straight to it, there's been a murder in Canterbury, and I want you to look into it. It happened, or was discovered, yesterday morning. If you check Kent Online, you'll find a few details, but so far, the police aren't saying much. I heard about it because I'm in the Labour Party and so is a member of the civilian staff at Canterbury Police Station, who thought I should be put in the picture as soon as possible.'

Sterling said nothing. He'd learnt to wait and listen. Even the most scatter-brained and incoherent clients came out with their stories eventually and with barely any prompting, at least not until towards the end, but he could tell that this one was going to be precise, articulate and comprehensive.

Even so, a murder. Surely that could be left to the police. What could he, Sterling, bring to the party?

June Selsdon took a sip of her tea. 'I expect you're thinking that it's a police matter, and wondering what you can contribute.'

Sterling didn't start exactly, but he felt the same butterflies as he'd had in earlier exchanges. This person seemed uncannily familiar with his thought processes.

'I'll come back to that in a few minutes. I need to give you some background first. I said I'm in the Labour Party. I've been in it for years, decades even, and I've held various senior positions on the constituency party executive, including as election agent for council and parliamentary elections. I've stepped back over the last couple of years because of this wretched arthritis' – she brandished her stick by the table – 'but since the Labour Party has been my passion and my life, I can't stand by and see it, and its reputation, besmirched, or any possibility of that.'

'The person who was murdered was called Jack Hankinson. He had a management job at one of the universities in Canterbury – the one in the centre, Corpus Christi. Although he was a Conservative councillor, he had once been a member of the Labour Party, and was very ambitious. He had various officer positions culminating in the role of vice-chair of the whole party. He put himself forward as a parliamentary candidate at the election before last. There were three of them at the hustings here in Whitstable – at our Labour Club. He wasn't successful in getting selected – but then, at the election itself, the person we did select didn't get very far.'

She frowned. 'That was disappointing of course, but we're used to it in this part of the world. That's not what's troubling me. I was never very sure about Jack. There was something about him, for all his debonair charm. As Ann Widdecombe said in a different context, "something of the night". He was entitled, certainly not short of cash, which he used liberally to buy drinks after meetings for our less well-off and sometimes more suggestible members, and not very reliable. I wasn't alone in my thinking. A few party colleagues and officers thought the same. I suppose we'd have had to put up with it, but after his failure at the hustings, it happened.'

Sterling leaned forward. This was getting interesting. June Selsdon's voice dropped. Into it crept an edge of contempt. 'He deserted us – the Labour Party. Even worse... he joined the Conservatives.'

Sterling forced himself not to lean back, and made a supreme effort to tighten the muscles in his face as they strained to make a smirk.

'You thought I might say that he'd embezzled all the party's funds, or was convicted for child abuse or something equally vile, didn't you?'

Again that prescience and insight into his way of thinking.

'Well, how bad *is* that in the scheme of things, Ms Selsdon?' Sterling maintained his deadpan expression steadfastly.

'I know, I know, we politico-obsessives can go over the top, but that's an absolutely unacceptable ideological journey, and, just to show I'm not entirely one-eyed about it, so is the reverse – Tory to Labour, as I'm sure any Tory would agree. Other switches, Labour to Green or to the LibDems, and vice versa, can raise suspicions but are generally acceptable. But this, after having been a candidate for election as our MP... even a private detective can surely see how unacceptable that is.'

Sterling reflected. He didn't follow politics closely. His father's socialist commitment had put paid to that, and his own innate tendency to think and do the opposite from what his father hoped and planned on his behalf. Sterling had been on plenty of rallies as a kid – 'Stop this or that', 'Solidarity with this or that group', meetings across the channel with the Confédération Générale du Travail. His father, a customs officer and trade unionist originally from the Cambridgeshire Fens, had expected his son to be a true socialist believer as strongly as he'd expected him to go and get a university education. Sterling had rebelled, sure enough, but it hadn't made him a Tory. More, it made him sceptical, and his father had been horrified when he'd forsworn university for the police.

On the other hand, loyalty – that was important. If you nailed your colours to a mast, you had to keep them there. Flip-flopping was unacceptable, he certainly got that. That's why, when he did read the papers, he couldn't understand why journalists were so tolerant of MPs resigning the whip and joining another party, sometimes not once but twice, often under pretexts that didn't ring true.

'Actually, Ms Selsdon, thinking about it, you've got a point. It's not just politics. Friendships, family.'

'Exactly, Mr Sterling. I'm glad you see it that way. That mindset, along with your skills and experience, is what I'm looking for. There's more, though, about Hankinson. He wasn't just a turncoat. He was corrupt. I can't give you proof, but he had his finger in a lot of illegal pies – land development, drugs, maybe prostitution. There has even been talk swirling around of rape.'

'OK, interesting. All noted. But I'm still not sure what you want me to do. The police have all the resources to investigate the murder and find out who did it. What can I add?' He needed this gig, but what exactly did it consist of?

'Essentially, your assignment is this. I want you to do everything you can, as events unfold, to protect the reputation of the party. Now that we are strong, now that we have a Labour MP, now that our membership is active and buoyant, the project can't be ruined by scandal. You're a successful detective. If you were to find out who murdered Jack Hankinson, that would be a bonus. But more important is our reputation. Whatever he's done, it can't come back to us.'

'I go wherever the truth leads, Ms Selsdon. Often it goes to uncomfortable places. Supposing Hankinson, having been proved to be dodgy, is genuinely connected with the activities of the Party?'

'If I thought the latter – that the Labour Party was involved – I'd deal with that when you gave me your final report, but I'm hopeful that it isn't. Otherwise I might not have got in touch in the first place. Employing you will provide insurance, as it were.'

'Right, I think I get it.' What roles was he going to play in this case? He articulated them to his would-be principal. 'If I take this on, I reckon I'll be a sewage worker, a fixer and a tidier-up, as well as an investigator.'

'Exactly, Mr Sterling. In short' – June Selsdon's eyes twinkled – 'a politician.'

'Hmm,' he said. 'It's new. To be honest, I've still got my doubts.'

'Do you want the job, Mr Sterling?'

Now there was a hint of steel, and Sterling realised another thing about the woman opposite him at the table: she was formidable. The review of his prospects and finances took a nano-second. 'Yes,' he said. He explained his terms and conditions, fees, including expenses, and, vitally, the pre-investigation advance. 'I suggest you engage me initially for eight days, with updates every two days and a final report. I'll do a timesheet so you can see when I've been working in those days, and I'll charge on an hourly basis.'

Eight days was pushing it. So was the advance. He knew he was chancing his arm, but June Selsdon agreed without a quibble. 'My enemies would call me a champagne socialist, or at least a prosecco one. I do have to check my privilege, and I have been lucky. When my husband died, he left me very comfortably off...'

Sterling nodded. It seemed strange for her to share that. He certainly didn't care where his money came from.

'Anyway... I have a couple of conditions for you in your guise as investigator-politician. They are necessary, in my opinion, for you to be able to take on this assignment. There's an important meeting coming up. Everyone who is anyone within the local Party will be attending. You need to join to be able to go. It will be invaluable. Connected to that, I've arranged an assistant for you, to help you get clued up into the ways of the Party and to give you an entrée as it were.'

'Whoa,' said Sterling. 'I do things my own way. I'm not sure...'

June Selsdon shrugged.

'OK.' Joining something, even the something being the Labour Party, wasn't a big deal. He could just as quickly leave when the case was over. It wouldn't be hard to sideline the *assistant*. Expenses could be inflated as extra compensation. Sterling laughed. 'You know, you're managing to get me to do something that my leftie father never could.'

'Needs must, Mr Sterling.' Another curious, unreadable expression flitted across the woman's face. 'Your assistant only lives a couple of streets away, and she's back from uni for the summer. I'll summon her over if that's alright with you. It will get you off to a flying start.'

A start, anyway, thought Sterling.

Chapter 5

'She's right,' said Murphy.

There were nods from one or two around the Major Incident Room.

'Well done, Sophie,' said Nolan. 'This gives us momentum. Let's do one or two quick things to confirm it, find out where he lives and his family circumstances, and then you and I, Bill, will have to go and see next of kin.

'In the meantime, how did he get to the river path in the first place? There's the Sainsbury's car park and then that other one a bit further along towards the city centre – St Radigund's. He might have left a car in one of those places and walked along the path. If he did, his waiting time will have expired, and the car might have received a warning or a ticket, even a clamp. What do we know about Jack Hankinson? Let's start a victim profile.

'What was his lifestyle like? If we find a car, that might start us off. What routines was he into? What were his hobbies? Any criminality in the profile? Not likely I suppose, for a councillor, but don't overlook anything. What about associates – friends, family, business links? He seemed quite smart when I saw the body, despite a night in the open. But what was he like in terms of personality? In a word, who is this man? I'll leave all that with you, Sophie, and you can delegate as you see fit. Make it an important focus. When you've got his home address, let me know. Remember, everyone, what the old hands say in a murder enquiry – "find out how a person lived and you will find out how they died" – no assumptions, but the victim probably knew the offender.'

'On it, guv,' replied the office manager as Nolan retreated to his office. With the door and blinds closed, he flopped into his chair. He rubbed his eyes. It felt as if he had grit in them, or a stray eyelash, but experience told him that blepharitis was recurring, just as it always did at times of high tension and excitement.

He had forced himself back to his office. Let Bill Murphy and Sophie Stephens get on with the tasks in hand, and delegate according to the skillset and competence of the team. He hoped for a quick conclusion – a suspect or suspects charged after a couple of days, or, short of that, some key breakthroughs that would maintain momentum and satisfy his superiors. They always got twitchy if things stalled, and that led to anxiety in the team, and then mistakes.

There was a knock on the door and Murphy's head appeared again. 'We've got some family details and an address, guv. Hankinson was married and lives up on South Canterbury Road. We have the wife's mobile number.'

'Let's head up there, Bill. Don't phone ahead. If she's not in, we'll review then. Next-of-kin notification has to be face to face.'

Ten minutes later, the unmarked police car pulled up outside a gracious, detached Edwardian house two hundred metres down from the hospital. Parking was difficult in a controlled zone, but Murphy, seeing a car already in the short driveway, squeezed in over the entrance and propped the police business authorisation card on the back window ledge. The two detectives looked at the immaculately kept house and compact front garden shaded by two small sycamores.

'How old was Hankinson?' said Nolan.

'Thirty-six,' said Murphy. 'Worked as an events and centre manager at Corpus Christi down in St Andrews Place.'

'He's done well then, or his wife gets a good salary. That Mercedes' – Nolan gave a nod to the nearly new two-litre they had just blocked in – 'is worth a bob or two, and I doubt this house would go for much less than £800,000 in the current market. Come on. We'd better get it over with.'

At the front door, the bell chimes echoed tinnily – it might have been a snatch of a rock anthem – *Everybody Hurts* or some such – out towards the back of the house. There was a rattle of keys and bolts and then the door was flung open.

'You're parked right in front of my car, for goodness' sake. How am I supposed to get out?' The voice, shrill and harsh, belonged to a tall, slender young woman with long, fine, straight chestnut hair and matching brown eyes, set in a delicate, pale, perfectly proportioned face. At that moment, the face was puckered by a fierce frown, and the frown was matched by a surly, ugly manner.

Nolan and Murphy showed their warrant cards. 'I'm sorry, ma'am, police – DCI Nolan and DS Murphy,' said Nolan in a calm tone. 'We parked there because our business is with you, and realistically, and unfortunately, no one will be going anywhere until we've finished. May we come in?'

Having examined the cards closely, taking each in her hand, the woman cocked her head and motioned the policemen forward. 'Brush your feet and turn left into the front room,' she said.

As they entered a bright space, all pale-yellow walls and grey, angular sofa and armchairs, with matching lamps and square lampshades, Nolan couldn't decide if the young woman's manner was going to make their job harder or easier. He and Murphy perched uncomfortably together on the sofa, while Jack Hankinson's wife swept beyond them to one of the armchairs, plumped herself down and crossed her legs.

'So, what's this about?' she said.

Nolan opened his notebook and looked down, more to compose himself for a couple of seconds, and not because he wasn't prepared. He wasn't taking any chances. Stories about misidentification of victims and related cock-ups were real and not infrequent. 'Just to confirm, you are Charlotte Hankinson, wife of Jack Hankinson?'

The woman nodded, almost imperceptibly. She uncrossed her legs and leaned forward, but tucked her arms under her chest. The atmosphere in the room changed subtly – a kind of power shift. Nolan got out the enlarged photo he'd picked up on the way out of the Major Incident Room, the best version of the dead victim – the one in which he looked slightly surprised while lightly asleep, the one that didn't include the matted, gory hair, and blood pool at the back. 'And is this your husband?' He pushed the large colour photo across the rectangular glass and metal coffee table.

Charlotte Hankinson looked down and nodded again. Her hand went sharply up to her mouth. Murphy, straight-backed and blank-faced, sat still.

Nolan swallowed and looked up. 'I'm very sorry to have to tell you that your husband...' - (has passed away? is no longer with us? Has fallen victim to...?) – Nolan plumped for plain speaking – 'is dead. He was found this morning with a head injury on the river path between Sainsbury's and Barton Student Village. At this stage, we're treating his death as suspicious.'

A tiny tear welled up in the corner of Charlotte Hankinson's right eye, and Nolan sensed a tremor run through her. Then she shook her head as if waving off a buzzing wasp.

'Unbelievable,' she muttered. She stared off into space.

Now Nolan watched her lower jaw working, and, curiously, a narrowing of those large brown eyes. She was struggling hard for control, certainly, but there was something else going on that Nolan couldn't identify.

He knew how shock and grief affected people in different ways. It was an opportune and crucial time, from an investigative point of view, to ask questions, but not all relatives of victims were in a fit state to cooperate.

The young woman was a thought reader. 'I'll answer any questions you've got now. We'll get it over with.'

'If you're sure...' said Nolan. He turned to Murphy. They'd planned it in the car. A different speaker could relax a witness... or suspect.

'Your husband was found early this morning, but the incident happened sometime last night. When did you last see him?' asked Murphy.

'We were together in the early evening, about six o'clock. He was having a bite to eat and I was having a cup of tea as I was having dinner later with my mother. He said he had a council meeting. One of his committees. They generally start at 7.30 in the Guildhall.'

'And you didn't notice that he hadn't come home?'

The young woman had resumed staring emptily at something neither of the detectives could see. Now she turned smouldering eyes back to Murphy.

'We don't live in each other's pockets, sergeant. We never have. We both work our socks off – work, worked…' – she stumbled – '… he usually went for a few drinks after a meeting. He could get home late. The house is big enough for us to… if he were really late he'd not want to disturb me, and then I'm out of the door really early. It's half-past ten now. I popped back here to get something. We'd have been exchanging texts around about now, and then I'd have noticed.'

'Where is work, Mrs Hankinson, for our records?'

'I run Jensen and Partners, the estate agents, on Castle Street. I own it too.'

'Right, and Mr Hankinson…?

'…Is the Events and Centre Manager down at Corpus Christi.'

'Right. I think we knew that. And does – did – your husband have a car?'

'Yes, the same year and model as mine, but silver instead of red.'

'It's not in the driveway.'

'He'd have driven down to the meeting. If he'd been drinking afterwards, he'd have got a taxi back and retrieved it in the morning. You might find it in the council car park at the Guildhall.'

'OK, we'll check. Do you need to contact any relatives?' Murphy paused. 'Children...?'

'No kids, thank goodness, given... this.'

'Why do you think your husband was on the river path last night?'

'I've no idea.'

Murphy was scribbling furiously.

'I have to ask this, Mrs Hankinson,' said Nolan, taking over. 'It looks as though your husband was murdered. Some personal effects – the things people normally carry – seemed to be missing – wallet, keys, cards, cash and so on, so robbery is a possible motive. But did he have any enemies? Is there anyone you can think of who might have done this?'

'No.' Charlotte Hankinson's eyes met Nolan's and held them.

Nolan waited for her to add something. Usually, loved ones and families elevated victims to sainthood. 'Maybe Jack was involved in unpopular decisions because of his role as a councillor,' prompted Nolan. 'Or he had a run-in with someone in his job at the university. He didn't say anything or mention anyone?'

'No.'

'OK. We might have to come back to that theme at some future point. We haven't got his mobile yet, but we'll need access to his phone records, his computer and his car, when we find it. Will that be alright?'

'Fine. Do what you need to do. He only had a laptop. I'll give that to you before you go, and he made sure I knew where all his passwords are.'

'Good. That will be very helpful.' Nolan ploughed on. 'And for the case file – a technicality really – where were you yesterday evening from around 8 pm onwards?'

'I know how it works, Detective Chief Inspector. I've watched the cop shows. As I said before, I was with my mother. We had dinner at The Old Coach and Horses in Harbledown. She's a co-director of my company. We had some accounts to go through. We left at about 11 pm, near closing time anyway.'

'Thank you. I had to ask. Now, we'll also need to allocate you a family liaison officer...'

'No,' said Charlotte Hankinson, shaking her head vigorously.

'I'm sorry...?'

'No, I'm not having one of those. I don't need one. I'll sort myself out with family and friends.'

'Mrs Hankinson – Charlotte – may I call you Charlotte? – you want us to find, arrest and charge who did this, don't you? We'll be ploughing a huge amount of resources into the investigation. In cases like this, we regard the victim's spouse and family as our partners in that work, and at the same time you have the right to know, via the family liaison officer, how we are getting on. It's crucial to the process that we have good, direct communication. There will be things you know but which haven't occurred to you as important, and other material, that an FLO will help you bring out. An FLO is a vital part of our team.'

'I don't care. You can communicate directly with me, or go through my solicitor.'

'Can I ask you to think about it and we'll get back to you?'

'You can, but I'm not going to change my mind.'

*

When the policemen had gone, the detective sergeant carrying Jack Hankinson's laptop, the detective chief inspector taking care to establish that someone would be returning to look for evidence in the house, Charlotte Hankinson sank onto the sofa. She leaned forward and hugged her knees, sobbing quietly. Then she moved to a room in the back of the house and opened the top right-hand side drawer of a desk. The prepaid mobile was under an envelope of paper clips and elastic bands. Sweeping her hair back behind her ear, she keyed in a number and waited.

A subtle transformation had stolen over her features. Her eyes narrowed. The knuckles on the hand that clenched the phone were white.

Chapter 6

His father had been a gardener, green-fingered in every aspect, manifested in the immaculately tended small front gardens at all the terraced houses he and his son had inhabited in Sterling's restless, nomadic upbringing down the east Kent coast. There had been hanging baskets over the doorways and vegetable gardens out back – or allotments if there had been no 'out back'. At every move, digging and prep, and Sterling's first planting always nasturtiums for colour, and spuds for sustenance. His father had always complained about the sticky Kentish clay soil compared to the rich, loamy earth of his native Fenland.

June Selsdon had none of those preoccupations. Her back yard had the same scrubby, failed air as the front, with wisps of grass struggling between the paving stones and weather-battered garden table and chairs, cracked and faded with neglect. Sterling was no expert horticulturalist but he'd inherited enough gardening genes to cleave to neatness, tidiness and colour. The little enclosed wilderness unsettled him. Gardens told stories about their owners.

There was a faint exchange of voices at the front door, and Sterling turned away from the yard to meet his *assistant*. He half-rose from his chair as she came into the dining area.

June Selsdon creaked along behind the girl and did the introductions. 'Frank Sterling – Maria Goodburn. Maria – Frank.'

'How do you do?' said PI and assistant, faces blank and posture stiff as they gazed at each other and shook hands. The girl's fingers were slender and cool.

Sterling reflected rapidly, and, he admitted to himself, sheepishly. If he had to have an assistant, it could have been much worse. He calculated that she was about twenty, an estimate bolstered by knowing that she was on holiday from university, and probably an undergraduate. Thick, straight, dark blonde, shoulder-length hair framed an alert face with a smooth and flawless complexion. Her eyes were pale blue, and her hairline was low. Her mouth, given that she was grave and unsmiling, was a straight red, pursed slash. Dimples were suggested in her cheeks, to be confirmed if she were to smile. The smallness of her features suggested a squashed-up look as if there wasn't quite enough room for all the face's essentials.

Sterling had noted the faded blue denim mini-skirt and coordinated darker blue T-shirt as she'd walked the length of the house. Her arms and legs were slim and pale brown from summery Whitstable sunshine. There was a neatness and compactness about her.

There was silence for a few moments.

'I've briefed Maria about what I want you to do, Mr Sterling. She's as keen as I am that the Party's reputation is protected. She's intrigued, as I am, about who might have finished Jack Hankinson off. I suppose it's inevitable that Party reputation and who did the murder are intertwined. Maria will be absolutely invaluable in helping with that part of your investigation involving the Party.'

The girl smiled, a tiny movement that revealed her dimples but didn't get as far as her eyes.

'I'm rather tired now,' said June Selsdon. 'The ache of the arthritis and all this excitement have taken their toll.'

'Understood,' said Sterling. He did understand too, about the tiredness, but not so much what seemed to be a welling of tears in the woman's grey-blue eyes, which he pretended not to notice. 'Maria and I can stroll into the town and sort out a plan of action. I'll do the application form for the Labour Party and report back in a couple of days.'

*

'Where are you parked?' said Maria Goodburn as she and Sterling strolled down Clare Road towards the main road at the bottom.

'I'm not. I came over from Sandley by bus.'

'Really? I thought private investigators had cars – ready for all that late-night surveillance.'

Sterling detected something – a challenge, stroppiness. 'Not all PIs are the same. Not all of them go about things in the same way.' He kept his tone even. The assignment was difficult. He'd make more progress if he kept her on side. She could be side-lined later if she was of no further use. 'I thought we'd have a coffee before I catch the bus home.'

They fell silent as they walked into the centre back along the bus route. Sterling thought again of Stacey. During a turbulent period of her early childhood, she'd been fostered in an informal arrangement, under Social Services' radar, to an Evangelical family in the town. She'd never had a good word for Whitstable since.

In the café, a national chain squeezed between a children's clothes boutique and a deli, he was careful to get a receipt for the cappuccino and latte as they made their way to the back where it was quiet. He noted, and ignored, the girl's slightly raised eyebrows as he put the receipt in his wallet. 'I've not had a case quite like this, or assistance like this.'

'Foisted on you, you mean. Me. The "assistance".'

Sterling opened his palms. 'I was a copper back in the day. In the end, I left before I was kicked out. Not a very good team worker, it was said. Among other things. Right. Let's get cracking. Unlike the police, who'll have a whole big team crawling over every aspect of this, we only have one way to go. We focus on the victim, and whatever comes out of that. The big advantage for us is that unlike the police, we don't have to do things by the book. If we know that it's going to have a bad effect on the Labour Party, we cross that bridge when we come to it. So, Jack Hankinson. What can you tell me about him?'

A baby keened somewhere at the front of the café, causing the girl to pause. The pause extended while a plump woman in a sleeveless flowery blouse, her arms lardy-white, went into the toilet.

'He was a bastard, that's the main thing.' Maria's eyes glittered, and a glower shrank her forehead even more. 'A turncoat. A switcher.'

'Ms Selsdon told me. Labour to Tory. Not done, apparently.' But to Sterling, the girl's vehemence about someone switching political allegiance seemed excessive.

Her loathing had a personal edge. He waited for her to continue.

'Absolutely right. While he was in the Party, he talked the talk. How he'd joined at fifteen, and campaigned tirelessly up in Gravesend before he came down here – canvassing and leafletting and street-stalling all day every day if you believed him. Then, when he put himself up for selection to be our next general election candidate and didn't get the nomination, he was off. And of course the Tories – via one of the wards in the villages – were the best option for him to become a city councillor. No doubt the Judas saw that as a better route to becoming an MP. I just don't get it. How come one week you're all for social equality, decent housing, fair education, fair wages, re-nationalisation of key industries, the abolition of private schools, and the next, you're a bloody Tory?'

'Bewildering,' said Sterling.

The girl's eyes narrowed.

He kept his face deadpan. 'Anyway, have you got a tablet in that bag? You can help do that application for "the Party", as required by my principal.'

It was done in minutes, the girl's fingers quick and deft over the keyboard compared to Sterling's more plodding, forefinger only style. He made a mental note to print off the subscription details for his expenses file. June Selsdon could pay for that as well.

'Now that you're a member, where do you stand on things, coming from the patriarchy?' Maria Goodburn's smile was mischievous but curiously humourless. Yet again, the expression didn't seem to extend to her eyes.

Sterling was glad of all Angela Wilson's tutelage as they grappled daily with the *Times* crossword in the Cinq

Port Arms. He reckoned he'd be able to hold his own. 'I might come from the patriarchy, but I wouldn't say I was *of* it. I can't see that I've got any power at all, even if I'm a decently educated white bloke, getting on a bit.'

The girl nodded as if it was an interview and the answer was satisfactory. 'What about the fact that the richest 10% of households in the UK have 44% of the wealth, and the poorest 50% only 9% - even worse if you think globally. What about the fact 74% of our judges were educated in private schools, and that our government is dominated by the privately educated? What about ten years of austerity, and–'

'Whoa,' said Sterling. 'I don't need a lecture. What do you want me to say? I got all that, one way or the other, from my father most days of my upbringing. Not always directly but I certainly got it. But what can I do about it? Nothing. The rich have always been rich. The poor have always been poor. Fact of life. You do the best you can with the hand you're dealt. I haven't got time for this. I need to get on with the case. So, if you can get off your high horse...'

The girl shook her head, eyes rolling. Then she gathered herself, a kind of physical drawing in. 'There were rumours about Hankinson, well beyond the political stuff. I expect June told you. He always splashed the cash, but he probably wasn't that well paid at the uni. We could find out more at the All Members Meeting on Monday evening. That's in Canterbury. You won't have a membership card in time, but I can get you in. You won't be able to vote either, if there are any motions – not that you'd care, eh? We had someone come to talk to us from a Sex Workers Collective not that long ago, after Hankinson had left the Party. She seemed to know something. She's based in Canterbury. I could set up a meeting with her, perhaps tomorrow or on the weekend if she were around.'

'That would be handy. A decent starting point. Do you know anyone in the Party who might have Hankinson's personal details and family circumstances? His home address?'

'I might. I'll see what I can do.'

'Here's my card. You can phone, text or e-mail. I could be in Canterbury any time on Saturday or Sunday. I'd be happy for you to come with me if your contact would feel more comfortable.' Sterling should have stopped there but he couldn't help himself. 'Someone from the sisterhood to support another sister.'

If the girl recognised the provocation, she didn't react. 'I'll come if I'm around, but I can tell you, she can look after herself.'

'Good. Well, I'm off to catch my bus.'

The child started keening again as the PI and his new assistant left the café. Sterling looked sidelong at the girl. She seemed alert and clever, but if she had a sense of humour, he hadn't spotted it yet. He hoped her company, in the days ahead, wasn't going to become tedious.

He called her back as she turned away from the bus stop. 'I forgot to ask – what are you studying at university?'

'Politics.'

The double-decker swept majestically into the lay-by, and the doors folded open. A tiny woman in black with a chihuahua in her arms tottered off and a lad with large headphones stepped on before Sterling. On the platform, Sterling looked over his shoulder.

'Of course you are,' he said.

Chapter 7

'Just pull up here for a few moments,' said Nolan.

Murphy drew in on a double yellow line down the hill from the Hankinson house. They were behind a delivery van whose driver had leapt from the front seat and dashed to a house a few doors down with a parcel from the back, his eyes fixed on the recording device in his other hand.

Nolan turned to his colleague. 'What did you make of that, Bill?'

Murphy shifted sideways in his seat to face his boss. 'Not like any other next-of-kin I've done. That was a really strong character, guv. You could feel her willpower. Cold, too. Icy, even. But... curiously vulnerable.'

'Agreed. I couldn't work out how she actually felt about her husband or his murder. There were all kinds of mixed signals. And the fact that she didn't seem to have missed him overnight. All marriages are different but that didn't quite stack up. Why did she refuse an FLO? I got the impression that something else was going on. I'll have to think about a strategy for her. We'll check her alibi, but we won't treat her as a suspect for the moment. The team needs to know about that interview and the vibes.'

There was a knock on the window. Nolan was so engrossed he jumped. The electric window didn't work with the ignition off. Murphy turned the key and the window motor whirred.

'You can't park here,' said a whining voice coming from the small mouth of an elderly woman with a tight blue rinse perm. It looked as if she had emerged from the front gate of a neighbouring house, and it felt as if she had used the phrase before.

Nolan rubbed his eyes. He felt an itch in his back. The eczema was starting. He fumbled for his warrant card. 'Police business, madam.'

'The police have no more right to park on double yellow lines than any ordinary citizen.'

'Right. Noted. Sorry for the inconvenience, madam. Let's go, Bill.'

Murphy rolled his eyes as they pulled away. 'Life goes on, eh?'

'As banal as ever,' said Nolan.

*

At 6 o'clock, the first major crime-review meeting started. Nolan had spent the day refining the case strategy, while Murphy worked to ensure that the growing enquiry team was working efficiently and harmoniously.

'Right,' said Nolan, in front of the large whiteboard, 'listen up. We need to get to it so we keep up the momentum. I'll start, and then I'm going to go around the room asking for updates from each sub-team manager. Make sure not only that you're ready but that you finish off your report with one or two key points. So... Detective Sergeant Murphy and I went to inform the victim's wife about her husband's murder. One of you has been going through his laptop, which the wife was happy to hand over. The interview wasn't entirely straightforward, and not because Mrs Hankinson was overwhelmed with grief. We both felt that something wasn't quite right, and in a way that was confirmed when she completely rejected the appointment of a family liaison officer. We're not treating her as a suspect, but we're keeping our options open, shall we say. We checked where she was at and around the time of her husband's death, and that was OK – dinner with her mother at The Old Coach and Horses in Harbledown.

'That's it from me for the moment. Write down any questions you have, and we'll deal with them all at the end. As we've now got some new team members, make sure you introduce yourselves at the beginning of your input.'

Three-quarters of an hour later, Nolan was referring to his notes. 'Crime scene and forensics: unusually, the offender seems to have left virtually nothing in the way of traces and evidence. How do we explain that? CCTV and lighting: there's no CCTV covering the actual scene, and the scene is between two lamp-posts, one of whose lamps isn't working.

'The CCTV we do have shows Hankinson walking along the river path, and lots of other people, mostly in hoodies, during the time frame – probably students walking to and from the student village. So, any number of potential candidates to be tracked down.

'House to house: basically, no one seems to have seen or heard anything, but in addition' – Nolan turned a page for the next point – 'some of the students canvassed are scared. Not the normal *scared* but scared because of who the victim was. It seems that the grapevine didn't take long to identify him.'

At the press conference shortly after the meeting, and ten hours after the murder, Nolan had dealt with all the questions with all the usual jargon. Now he looked stonily on as a local hack, a small man with a narrow, pinched face who had the knack of making Nolan's job title sound like an insult, turned his final question into a statement.

'So to confirm, Detective Chief Inspector, you have no clues, no firm lines of enquiry, no suspects and only the name of the victim.'

Nolan shuffled and straightened his papers. 'Thank you everyone,' he said with a forced smile. 'We'll keep you informed about the next conference and briefing.' Unwelcome as it was, the hack's statement was a perfect summary.

*

Charlotte Hankinson had refused to attend the press conference. Now she was sitting on a small bench at the Simmons Memorial, an ugly, grey Victorian monument set high on a mound on the edge of Dane John Gardens. She'd done her make-up and was wearing an expensive flowery knee-length summer dress, showing off her slender arms and shoulders. She'd plaited her long, thick chestnut hair, which reached down to the small of her back. Just because she'd lost a husband, it didn't mean that standards were going to slip. While she waited, she treated herself to a rare cigarette and took in the glorious early evening view, where, to the northeast, the main tower of the cathedral dominated the cityscape. To the south east, and much closer, she could see the police station on the other side of the ring road, where she knew the press conference was going on. It looked shabby, small and mean compared to the magnificence elsewhere.

The mound was a favourite spot when her husband had been courting her, not long after he'd moved down from the north of the county. They'd laughed at the ridiculous, thin stone barrel poking up at the sky from its heavy plinth. At the house, she hadn't given much thought to why she'd chosen this spot for the meeting, given that she'd stopped loving, or even liking, her husband a while ago, but sitting here she knew. Now that Jack was gone, she had to overlay old memories with new ones. This would be where the new regime took over. Looking down at the police station and cocking a snook at the officers who'd visited her that morning was an extra, unanticipated benefit.

She started slightly as a man slipped onto the bench next to her. He was small – no more than five feet six – and wiry, dressed in dark blue jeans, maroon, short-sleeved polo shirt, and grey canvas shoes that had once been white. Despite his slightness, the jeans hung loose and baggy around waist and backside. The sun had caught his arms, face and neck, which were a pale, lobster pink. A pair of black, old-fashioned square spectacles dominated the top half of his face. Despite the steepness of the spiral path to the top of the mound, the man showed no signs of being out of breath. He was ex-army and kept himself fit. There was a faint smell of cologne about him – Chanel Bleu? Armani Code?

'Good spot this time of day,' he said. 'All the poxy foreign kids have long gone on their poxy coaches. I'm sorry about Mr H.'

It sounded genuine, but Charlotte Hankinson knew that Jimmy Jarvis was virtually a psychopath. He could only pretend. 'Thanks,' she said. He didn't need to know her true feelings – that she had no longer cared much for her husband and was more concerned with the ramifications of his murder on the business and herself. 'The thing is, I don't want whoever's done this to get away with it, and they will if we leave it to the police. So we need to do our own poking around via our own... networks.'

Jarvis was rubbing his hands together, and a tremor had started in his left leg.

'In addition,' she continued, 'we need to keep the police investigation off-balance, which means that people need to keep their mouths shut. And most important of all, Jack was robbed. The police haven't found his wallet, his phone or his keys. So they won't have found his flash drive either.'

'The memory stick,' said Jarvis. 'Christ...'

'Exactly. The police have got his laptop, and they won't find anything on that, but the stick...'

'Right,' said Jarvis. 'Identification of perp, diversion, persuasion, memory stick. I can do all that.'

'Urgently. Start tonight. We can meet discreetly sometimes I suppose, but otherwise no communication except by the burners. And Jimmy...'

He stopped.

'No guns.' She knew Jarvis's wild streak well.

''Course not,' said Jarvis. 'Mr H didn't believe in them, you know that. They attract far too much attention. And other... methods are more effective. He always said that.'

She watched him pad away back down the path. She knew she could rely on him – mostly, anyway. So he didn't give a damn about her husband, but, after his army years, he'd gone virtually from skid row and St Benedict's, the local homeless charity, to a comfortable flat in St Stephen's and all the perks under her and Jack's wing. And if the truth got out, he'd go down with her. But most of all, he loved the work, if you could call it that. So far, so good with the new arrangements. The trouble was that Charlotte Hankinson was already beginning to be troubled by doubts. Should she not be trying to extricate herself from her husband's sordid business rather than getting more deeply in?

*

It had only been a short wait at Canterbury Bus Station for the Sandley bus, and three-quarters of an hour after that, Sterling arrived at Sandley Guildhall. He slipped through the archway and then into his house. Thankfully, Angela, whose own terrace was just two doors down, was nowhere to be seen. He wondered if the Hankinson murder would be on the BBC South East News.

He caught the tail end of the national weather forecast as he sat down in front of the television with a cup of tea. Yes, there it was.

'The body of a man was found on a riverside path in Canterbury early this morning,' started the presenter. 'We go over to our reporter, Michael Smith, at this afternoon's press conference. Michael, what can you tell us?'

Not much, thought Sterling, but he perked up as footage appeared of the police press conference. This is where the meat would be, if any.

And there he was, Andy Nolan, his old mucker, sharer of late-night chips and squad cars in Folkestone all those years ago, conciliatory to Sterling's abrasive, whether in 'domestics' or seafront brawls. There he was, not entirely surprisingly, fronting the conference and therefore, by default, leading the investigation.

In those days, it had been PC Nolan and PC Sterling. Now it was DCI Nolan and PI Sterling. Sterling almost winced, but he knew that his friend was as good a politician as he was a police officer and investigator, whereas he rated himself as an investigator but had no time or talent for the politics. And his rash temperament, he reminded himself, meant that he'd jumped out of the Kent force just before he was pushed. He wondered if he envied Andy. Jane, his wife, was attractive and competent, and always kind to Sterling when their paths crossed, and the two kids, Poppy and John, were fond of him when he showed up. On the other hand, his own life was precarious, especially recently. He'd been divorced for years, and who knew where his ex-wife was. Stacey had gone, and so had all the others…

He snapped back to the conference. Andy Nolan was playing a blinder, saying a lot while saying nothing – nothing that he didn't want the press pack to hear anyway. Sterling deemed it a stroke of luck. Nolan was one of his best and oldest mates. He'd be sympathetic to his side-investigation, and that would help him get the outcome he needed.

After dinner, he made the short walk to his office for some background work on Jack Hankinson and to sort out a schedule. He still wasn't sure he had the subtlety to protect the Labour Party's reputation – if it turned out to need protecting – but he'd got his advance and the rest of the cash was all but guaranteed.

Chapter 8

They were just two workmen, gardeners perhaps for the city council on their way home after a solid week's work. They'd cycled in together in the morning, and now they were cycling home along the Sturry road to one of the villages – Sturry itself maybe, or beyond that Hoath, or Maypole, or Hersden. Their bikes were sturdy and nothing fancy – road bikes, not tourers or those fat-rimmed, knobbly-tyred mountain bike contraptions. They'd probably pop into the *Middle of the Road* pub on the way home for a loosener before dinner. As you'd expect, they had little backpacks strapped on for their lunch boxes, tobacco and roll-up papers. The wooden handle sticking out of the pack of the lead rider, bobbing in rhythm with his pedalling, would be part of a specialist tool needed for weekend garden work, borrowed with the permission of the supervisor, and recorded in the notebook.

That impression was Jimmy Jarvis's intention at least, if any observer, casual or otherwise, took any interest. But when they got to the Barton Student Village traffic lights, they turned left, going down towards the river path parallel to the main road. Jimmy and his companion locked their bikes at the little bike park, and made for one of the tenements. Against the bulk of his enormous associate, an occasional nightclub door supervisor called the Fridge, or more often simply Fridge, Jarvis looked even smaller. He pressed the door code, listened for the buzzer and slipped in. The Fridge clumped in behind, too big and clumsy for delicate footwork.

Jarvis pushed the bell button of a flat on the second floor – two short rings and a longer one that echoed down the hallway. He and Fridge stepped away from the peephole and waited either side of the door. The security chain rattled, two bolts were released, top and bottom, and the door opened a sliver.

Jarvis swung into view. 'Stevie, my old china, I've come for a visit. And so has the Fridge.'

Fridge stepped behind Jarvis and loomed over him, silent and dead-eyed.

Stevie blinked rapidly and swallowed. 'It's not really a good time, Jimmy.' He tried to smile and failed miserably. 'It's Friday night. You know, one of my really busy times, what with the weekend coming up.'

'Stevie, if you don't open this door, we'll kick it in.'

There were some shuffling and movements on the other side. Jarvis could wait. He knew what would be going on. Then, the security chain was released and the door opened, and there was Stevie, sheepishly at the side, tentatively ushering the visitors in. He and they knew that they would have had a hard time kicking the door in, which was surprisingly solid and sturdy among the other cheap and cheerful doors in the corridor, and they all knew why. But Stevie also knew that Jarvis and the Fridge would be able to catch up with him sooner or later. He'd take his medicine now rather than have a surprise and inevitably unpleasant dose down the line.

Jarvis sauntered across the threshold with his bag and looked around to check how much things had changed since last time. The Fridge lumbered in, having to duck under the lintel, and took station by the door. The smaller man wandered around the flat doing inventory, opening the drawers of a Welsh dresser next to the door and nodding at the contents – burner phones, a small set of digital scales, drugs bags and wraps. Crack pipes and other paraphernalia clattered as he rummaged.

'You've heard about JH then, Stevie boy?'

'Hard not to. Everyone's talking about it around here.'

'And does anyone know who did the deed?'

'I haven't heard anything. There haven't been any rumours so far.'

Jarvis nodded and continued his inspection. The flat was spacious, and took up one corner of the large rectangular block. Half of it consisted of a large living space with French windows in front of a false balcony with railings that looked out up to the main Sturry Road – the one that Jarvis and the Fridge had cycled down. Off this space was a galley-style kitchen with a breakfast bar, a door leading into the bathroom, and next to it, a door leading into the bedroom. Near the French windows, cheap mass-produced furniture – a large black faux leather sofa and matching armchairs encircling a glass-topped coffee table, and abstract expressionist prints on the walls – gave the space a faint hint of homeliness. They came with the lease, and Stevie had merely adapted himself to the already installed décor. Only the large, flat-screen television affixed to the same wall as the Welsh dresser, a Peloton cycling machine by the kitchen area, some weights next to it, and a couple of faded Moroccan-style rugs to cover the scratched parquet floor, likely belonged to Stevie.

The flat was neat and sparse but with a grubby air, as if its tenant had OCD tendencies but little sense of housework. The strong scent of patchouli pervaded throughout.

Stevie himself perched on the arm of the chair closest to the French windows, not objecting to Jarvis's poking about. He looked about twenty-two, with thick, black, sleek hair, long on top and with a strand at the front that flopped into his dark eyes. He'd probably stopped realising how he occasionally flicked it back with a short toss of his head. His complexion looked Mediterranean, and on his wrists were multi-coloured braids. His legs were encased in skinny blue jeans and his torso in a black T-shirt emblazoned with an image of the rock band Greta Van Fleet.

'This is nice,' said Jarvis, as he sat on the cycling machine and did a few pedals. 'Must be costing a bob or two.' He hopped off and continued his tour of the room, like a dog cocking its leg. Having confirmed who was boss, he flopped on the sofa, leaned back, spread himself out in a wide-armed, wide-legged sprawl and turned to Stevie.

'How's the course going, mate? Physiotherapy, isn't it? Bachelor of Science.' Jarvis rolled the phrase off his tongue, simultaneously managing to acknowledge the nobility of the aspiration while showing he didn't care a jot for it.

Stevie managed a small grin. That's not why he was living in Barton Student Village. 'Alright. Doing enough to get by.'

Jarvis nodded. 'And how's business?'

'Yeah. Good. Steady.' Stevie was silent for a beat or two. 'It's not time yet – you know – for the next instalment. It's only about ten days since I did the last one. Anyway...'

'Yeah, anyway,' said Jarvis. 'Anyway, JH is no more, so that disrupts things. That's what you're thinking, eh?'

'Well...'

'You're right and you're wrong. Obviously some things are going to be a bit different, but overall, everything's going to be much as before – monthly payments and that – the same enterprise, as it were. More to the point though, have the busies been around yet, asking questions? "Did you see anything?" and all that?'

'Yeah. The day after it was supposed to have happened. They were doing house to house, like.'

'*That's* what this is about, Stevie. Which reminds me...' Jarvis leaned forward on the sofa and undid the drawstrings of his bag. From it he carefully pulled out a baseball bat tightly wrapped round with barbed wire, which glinted dully in the flat's light.

In the corner near the front door, the Fridge shifted his bulk from one foot to the other as he slouched against the wall. Stevie tensed, his rich Mediterranean complexion turning to a strange pallor.

'This is Barbie. I know, mate – bit of a cliché, but I had a good think, and I couldn't come up with anything better. Nor could the Fridge, could you, Fridge?'

The big man shook his head.

Jarvis started swishing the bat like Darth Vader's lightsabre. There was a swooshing sound as it moved through the flat's close air. Stevie gulped and leaned back on his armchair perch.

'The message is, do not say a word to the fuzz about anything to do with Jack Hankinson, either the murder or his business. The message is, make sure all your clients and customers in this block and this student village don't say a word either. If some residents are straight and clean, they don't say a word either. The message is, if you get busted, there is no connection between your little operation and JH or anyone associated with him. Otherwise...' Jarvis suddenly got to his feet and smashed the bat savagely into the arm of the sofa where he'd just been sitting. He smashed it down and smashed it down, grunting very slightly with the effort, his face reddening even further than from the sunburn. The final time he left it in the ripped fabric of the arm and pulled it towards him, fabric and barbed wire combining to make a blood-curdling, tearing noise as the white stuffing bunched and spilt out.

'Does that make everything clear? Any questions? No? Well, thanks for your hospitality. Fridge and I will be on our way. We've got a busy evening ahead of us.'

Pubs, clubs, private houses, not-so-private houses, restaurants, takeaways – the visits were the same even if the technique varied. Sometimes Jimmy Jarvis and the Fridge received welcomes that were almost warm; sometimes they simply relayed their message on doorsteps, and the handle of the baseball bat protruding from Jarvis's backpack was sufficient reinforcement; sometimes they were ushered through to managers' offices at the back. Sometimes, *in extremis*, as at the student village to the north of the city, out came Barbie.

At half-past nine, Jarvis and the Fridge stashed their bikes away in the dingy narrow hallway of the Fridge's billet in the Borough. They strolled (or in the Fridge's case lumbered) up Palace Street, past the wonky door of the antiquarian bookshop on the corner and the King's

School opposite. At the other end, they passed a hippy shop, and then ducked right a few yards down Orange Street and into The Moon under Water, Jarvis's watering-hole of choice and habit. Other members of his crew were already occupying bar stools and ogling the milky-white décolletage of the cheerful new barmaid, the shade of the bosom on show slightly at odds with the foundation and make up on her jolly, open face.

'Mine's a pint of London Pride, Fridge,' said Jarvis, after a short leer of his own. He wasn't that interested because there was always Lucija, his favourite little Slovenian girl up at the brothel in Westgate Close.

He leaned on his elbows with his back to the bar and surveyed the Friday evening clientele sitting at the crude wooden tables on the shiny, slate-grey stone floor, and the footfall outside through the plate glass windows. A knot of students on one scarred table had an orange cocktail jug and were rowdily toasting the birthday of a pink-haired girl with a nose ring who tossed back a slug of the garish liquid, to ragged cheers. A tourist couple, possibly American with their baseball caps, shorts, white socks and chunky trainers, walked past while peering in, faintly bewildered expressions on their faces. The TV screens were off, so there was no sport of note. From the speakers, Metallica's *Master of Puppets* boomed out, and Jarvis's head bobbed approvingly to the sound. He clapped the huge expanse of the Fridge's back as the big man got in the drinks.

'That chink,' he laughed, 'at the takeaway by the level crossing, when I smashed the counter. He remembered his English pretty sharp fucking quick then, didn't he?' Jarvis hadn't heard any rumours or received any hints about who might have despatched

Jack Hankinson, but the joy of the work – an evening of menace and intimidation – hadn't dampened his mood about the failure in that department.

The Fridge nodded. Towards the end of the little intra-city cycle tour, the arthritis around his arms and shoulders had started troubling him. He took a hefty couple of swallows of his pilsner, feeling the alcohol start its numbing. He wondered, with a morose look at the pitted bar top, if Jimmy would ever get in the first round, or even the second or third. He wondered how long their little expedition would keep up the wall of silence among all the various operations now that JH was gone. And he wondered, if and when the fallout happened, whether he'd be able to keep his distance from it.

*

Back in Barton Student Village, Stevie was on the phone. 'They came,' he said, 'as you predicted, and I made myself look suitably scared. Bloody hell, it wasn't all an act. Jarvis got out a baseball bat wrapped in barbed wire. I need a new sofa.' He listened. 'And I'm going to get this extra money when?' He listened again. 'Twenty-five grand isn't enough for what I've already done, never mind the next bit.' Finally, the negotiation ended. 'OK, I'll do it. Yeah, all of it.'

Chapter 9

Nolan and Murphy came in for the post-mortem around the back, far away from the Outpatients entrance, with their unmarked police car parked in a specially designated slot next to the ambulances. They strode through the rabbit warren of corridors in one of the older sections of the dilapidated Kent and Canterbury Hospital. The hospital sprawled at the top of South Canterbury Road over a large acreage abutting open countryside leading to the North Downs. Going to the mortuary always felt sneaky to Nolan, like a dirty secret, and the discreetly tucked-away location enhanced the sensation. As they got closer, the temperature dropped until they went through into the cool room itself, all pale green walls, cushioned silence and stainless steel, redolent in one respect of the reverential atmosphere of a church.

Anthea Tilson, the Home Office forensic pathologist, was already masked, gowned and booted. A couple of assistants, also fully prepared, hovered expectantly. Re-introductions took a few seconds, preparation by the police officers a minute or two, and then they were ready. Nolan had been to enough autopsies to have everything under control, his breathing, his knack of distancing himself from the cutting and blood and viscera and miscellaneous other matter he knew he'd be viewing. He'd found it helpful in the past to imagine himself in an old-fashioned butcher's shop, but instead of the sawdust, runnels to catch the blood running from the body on the slab. Murphy had never seemed troubled by the view and the ambience.

Tilson was clearly highly competent and experienced. She went about her gory work efficiently, videoed at every stage by one of the technicians. Nolan switched off from the technical vocabulary. It was the summary, and after that, the written autopsy report, which would be most important. It had crossed his mind that this was a task he could simply have assigned to colleagues, but in his view it was one of the aspects of the job a leader had to participate in. There was any number of other more suitably delegable duties.

'Right, DCI Nolan,' said the pathologist. 'My oral summary in plain-ish English.' Her brisk tone suggested that she might have mistaken his vacant look, ruminating on the case in general, as squeamishness. 'Ready?'

His eyes re-focused. 'Ready,' he said.

'Mr Hankinson was a healthy young man in his thirties. There is evidence of a diligent, one might say sensible rather than obsessive, fitness regime in his muscle definition and related evidence. There is no evidence of any morbidity or issues in any of his major organs. His skin is clear and lightly tanned, as if he had recently been on holiday. His teeth are in excellent shape – even, and with clear signs of professional whitening. So, overall in very good physical shape. He was very clean, and so, incidentally, were the clothes we took off him. His jacket was dry cleaned. His shirt, going beyond my specialised expertise to my general knowledge, is Oxford button-down in style, white and crisply ironed.

His jeans are designer – Diesel by the label – and ironed in lines between the seams. Mr Hankinson showered and washed his hair before he went out on Wednesday evening. All this is important for our purposes, because it means that there is very little in the way of fibres and materials on his body or clothes. We carried out extensive swabbing, penile, pubic, anal, head and fingernail. There were no signs of recent sexual activity, including perimortem, although his showering will have removed them if they were there.'

'Blood and urine samples have revealed no presence of drugs and only a little alcohol, well below drink driving limits and suggestive of, say, a glass of wine. We were able to get partially digested stomach contents – pasta with a tomato sauce, and some salad. We also managed to detect signs of shaving and aftershave – my technician, an authority on these matters' – again the sparkling eyes – 'hazards Man by Jimmy Choo, but we are investigating further. All the indications are, gentlemen, of a healthy, prosperous and indeed successful young man.

'Time of death: you will probably have independent corroboration of this, but all the indications are that he died at around 10 pm on Wednesday, 9th June. Cause of death: now we're getting to it, what you really want to know…'

Nolan couldn't see Dr Tilson's mouth, but her eyes were smiling.

'… Were two blows to the back of Mr Hankinson's head.' Since the body was lying supine on the slab, the pathologist referred to photos on a side counter. 'Both were heavy and violent. The first was when Mr Hankinson was seated on the bench. The evidence, which I think your crime-scene manager will confirm, suggests that this blow to the base of his skull propelled his whole body across the bench. The second blow, to roughly the same place, stove in the skull and was the *coup de grace*, as it were. It was a determined and, I think, effective attack. Mr Hankinson will have died very shortly after the second blow. His sprawl along the bench was the final position – that is, he wasn't moved after death.'

'I'm happy to give you some informal extra advice if you'd like to have it.' The pathologist's left eyebrow went up.

'Please,' said Nolan.

'What do the death blows mean? What does the state of the body mean? State of the body first. The fresh clothes. The showering. The shaving and aftershave…'

'He was meeting someone,' said Murphy, 'but not just meeting – it was a date.'

'That would be my cautiously expressed view.'

'And what you called the death blows?' said Nolan.

'It was a measured attack, not a frenzied one. That doesn't exactly mean there wasn't anger or passion, but the perpetrator knew how to kill. I'd suggest that he had despatched animals or even fish – large fish. I say "he" but there was a certain amount of… skill to the attack, which obviated the need for pure brute force. It's possible that the killer was female. The fact that Mr Hankinson was struck twice from behind suggests–'

'Ambush,' said Murphy.

The pathologist nodded.

'So Mr Hankinson's tryst could have been with a man or a woman who lured him there,' said Nolan. 'Could there have been an accomplice, Dr Tilson?'

'It's possible. That's beyond my remit really.'

'What about the murder weapon?'

'A large stone, something that could be fitted in the hand, or a mallet…'

After some more desultory questions and answers, Nolan thanked the pathologist, and the two officers made their way out. In the open air and bright sunshine, they took greedy breaths. Release from the oppression of the pathology suite didn't last long. As he got in the car, Nolan sighed. *How much further have we got?* he silently asked himself. *Exactly nowhere.*

Murphy's muted actions and expressions confirmed it.

Chapter 10

Sterling reviewed his to-do list over a bacon sandwich and a mug of builder's tea, not altogether successful in keeping globules of fat from the page. He went for a square of kitchen towel, wiped his fingers, and sat back down. He'd achieved the first item at his office last night – a desktop search and investigation of Jack Hankinson. It didn't turn up much. As well as his marketing job at the university, he'd had a sideline, with his wife, in renovating and refurbishing a former pub in Dover Street a hundred metres the other side of the inner ring road.

The new premises, going by the name The Lotus Blossom, had been done out in a far-eastern theme – pastel shades, bamboo and murals of oriental gardens. From the pictures and accompanying report in the local rag, the new offering occupied the ground between an upmarket bar and a nightclub.

On the city council website were details of the ward Hankinson represented in the villages, contact details via the local Conservative office and a council e-mail address, and a headshot of a confident young man with an immaculate short back and sides haircut, and the glimmerings of a smile. For a relatively prominent local businessman and politician, there was, to Sterling's eye, surprisingly little online information. He'd obviously need to carry on digging in the more conventional way, through foot leather and interviews.

He scanned his list again. What else? There was Maria Goodburn's contact from the Women Sex Workers' Collective. He was waiting to hear about that. Andy Nolan was on his list. Andy was bound to be working around the clock so he'd be in Canterbury next time Sterling bussed over. There was the Labour Party meeting on Monday evening. He'd walk the river path where Hankinson's body was found, and he knew that at some stage he'd have to try and arrange to meet Hankinson's wife. It would be good to get a feel about where and how the murder victim lived. The Lotus Blossom obviously needed a follow-up. Yup, plenty of directions to go in, even if the focus was narrow.

His phone chirruped – Maria Goodburn on ID. 'Hello,' he said.

'Mr Sterling, it's Maria,' said the girl superfluously.

Sterling noticed that neither of them had got beyond stilted formality. He didn't even remember addressing her by any name at all. If they were a partnership.... 'Maria,' he forced himself to say, 'you can call me Frank.'

'Right... Frank. I've heard from Janice Wray.'

'Janice Wray.'

'From the Women Sex Workers' Collective. She can meet us in Canterbury later this morning.'

'Are you going to come over from Whitstable?'

'She won't meet you without me, as it turns out.'

'OK, this morning will suit me well enough. What time?'

'11 o'clock at the Martyrs' Field Memorial in Canterbury. It's apparently behind Canterbury East

Station. If I meet you at Canterbury Bus Station at 10.30, that will give us time to walk through. I can sort all that out.'

'Why not somewhere in the centre – a Starbucks or Caffé Nero? It's a faff.'

'She's doing us a favour, isn't she? She lives around there. Why should she have to put herself out?'

'Alright. See you then, Maria.'

Sterling looked at his watch. He had half an hour to get to the Guildhall bus stop. He was beginning to see advantages in having an assistant, and it was handy that something on his list had come up so quickly.

Maria was waiting for him as he got off the Sandley bus, in the same denim mini that she'd been wearing the day before, some complicated lace-up beige sandals, and a pale blue T-shirt with 'Resist' in small letters stencilled across the front. Her tiny backpack-cum-satchel matched the sandals in shade and style. His own khaki chinos, desert boots and thin blue flower-printed shirt gave them a loose kind of matching look. Were it not for the age gap, they would have been girlfriend and boyfriend meeting for a day out. *Uncle and niece, maybe.*

'The walk's a bit complicated, but I've got the route on my phone, so we should be alright.'

'I'm in your hands,' said Sterling as they set off back the way the buses had come in. They turned left in Watling Street, passed under the city wall and down into the underpass. This was convenient. The police station was on the corner of Rhodaus Town and the Old Dover Road. After they had met Janice Wray, they could call in at the police station and Sterling could have a conversation with Andy Nolan.

Beyond the centre, the city became bedraggled, with a hotchpotch of different architectural styles according to the era of construction. Soon they were walking along an obscure narrow street of mid-Victorian terraces which petered out into a path running parallel to the Canterbury-Dover railway line. Bramble tendrils insinuated themselves across the path from both sides, and every so often there were little shards of broken glass and other detritus.

'Watch your feet in those sandals,' said Sterling.

'I know,' said the girl. 'We cross here.'

There was a walkway over the tracks. Maria looked at her phone on the other side. Now they were on the edge of a large ex-council estate. They turned right and made their way past a square with patchy, dingy grass, some shabby trees and a line of cars.

'Down here,' said Maria, turning down another pathway between the houses.

'Are you sure? This is getting silly.'

Maria ignored the complaint. 'Now left. We're almost there.'

Soon, along the scruffy road sandwiched between the fences of back gardens either side, the walkers could see the railings and then the monument in the small garden, an obelisk with a Canterbury cross on top, resting on a bed of broken granite. They walked in through the metal gate shortly before eleven. If Janice Wray was coming, she hadn't arrived yet. While Sterling slouched on a bench in the welcome shade of the garden's trees, Maria went up close to the monument and busied herself reading the rubric.

'I didn't know about this,' said Maria. She read the inscription on one of the stone panels. '"In memory of forty-one Kentish martyrs who were burned at the stake on this spot in the reign of Queen Mary, A.D. 1555–1558. For themselves they earned the martyrs' crown. By their heroic fidelity they helped to secure for succeeding generations the priceless blessing of religious freedom. Precious in the sight of the Lord is the death of his saints." So, if I remember rightly, Mary was Henry VIII's Catholic daughter and these were Protestant martyrs. Elizabeth I, Henry VIII's Protestant daughter, succeeded her.'

'I expect Elizabeth made a few Catholic martyrs in her turn,' said Sterling. 'People killing each other down the ages for this and that. Religion, politics. I don't get it. Never have.'

Maria didn't respond. 'Plenty of women on here dying for their beliefs.' She was looking at the other panels. 'A couple of them didn't even merit their Christian names – 'Bradbridge's widow, Wilson's wife – typical – women defined by their relationship to men.'

'Always an angle… It's tiring,' said Sterling.

Now she did rise to the bait. 'At least I believe in something – equality for men and women after years of women's oppression. We didn't get the vote till 1928. Equality for everyone so that poor people aren't ground into the dust while the rich just get richer. Properly funded public services. Everybody paying their fair share of taxes. Decent educational opportunities for everyone. Decent jobs and decent housing. An end to vulture capitalism. I'd hate to be someone like you. You don't seem to believe in anything. You seem to just drift through life thinking that it's got to be like this – that no change is possible. It's the worst kind of determinism.'

Sterling smirked. He'd got a rise out of her, just as he used to do with his father, and it could be satisfying. Mind you, his father had needled him too. 'So cynical for one so young' had been his mantra.

They'd entered the memorial garden at the top, and the path sloped down to the monument in a diagonal, continuing in the same diagonal to an identical railed gate at the bottom. Sterling was about to respond when they both heard the clang of the bottom gate, and a slight figure slipped into the space. She was around thirty and had a careworn air, with blue-blond hair cut elfin style, heavy eye shadow and winged eyeliner giving her face a widened, stretched-out look. The day was warm and bright, approaching midday, but Sterling could see the goosebumps on her sun-starved forearms. She wore close-fitting blue jeans, slightly flared, and a cold shoulder top in a slightly darker shade than her hair. She approached the monument with her hands hugging each elbow, as if rocking a baby or caught in a draught, exuding a restless, nervous energy. A cigarette smouldered from the two forefingers of her right hand, the nails bitten down to the quick. She and Maria hugged, two sisters showing solidarity. Sterling felt the stirrings of resentment at an exclusion he'd experienced before in the company of women.

The young women exchanged a few quiet words at the monument before turning to Sterling on the bench. He shifted up to the left and turned towards Janice Wray, who sat at the other end and faced him. Maria stood in front of them, closer to the woman than Sterling, the solidarity continuing. Introductions were brief.

'I've been asked to look independently into the murder of Jack Hankinson,' began Sterling, 'or, more accurately, to make sure that my principal's organisation isn't tainted by the business. Maria has been designated to help me. She tells me you might know something that will help us.'

Wray nodded. 'Well, I run the Collective part-time, which supports female sex workers locally, as Maria has probably told you. I haven't been down here long. I was in London and I got out of the life...' Her eyes took on a faraway look and she took a draw from her cigarette, tipping her head upwards to expel the smoke.

'So why Canterbury?' said Sterling.

The young woman's eyes focused back. 'I found an Access course at Canterbury College and then got a place at Corpus Christi. Sociology and social policy. I live a few streets from here. Anyway, Hankinson, and what the Collective had to do with him... His name came up occasionally in our work. It was all hearsay and rumour, and certainly nothing that was going to come out publicly, but he was said to be connected with three dodgy activities in the area. The first is a brothel somewhere up by the cemetery, where there's talk of trafficked girls from Eastern Europe. The second is somehow linked – a sugar daddy organisation recruiting sugar babies from the universities...'

'Wait,' said Sterling. 'Wait. I'm missing something. Brothels. I know about them. Sugar daddies. I've heard of them. But sugar babies? You're involved in this agenda. I'm not.'

'Well, I'd recommend some research, which wouldn't be too tricky, but basically, sugar babies are young students funded through college by wealthy older men and sometimes women – sugar daddies and mamas – in return for... benefits. Oh, it's dressed up in fancy language and the benefits are meant to be mutual, but more often than not it's just plain exploitation in the age-old way.

'Of course, just like nationally and internationally, the process was developed and streamlined through a website, Canterburysugar.com, which draws in young people and the kind of wealthy folk who live around here. It's not certain that Hankinson was behind it, but the rumours are strong. The kids make the connections and the initial innocent-seeming contacts, and then it gets far darker – rape, illegal imprisonment, stalking…'

'The seaside towns around here have their sleazy sides, but Canterbury…' Sterling's words trailed off.

'I know,' said Wray. 'That's exactly what I thought coming down from London. I thought could leave all the crap behind, but it's as bad here as up there – terrified girls, horrible punters, a whole underworld of darkness under the surface.'

'You said three dodgy activities…'

'Yes, I was getting to that. Through the data on the website, there's blackmail – a completely new variant of nasty practice. Blackmail, I think, involving both parties in the transaction. Everything's meant to be out in the open and above board, but you'd be surprised at how many people don't want their friends and family to know about their "sugaring" activities.'

Sterling leaned forward and clasped his hands on his knees. 'It's all vague, isn't it? All ifs and buts and supposing. But if Hankinson was involved, do you think it might be someone from those worlds who bumped him off?'

Janice Wray shrugged. 'There's a lot of violence in them. Yes, it's possible. I didn't say to Maria that I had any specific information. I'm just telling you what someone relatively new to Canterbury, and involved in the sex worker agenda, has heard. If you have other sources, you'll probably hear the same. There's something else – as if all that isn't bad enough – it went beyond criminal enterprises. He was a rapist too, apparently, using his "charm" and taking advantage. I've heard that it wasn't just vulnerable women he preyed on, either. I expect he would have used the usual defences and pressure – "the sex was consensual", "I'm a councillor – you'll never get it to stick" – that kind of rubbish.'

Sterling was concentrating on what Janice Wray was saying beside him, but in his peripheral vision, he saw Maria shuffle from one foot to the other and sensed a change of atmosphere. He forced his eyes upwards. She looked angry and preoccupied. He turned back to Janice Wray. 'No shortage of motives in any of it,' he said.

His experience in the police had inured him to awful stories. He well knew how horrible humans could be to each other, but he didn't want to appear casual or dismissive. After a respectable interval of contemplation, digesting what he'd been told, he reminded himself of his brief to protect the reputation of the Labour Party. 'What about politics? Could there have been a political motive?'

'Not anything I know about. A group like mine doesn't have much faith in or connection with conventional politicians. We might sometimes get local or national funding, but bitter experience is that some politicians are corrupt, and the corrupt ones are the ones who gravitate to our orbit. It could be political. Who knows? The only absolutely certain thing is that Hankinson was a prize shit.' Then the young woman went still. 'Wait a second. I've just remembered something. In fact, **someone**, a specific individual, a punter, Logan Seymour. Nasty piece of work. Off the same block as Hankinson. A couple of girls have come to the Collective about him. He'd knocked them about, and worse. It was vicious.'

'Why didn't they go to the police?' said Maria.

Sterling and Janice Wray looked at her.

'Sorry. Naïve.'

'Right. Sex workers and the police don't mix,' said Wray. 'The Collective is in a better position to give the protection they need. The word was that he was trying to start up in the business himself, pimping and building up a "string" of girls, for want of a better expression. Hankinson would have been a rival. Seymour is a fantasist with a high opinion of himself, but he's clever too, in a shrewd kind of way. He's certainly violent – violent enough, from what I've heard, for murder. He'd be worth looking at.'

Sterling made a note. 'Do you know where he lives or if he has a job or any other details?'

'He lives locally – somewhere in the city. Otherwise, he's a mystery. I overlooked him because he's relatively new on the scene. He might have come down from London.' Wray smiled wanly. 'Like me. Who knew Canterbury would be such a draw for the sex trade and those associated with it?'

Soon, she and Sterling got up from the bench, business completed.

'Here's my card,' said the PI. 'If you think of anything else, or hear anything else, can you get in touch? Anything you'd like to add, Maria?' The girl shook her head, still preoccupied. He turned back to Janice Wray. 'Thank you for meeting us. It's been helpful. We can add all you've said to our lines of enquiry, as the cops would say, especially the Logan Seymour angle. Good luck with your studies and with the Collective. It's important work, I reckon.'

The young woman's eyebrows went up like insincerity detectors. Antennae. Sterling offered his hand and a steady gaze. Her eyes searched his. Then her face did a small upward tilt. She bent down, stubbed out her cigarette on the bench's hard standing, straightened up and presented her own hand in one smooth movement. Sterling had got the verdict. Having given him one delicate shake, fingers only, she hugged Maria and slipped away through the bottom gate.

The PI and his assistant went in the opposite direction, back the way they'd come. Neither they nor Janice Wray noticed the scruffy man shuffling down Martyrs Field Road just beyond the gate that Wray had gone through. His phone, gleaming and new, belied his down-at-heel, grubby suit, scuffed shoes and stubbled red face. He pressed speed-dial and put the phone to his ear. 'The woman you told me to keep an eye on, my neighbour: she just met a bloke and a girl in the Martyrs' Memorial Garden.'

He pulled up and listened. 'What about my drink?'

A smile broke across his features as he listened to the reply. 'Tidy,' he said.

Chapter 11

They were passing the launderette at the bottom of Nunnery Fields when Sterling and the girl next spoke.

Sterling was thinking of the enterprises Wray had raised, and the angles he and Maria could explore. Logan Seymour was an interesting one. Even if he hadn't been involved in the murder, investigating him might lead on to something else.

'How are your research skills, Maria?'

'OK. I'll be doing a thesis shortly.'

'Well, it might not be the same kind of research, but can you do some digging on this Logan Seymour? It's a long shot but still worth it.'

The girl nodded vaguely. Something was still distracting her.

'Are you alright?' said Sterling. 'You've gone a bit quiet.'

'Well, Janice's story was pretty dreadful, wasn't it?'

'Yeah, but…'

'I'm fine. I'll try and find out about Seymour, OK? But can we talk about something else for a little while? For example, I didn't think it would be like this,' said Maria.

'What? Being a private investigator?' If the girl didn't want to open up or discuss leads, it didn't matter to him. 'What were you expecting? The walks down mean streets? Non-stop action? Guns, fights? Car chases? Pistol-whipping the bad guys for vital information? And them coughing it up every time?'

'Well, not bussing everywhere and walking, anyway. I thought you'd at least have wheels.'

'"Wheels?"' Sterling guffawed. 'You've probably been reading too much pulp.' Looking from the corner of his eye, he caught the girl's sly smile. 'Touché,' he said.

'Actually… it's not all politics at uni. We can choose one or two other modules to get degree credits. I did one on detective fiction last term. Hard-boiled US; British Golden Age…'

'A bit of light relief, then. Which uni is it anyway? I never asked the other day.'

'Birmingham. Second year, if you're interested. We're the only university in the country with our own railway station. Handy for quiz nights.'

'Right, thanks for that. So, this case, you think we should be doing it differently. But with what we've been asked to do – vague when you think about it – and the resources we've got, there's not much choice. You can't bash people or beat answers out of them, or only in the very last resort. You listen. You value. You respect. When it's only you and an offsider, you rely on trust and people telling you stuff, like Janice did. We certainly haven't got the heft of the plods, but we haven't got their disadvantages either. We'll find things out from left field that they'll never get.'

'Not much respect for the police then.'

'I know what the force is like, that's all. I was in it for sixteen years. I've had a bit of excitement now and then.

But most of the time, the work is dull and often sordid. People ask me to check their spouses or investigate their kids' allegedly dodgy girlfriends or boyfriends. I've been asked to stake out allotments because of petty little feuds over potatoes or seedlings or whatever. Occasionally, an insurance company will get me to look at something… It's feast or famine, this line of work, too. Currently feast, but famine will come back soon enough, I expect.'

'Why do it then? A man like you could do loads of other things. June told me she thought you were single. If you've got no ties, it makes it easier, doesn't it?'

'You and June have been talking about me, eh? Very cosy.'

Maria shrugged. 'Why wouldn't we?'

'I could do security work, I expect. I did weapons training when I was in the job. Door work. Bodyguard-chauffeur. Yuk. I didn't leave the police to join another team. I like working by myself, for all the ups and downs, and actually, generally speaking, it calms me down. I had a rep in the Kent police. The Police Federation bloke spent more time defending me for the scrapes I got in than on any other case. So he said.'

They'd reached the inner ring road again, with the police station at the corner on the outside of the city. Sterling realised why he'd opened up. Maria had been foisted on him, but if they also had to work together, he'd make the best of it. And to do that, they needed a rapport.

'Next on the list: pop into the police station to see Andy Nolan,' said Sterling.

'Andy Nolan?'

'I didn't tell you, but Detective Chief Inspector Nolan is the senior investigating officer for Hankinson's murder. He did the press conference yesterday. He also happens to be an old friend of mine, back in the days when we were in a squad car together in Folkestone. The only one I've really kept in touch with since I left. I'm going to offer our extracurricular services to help him. That way, we might get something back.'

Sterling and Maria ducked in through successive heavily reinforced plate glass doors of the station, going up to the reception desk beyond the lobby. Sterling gestured towards the reception bell on the desk nearest to Maria and she pinged it once. A civilian appeared from behind a heavy door, severe in heavy, dark-framed glasses and gun-metal grey hair in a tidy bun. She set a referral pad on the battle-scarred desk. 'Yes, may I help you?'

'Can you tell DCI Nolan, who I understand is leading the investigation into the murder of Jack Hankinson, that Frank Sterling – that's S-T-E-R-L-I-N-G – is here to see him.'

The woman scribbled on the pad – date, time, enquiry. She looked up. 'You have an appointment?'

'No. My colleague and I had business in the city and we were passing. We might have information useful to the investigation.'

'I see. DCI Nolan is very busy, as you can probably understand.'

'I'm certain he'll see me if you let him know I'm here. He knows me very well.'

'I'll go and check.' The woman disappeared through the heavy door.

Five minutes elapsed. Then ten. Then twenty.

'This is going well,' murmured Maria. Sterling was pacing as she sat on one of the reception's battered plastic chairs.

The heavy door opened again, and someone different appeared, a small, compact young woman whose thick brown hair reached just below her shoulders.

Sterling looked up. His face darkened. 'Andy,' he said. 'Sex change. Suits you. They lopped a few inches off your height as well.'

Shock registered on Maria's face. The woman pursed her lips. 'DCI Nolan is very busy. He's just got back from the post-mortem and there's a whole pile of stuff on his desk. What's this about?'

'If I'd wanted the monkey I'd have asked. I need the organ grinder. Come on, Maria. If we've got to spin our wheels, we can do it somewhere more comfortable, serving coffee maybe.'

'A second,' frowned the woman as she disappeared into the back.

'Not ten minutes,' Sterling called out.

'So much for trust and respect,' said Maria, 'and keeping people onside.'

'She'll have heard much worse on a Saturday night in the city centre, where there'll have been spitting and punching as well. My patience has limits. In the case of my former employers, the limits are... limited.'

'Still, I would have thought the police were exactly the people not to fall out with.'

'Are you assisting me or just doing the nagging?'

'"Nag"... such a sexist word...'

Sterling was realising that the girl could give as good as she got. Who was getting a rise out of whom now? Firmly on the back foot, he was rescued by Andy Nolan's appearance through the heavy door.

Nolan was well turned out, as always, in light linen trousers, the bottom half of a suit, and a crisp, brilliant white shirt and plain, light-blue tie. He nodded. 'Frank.'

'Andy.'

Nolan gestured to Maria. 'And this is...?'

'Maria Goodburn,' said the girl. 'Helping with Mr Sterling's enquiries.' Sterling couldn't be certain, but he thought he detected a mocking quality in the statement. Nolan's gaze held hers.

'I can only see Frank, miss, if you'd like to wait here. Frank, come through.' He unlocked the reception door and stepped aside. 'Interview room number 1. You know the way.'

The room was bare and starkly functional, painted two decades ago in a white colour that had long faded. No one would have smoked in there for years, but there was still a stale, musty, smoky atmosphere. A dirty window, high up, let in the only natural light. The men selected their chairs out of the three in the room, Sterling checking that he hadn't got the one whose front legs were an inch shorter than the back ones, causing the user to slip forward constantly. They settled themselves at either end of a table. On a ledge next to them, interview recording equipment stayed blank and silent. Sterling knew that Nolan's devoted, vicariously ambitious wife made sure his clothes were clean and sharply pressed, and his shoes polished to a bright shine, but she couldn't do anything about his red-rimmed eyes, and the way, every so often, his hand went up to scratch his scalp.

'You've ruffled a few feathers, Frank. That young woman was my MIR office manager. She's competent, and, for one so relatively young, experienced, but she didn't appreciate being characterised as "the monkey", any more than I like being "the organ grinder". And the reason she came out originally, and not me, is because part of her job is to stop me getting diverted from my strategic oversight of a murder investigation.'

Sterling thought of his lecture to Maria about trust and respect, and her response. The girl was right on all counts. 'What's your office manager's name?'

'Sophie Stephens.'

'Please convey my apologies to her. I was out of order.'

'Will do. Now, what's this about, Frank? You know what it's like when you get a suspicious death. I've got a million things to do.'

'Yeah, of course, Detective Chief Inspector. Well, I've got an interest in Jack Hankinson as well. I've been engaged not exactly to run my own investigation into his death, but to make sure that my principal's organisation is not tainted by anything that comes out.'

'Your principal's organisation? Who's your principal? What's the organisation? What if the organisation is tainted? And, while we're on the subject of mysteries, who's that girl in reception?'

'You know my principal's details are confidential, but the organisation's the Labour Party, and the girl is my temporary assistant as required by the conditions of my engagement.'

'The Labour Party. Why? And I thought you worked alone except when you needed Angela Wilson or Mike and Becky Strange.'

'Hankinson was apparently a member of the Party at one time. As for the girl, I'd prefer not to have her, but I don't have the luxury of a guaranteed monthly salary, so needs must. Anyway, we were passing so I thought we'd call in and establish contact. We could maybe cooperate as things unfold.'

'Cooperate, Frank? Let me get this right. A formal police murder investigation involving, oh... about twenty full-time professionals at one time or another, working twenty-four hours a day on multiple lines of enquiry teams up with a solitary private investigator from Sandley who happens to know the SIO, along with his... assistant. In what way is this cooperation going to be of any use to me?'

'No need to get uppity, Andy. You know I've got the knack of getting to the bottom of things. I've helped you out with a couple of cases. The incident down at Dungeness for instance – that did your reputation no harm. You were only a detective sergeant then, if I remember rightly. It hasn't taken you long to get to DCI.'

Nolan reddened. 'That "incident" as you call it – you didn't "help me out". As I remember it, you did your usual hot-headed lone-wolf act, ignoring any sane course of action and leaving a trail of havoc in your wake, while I was the one to put my head on the block, declare a major terrorist incident, and only escape a complete career trashing by the skin of my teeth. That could have gone either way for me, Frank, and you know it. Even when we were together on the job, you were the one wading in and messing up, and I was the one getting us out of it. I've had some luck to get to where I am, but I've had to work bloody hard as well.'

'Whatever,' said Sterling. 'Selective memory must come with every promotion.'

Nolan threw his hands up. 'Well, I can't listen to insults all day, Frank. I've got to get on. But before I do,

I need to remind you of a couple of things. Firstly, don't interfere with my investigation. There's enough for me and my team to do without having to factor in any interventions or cock-ups you're likely to produce. Secondly, if you do find something out that's pertinent to our enquiries, you must tell us. It would be an offence not to – obstructing a police officer or wasting police time.'

'I still know the law, Andy. And you know what, you can fuck off. While you're doing that, don't forget that apology to your office manager for me. I'm out of here.'

Chapter 11

Grim-faced, Sterling strode out of the police station with Maria, who knew when to pipe up and when to keep quiet. They were in the city centre before Sterling reached into a pocket and brought out his list. He scanned it and returned it to his pocket. 'We'll go down the river path and see if we can look at where Hankinson met his Maker.'

They turned into St Margaret's Street, a narrow, intimate thoroughfare of mainly local businesses. At the chippy in the middle, a group of young French students, two gangly boys and girls, chatted happily at one of the tables outside, enjoying something tastier than their packed lunches. Sterling and Maria turned left into the High Street, suddenly part of a less intimate throng of shoppers and visitors.

'Right here,' said Sterling, consulting the pop-up map of Canterbury he'd remembered to put in his pocket before he'd started out that morning. They took the turn past a dull Victorian pile that housed library, museum and tourist information point, and moved eastwards in zig-zags down the narrow streets towards the crime scene. 'Mill Lane,' he said. 'You know what, I could murder a pint, and if I remember rightly there's a pub just around the corner opposite the river.'

'You're right,' said Maria. 'It's where we all go after Labour Party meetings. Here it is.'

'Uh oh,' said Sterling. He pulled up, the muted roar of the water being regulated through the locks in the background.

'What?'

'Shit and scream.'

'Shit and...?'

The PI pointed at the sign, *The Millers Arms*, and then at the brewer's just beneath it.

The girl's puzzlement cleared. 'Shepherd Neame. What's wrong with that?'

'Find me a decent pint in that place, or any from that stable, and I'll revise my opinion. Still, a pint of lager won't do me any harm. Come on. What's your poison?'

'Half a cider, please. There's a kind of little walled garden out at the back. I'll get us seats in there.'

Sterling made his way with the drinks through the dark, homely pub interior and around the solid-oak tables. On the walls were faded black and white pictures of horses and drays, cellar doors opening up from pavements and draymen with handlebar moustaches manhandling barrels, or looking into the camera with curiously neutral faces. In the garden, sunshine and shade dappled Maria's face and the table in front of her, and vine-like plants cascaded over the brickwork, endowing the space with an insular coolness amid the midday heat.

Sterling took a long pull from his glass, needing the alcohol hit as much as to quench his thirst. 'I got fobbed off. Not just fobbed off, warned off. Clearly, a murder investigation trumps the old bonds of friendship, forged in crappy patrol cars in the early hours. I shouldn't be surprised really, and after my little lecture to you about trust and listening, I suppose I cocked up. My hot-headedness always comes out at some stage. I should be better at aligning what I say and what I do these days.'

Maria sipped at her cider. The girl still maintained a sense of restraint about her, at least from what Sterling had seen, as if matters – injustice, inequality – were too serious for her to be able to cut loose. 'At least you're honest about it and you can admit your mistake.'

'I've got a friend in Sandley, who kind of – what's the word she uses? – mentors me.'

'Right,' said Maria. 'Well, obviously I don't know much, but couldn't police hostility work to our advantage? If they're freezing us out and warning us off, doesn't that, in a way, give us carte blanche to go in any direction we want and talk to anyone we want? Can't we use methods that the police are banned from? Not stuff that's illegal, but…'

Sterling looked at her. 'You're picking things up quickly. There's something in that. And if the police don't want to talk to us, we won't be telling them anything.'

'Is that allowed, from a legal standpoint?'

'A very grey area, girl. I need another pint, and a sandwich to go with it. It's nice and comfy here. Do you want another – maybe a pint this time – let yourself go a bit.' He smiled, half-mocking, half-challenging.

'Aren't you… on the clock?' The girl was smiling too, mirroring the mocking and challenging, but, to Sterling, still buttoned up. He'd known pals of his father like that, so pure in their socialist beliefs that they were the new puritans.

'Well, you can report back to Ms Selsdon, can't you? The deal is pay for work done. She surely wouldn't begrudge me a couple of pints of Whitstable Blonde during my lunch hour though.'

By the time the sleuth and his assistant had eaten their ploughmen's and finished their drinks, Maria loosening up enough to graduate to a whole pint, Sterling had almost completely regained his equilibrium. Crossing the road from the pub, they started off down the path next to the river. The water level was low, but they could see the dark shapes of fish darting among the long green fingers of vegetation rippling with the current, and moorhens and ducks with rapidly maturing chicks foraging sedately.

'Why are we doing this again?' said Maria.

'We need to get the feel of things. It's not just about hearing what people say and doing everything second hand. We know Hankinson was bumped off further down here at ten o'clock at night. He doesn't live down here, as far as we know. He didn't have any connections down here, as far as we know. Apart from being quite a nice walk, there's nothing much at all down here. So why did he come this way?'

They walked along the underpass, following Nolan and Murphy's footsteps two days ago, and then came upon the crime-scene tape below the Stonebridge estate. A young constable was stopping passers-by, pointing to a path-side notice that read 'Major incident Wednesday evening, June 9th. Did you see or hear anything?' with hotline and e-mail contact details.

Beyond him, behind the tape, Sterling saw someone he thought he recognised, a uniformed sergeant in shirt sleeves whose cap did not hide his craggy face and long, bushy sideburns, fashionable circa 1972.

'Is that Sergeant Peterson, officer?' Sterling said to the constable, as the latest path walkers wandered off.

'Correct.'

'Can you call him over? He's an old colleague. It would be nice to have a word.'

The constable's face was open and conscientious. Sterling could see the quick calculations going on in it, and their conclusion.

'Sergeant Peterson? Someone to talk to you.'

The older policeman came over, slipping his phone into his pocket. A wide beam triggered a mass of creases around his weather-beaten mouth and eyes. 'Frank bloody Sterling. Who'd have thought it? What are you doing here?'

'Mick, good to see you. How're you doing? Is it possible to have a quiet word? This is my colleague, Maria.' Beside him, he could sense his assistant straighten up. He gave her a sideways glance and noticed a smile.

'Sure. Let's sit on the bench by the river. The crime-scene people won't be back. Another hour and Freddie' – he motioned to the young officer – 'and I will be clearing away the tape and heading off.'

They settled on the bench, an unlikely trio, Maria in the middle. The day was harshly bright and hot, but the coolness of the river dropped the temperature down a notch or two, and the placid current cast a beguiling, serene spell over the little jetty.

'Frank and I go a long way back, miss, even though I'm a bit older than him. There was a Police Federation rep, Jim Selsey. He was always having to come out to bat for one or other of us. At one time, someone in the force was running a book to see who'd have more disciplinaries over a two-year period. You were way out in front, Frank.'

'Yeah. I got out in the end, Mick, before I got booted out. But you've got your sergeant's stripes.'

'I calmed down. They gave me a kind of adviser. They told me I'd be a good cop if I concentrated on it. I listened. For once.'

Sterling nodded, letting the statement register. 'Mick, I need to be straight with you. Maria and I have got an interest in this case, which I can explain in a minute, but we've – I've – just fallen out with Andy Nolan, and I don't think he'd be very pleased if he had any idea that we were sitting here talking to you.'

Peterson waved his hand. 'The suits can get far too precious. Anyway, no one's going to know. Freddie's alright – graduate entrant – so a bit of flexibility already built into his thinking. He's certainly not a jobsworth, like some of them. Just to be clear, anything I might say won't be coming back to me, or getting in the papers, right? So, what's your interest?'

Sterling motioned to Maria and she explained. He noted how clearly and concisely she explained their brief and her role.

Peterson pressed his lips together. 'Interesting. Well, it will come out in the press and telly briefings anyway, so I can tell you that we haven't made much progress. Diddly squat in fact. Freddie and I have been up there on the path most of the day, and it's all "see no evil, hear no evil, speak no evil."'

'Nothing much from this crime scene either. As you can see, it's a good spot for bumping someone off in. You approach down from the path, and you have to make a little right-hand turn to get on this little jetty.

The bench backs on to bushes and foliage, which in turn blocks sightlines from anywhere on the path. Whichever way you're walking, you can't see the bench.

'Interestingly too, from what a foot soldier like me is hearing after our internal briefings, this crime scene gave up virtually no clues about the assailant. Hankinson was sitting on the bench. Two blows to the back of the head. No murder weapon. Virtually no traces. Baffling. No idea of motive yet, though it's early days. The only obvious thing is a meeting between victim and killer, who incidentally could have been a man or a woman.'

After ten minutes, the conversation came to a natural end. 'We'll be heading off then, Mick. Thanks for your input. Discretion is absolutely guaranteed.'

The two men shook hands, and then Peterson and Maria. 'Nice to meet you, miss.'

'Likewise,' said the girl.

'I've been involved in loads of these investigations,' said Peterson, as they walked back up to the path. 'They're often not very – how can I put this? – subtle. Someone bashes someone else, the offender is tied to the victim by circumstance, relationship, forensics, whatever. This one's different. It's complex. There's a lot in the background. As I said, no one says they've seen or heard anything. But that's not necessarily because it's true. There's a smell around this case, a smell of fear, and that's a big barrier. What does it amount to? I'd call it a wall of silence.' He liked the phrase and savoured it. 'Yep, a wall of silence.'

Chapter 12

A mile away on the same day, at Jensen and Partners Estate Agents in Castle Street, Charlotte Hankinson had let the secretaries and the sales negotiators go home just before five. It wasn't that business was slow, but there was nothing that couldn't wait till next week now that viewings had been organised for Sunday.

Naturally, there was a reason for her generosity. It came in the form of a procession of people she ushered through the door, past the serried desks of her staff and up the narrow stairs to the conference room next to her office on the first floor. At half-past five they were all assembled, ten of them, including Jimmy Jarvis, with Charlotte Hankinson at the head of the table.

It was a motley crew. The most casual, in dress and demeanour, was Jarvis, who slouched carelessly across his chair in characteristic jeans and T-shirt. The most elegant was a slim woman in her late thirties, Maddie Spedding, in a sleek, black, knee-length, satin dress, sheer light tights and luxurious dark mauve ankle boots, with delicate make-up and pencilled eyebrows on a pale, china-doll face – perfect for someone who spent so much time inside. Apart from Jarvis, the men wore light summer suits of a superior cut.

Hankinson offered no small talk and no refreshments. The meeting was all business, even when one of the men, a property developer, jowly and thick-necked through good living, tried to offer his condolences.

Hankinson put up her hand, like a policeman stopping traffic. 'Thank you, Mark, but let me deal with all that privately.' She didn't want false notes and hypocrisy. Jack had not been popular in any sphere of his life – she knew that. Towards the end, and even a year or two before that, she hadn't liked him herself. She had no illusions about his philandering, including sampling the goods in the brothel, which Spedding, its madam, encouraged. It was fortunate that the house had been big enough for them to live separate lives. Their business interests intertwined, and she had her own life. If it suited her that everyone thought differently, that the flame had still been bright, she didn't want it overdone.

Jarvis smirked. His own condolences two days before had received a similar brush-off.

'Let's get some things straight. Jack has gone, but of course the organisation carries on. I'm taking over all his functions. Instead of reporting to him, you report to me. It's not as much change as you might imagine. We shared the direction of the business but I thought it best to stay in the background, while, as we all know, he loved the limelight.

'This is what we'll be discussing. Jack… and who killed him – painful but necessary. Protecting our business from here on in the light of his… departure. A summary from each of you, as I requested before the meeting – in the usual format – income, expenditure, strengths, weaknesses, opportunities, threats, anything else that's urgent…'

'Hold up, hold up,' said one of the men, known only as Mac. He was barely thirty, with pallid skin, carroty red hair, a sharp nose and dark, cold brown eyes set a narrow, vulpine face. The suit was expensive, certainly, but he wore it poorly, and the collar of his shirt, small as it was, still left a gap at the large Adam's apple in his scrawny throat. He'd been a sometime groundsman and drug dealer, and was then discovered and elevated by Jack Hankinson to his current role as manager and coordinator of illegal drug deliveries in the city. His flat voice and Mancunian accent grated in a room of southerners. He was known for his barely concealed ambition and the rough way he treated his crew. 'Shouldn't the first item on the agenda be reviewing current organisational arrangements and structure, including leadership?'

Charlotte Hankinson looked at him, her face devoid of expression. Then she looked around the room, her gaze lingering on each person. Although outside the early evening still retained the heat of the day, the meeting room had been cool. Now the atmosphere became even chillier. Known, and feared, for her ice-queen qualities, it was as if Charlotte Hankinson had turned down the temperature even further by dint of her personality alone.

Maddy Spedding shivered.

'Do we need to dignify Mac's question with an answer or can we just move on?' She glanced at Jimmy Jarvis, who stopped slouching on his chair and leaned forward, clasping his hands, surprisingly slab-like for such a compact and wiry man, on the table. Mac stayed erect in his chair, his eyes fixed on the ice queen. Everyone else stared downwards.

Hankinson stayed quiet for a further twenty seconds. 'Thank you for raising that, Mac,' she said. 'A helpful...

clearing of the air. Moving on, then. Jack and his murder. Have you heard anything in your networks? From what I can gather from the police, they haven't made much, or indeed any, progress in the last few days.'

No one said a word, though there was plenty of head-shaking. The circumstances of the death were blurred – simply that he'd been found on the river path with his head stoved in. What could they know about means and opportunity? But everyone could sense the unspoken undercurrent: there were any number of motives to kill a crook like Hankinson, and therefore any number of suspects.

'Well, keep your ears to the ground. Ask around. It's in all our interests that the killer is found and we can get back to some kind of normality. Better that we find out and act rather than the police.'

The meeting moved on, rhythm and structure dictated by the reporting format from each associate.

She summed up. 'Things are stable to date, though the organisation's obviously had a jolt. We might struggle in the next few weeks as people take time to adjust. There might be some disruption and dissent. Keep me posted, and Jimmy can be brought in to deal with it where it occurs. You might have noticed that he's already done some work in that direction, and it might continue here and there over the next few days. We don't want anyone breaking ranks – not anyone in this room,' – she looked around pointedly – 'and not among the crews. We stand and fall together. Finally, a word about internal communication. The first rule is, no communication except in an emergency. The second rule is, no landline, mobile or social media usage on our business. Only Jimmy and I use phones, and those are burners. If you want to speak with me – or even, if you have to, among yourselves, you put a note through Jimmy's door – clear to us but impenetrable outside our circle. Then Jimmy will take the appropriate action. Any questions? Any other business? No? Thank you for coming. Enjoy the rest of your Saturday evening.'

Everyone got up and put their chairs under the table. Hankinson was notorious for her sense of tidiness. Before they shuffled off, and before the first person had reached the door, she spoke out, guaranteeing that she would be clearly heard. 'Jimmy, stay back for a few moments. We've still got one or two things to discuss.'

Jarvis grinned. He went back to his chair and his previous slouching posture, draped diagonally across it, one arm dangling to the floor.

'Mac,' said Hankinson, when only she and Jarvis were left. 'Keep an eye on him. He's got more ambition than sense, but it won't do any harm to know what he gets up to. Wait.' She shook her head slightly, and her eyes tilted upwards. 'You don't think Mac killed Jack, do you? Or arranged it with one of his crew? And while we're on that subject, what about one of the others – Mark Prideaux or Maggie Spedding. Any of them.'

Jarvis leaned back and clasped his hands behind his head. 'Well,' he said. 'Interesting question. There are plenty of nutters about who could actually do the deed on behalf of one of the team. Mac's always been too big for his boots, but what does he gain? The timing's off. He's still developing his part of the operation. Prideaux might be miffed that Ja... Mr H didn't pull off that big planning permission he needed, but why kill him? He'd need him for the appeal round of greasing palms. Spedding's just a madam. That's all she knows. It's the same story with the others. They could all have had it done, but why would they?' He smiled and leaned forward. 'The same applies to me.'

Hankinson's face stayed blank.

Jarvis became serious again. 'Mac's the most likely from those on the inside. I'll do as you say and keep an eye on him. Prideaux's a dark horse. There might be an angle we don't know about. I'll look at him too.'

'Right, moving on,' said Hankinson. 'The flash drive: I wasn't going to let any of that lot know that all Jack's dodgy dealing, including with them, had gone missing. I'm glad you had the sense not to mention it. Any news?'

'I haven't heard anything. I guess that's a good thing for the moment. It means it's out of circulation, or maybe whoever has got it doesn't realise what it is and what it's worth. That's another reason for thinking it wasn't Mac or anyone on the inside. There's the password too. I'm assuming there was a password.'

'I don't know. Jack had a reckless streak, and he could be stupid. Anyway, in the right hands, passwords can be broken. We can only carry on looking for it and trying to work out who attacked him. Aside from Jack's murder, Maddy Spedding is well turned out. I'm wondering if there's any skimming going on there. Drop in on Westgate Close sometime – off the cuff – and do a bit of poking around.'

Jimmy grinned. He'd be able to combine that with a session with Lucija, his little Slovenian cracker. 'Something else for you to think about, Mrs Hankinson. One of my street blokes was out and about and saw that busybody sex woman – from the what's-its-name collective – talking to a man and a girl in the Martyrs

Field Garden today. He said it looked a bit iffy, as if she was giving them information.'

'Were they police?'

'My bloke doesn't think so. He said they didn't look as though they were from any sort of... what? – agency. They were together, but not a natural fit. Maybe freelancers. Journos... muckraking or something, for a story. Want me to do anything?'

Hankinson drummed her manicured, blood-red nails on the conference table. 'Not for the moment. That woman – Wray, that's her name, isn't it? – is going to come a cropper one of these days, but we'll see how it works out. OK, that's it for now. I'm going down to The Lotus Blossom later tonight. That's where you'll find me if I'm needed.'

Jarvis unfolded himself from the chair, put two fingers to his forehead in a mock salute, and sloped off. Hankinson heard his feet clattering down the stairs and the office door close.

She sat quietly in the cool conference room. Outside, the light was leaching from the evening as the ancient gravestones in St Mary's Green almost shimmered below the darkening blue dusk sky. Never mind Jack's murder. Mac. All those other second-raters around the table. None of them with the balls or expertise to run the business or any true idea of its scope. OK, Jack had been competent enough, with the flair and personality to be a figurehead as well. He had a certain leadership panache. But she was the organised one, and she was the one with the technical competence and the qualifications – the accountancy degree, the MBA from the university up on the hill. She'd add all the other tasks to the bookkeeping. She'd pretty much been in charge behind the scenes anyway.

But then the doubts resurfaced. Why, and how, had she arrived at this point? Jack had corrupted her – his own wife – as smoothly and adeptly as he'd corrupted all the others in his sphere. If only she hadn't got drawn in.

For the moment, while she grappled with everything, Jimmy Jarvis had to be kept onside. He might not be that bright, but he was the most cunning individual she'd ever met. He wasn't exactly loyal or trustworthy either, but he knew which way his bread was buttered. She reckoned that as far as Jimmy was concerned, she was the best bet to keep him happy. She suspected that her dead husband's appeal for Jimmy Jarvis had a different, more dubious basis, including drinking and whoring. Not that it mattered anymore.

She shut up the office, left through the back door and headed into the car park to her Mercedes. She had time to go home, shower and change. Until she worked out what she really wanted, her appearance at The Lotus Blossom would send out a public message to any would-be rivals and opportunists in the local criminal fraternity – business as usual. For herself, there would be precious breathing space for the decisions ahead.

Chapter 13

Maggie Spedding walked briskly up Castle Street towards the Norman keep on the edge of the inner ring road. The meeting had left a bad taste. When old Jack had chaired them, they'd had a laugh and a joke – and a drink. But that... misery, and Mac trying to make a play... Still, now she had time to go and see Logan before getting back to the house. She always made the effort when she was in the city centre, and this time there was a particular reason.

She crossed the ring road through the underpass and skirted the front of Aldi. His flat was behind the supermarket and he buzzed her in promptly when she rang the entry bell outside the lobby. The lift pinged, the doors opened promptly and she went up.

From behind Logan's door on the fourth floor she could hear an intense bass beat, which stopped abruptly when she knocked, and then there he was, at the door, her darling boy. She reached up to give him a peck on the cheek and he leaned down to receive it. He wasn't much taller than five feet nine, but she barely cleared five feet herself.

The flat was large and spacious and looked out from the living room side across the marshes and over the railway track. A kitchen and dining area were part of the open plan to the back, with doors to the bathroom and the one bedroom also at the back.

Without even sitting down, Spedding started tidying up, moving around the generous space folding and stacking jackets, jeans and assorted other clothes, binning cartons and stacking cups and plates in the built-in dishwasher. She knew not to touch the laptop on the coffee table, just as she steered clear of the bedroom.

The young man lolled on the sofa and turned on the widescreen television fixed to the wall. His thick, dark, wavy hair was swept back from his face and unfashionably long – more nineties popstar than current immaculately groomed young Premier League footballer, and his arms bulged from a dazzlingly white, close-fitting T-shirt that enhanced tanned smooth skin. Not that he was bulky – he was simply muscular within a slender and lithe frame.

Spedding looked for a long moment at her son from the kitchen as he watched the reality show – her darling boy with his dark brown eyes, his flawless straight nose and his white, even teeth. That early battle with him about the brace, ten years ago now, had been worth it, even if he'd never acknowledged it himself. He'd be a wonderful candidate for *Love Island*... And when they went to dinner together in the city on her rare nights off, she watched the girls in the restaurant and in the streets as they ogled him.

'Cup of tea, Loges?' No one else called him that. He'd never stood for it.

'Yeah, thanks.' The young man's eyes didn't stray from the TV.

Absent-mindedly, she tidied the kitchen and wiped the surfaces as the kettle boiled. She had to rinse out a couple of mugs in the sink as there were no clean ones on the rack.

It hadn't been easy for her in the early days. Her foster care had been patchy and the Social Services supervision cursory. She'd got on the game early, and she'd liked it. She had been good at it too. And then she'd got pregnant with Logan when she was only sixteen. His father had been the only man she'd ever loved, despite his... exotic tastes in the bedroom, and he was long gone, leaving only his surname – Seymour – for his baby son.

Of course, Logan had seen too much of the sex trade life than was good for him, and from too young an age. There wasn't often what the bleeding hearts called "non-consensual" violence, but when it erupted... That, and inheriting his father's tastes... She closed her eyes and tried to expunge the memory of the shed they'd had in the garden of the London house. But what she'd discovered the only day she'd gone inside, looking for the boy, was not easy to forget. The cat with no head, nailed to the wall by its paws, the rats with no tails and no eyes, the matches, the screwdrivers and secateurs and the other tools, smeared with blood. Around that time, she'd started looking with new interest at the notices on lamp-posts of missing dogs, but had chosen also to ignore the little burial mounds by the fence at the back.

All that had been so much worse than the stash of skin magazines she'd once unearthed, depicting stuff that had been eye-opening and repulsive even for her. There were no mags now, now that there was the laptop...

There had been no shortage of girls in Logan's adolescence. When he turned on the charm, none of them could resist. The way they looked at him. The things they'd do for him – early on. But the turnover.

How quickly and abruptly, and almost always bitterly, they came and went…

She brewed the tea and took the mugs to the coffee table in front of the sofa, settling herself down next to her son. He had been in the flat for three months. She'd been thrilled when he'd decided to relocate from London.

No one was tougher than Maggie Spedding, she knew. Years in the sex business had done it. She'd seen, and done, so much that she was rarely shocked. Keeping the brothel going and profitable required the hardest of hard-nosed management. It was all for her boy. The well-being and happiness of her lovely boy were the only things that mattered.

'So, how's everything going, darling?'

'Yeah, alright.' The young man kept on looking at the TV. He sipped his tea and put the mug back on the coffee table.

She took a sip of her own and tried a casual tone. 'You're nicely settled in here. What are you up to?'

'This and that. Irons in the fire. You know me, Mum. Something always turns up.'

Spedding continued sipping her tea. She did know him, and how swiftly he would have enfolded himself into the fabric of Canterbury's dark side. She could guess what 'irons in the fire' were and what they involved.

On the screen, two beautifully sculpted, scantily clad creatures were having a bitter row on a sunny veranda.

She wondered whether the allowance she gave Logan was enough, and for how long he'd need it. After half an hour of companionable silence apart from the TV, she took the empty mugs and washed them up.

'I've got to get back, darling.' She still hadn't mustered the nerve to broach the main reason for her visit.

'OK, Mum. Thanks for popping in.'

At the door, she hugged him and then looked into those liquid brown eyes. 'Jack Hankinson,' she said. 'It wasn't yo... You didn't have anything to do with what happened, did you?'

There it was, that little twisted smile, that lopsided mouth that transformed his whole face into ugliness.

'Goodbye, Mum.' The door closed.

Chapter 14

As arranged at the riverside, Sterling and Maria met again later that day. They'd both returned home for a few hours to rest, have something to eat and change. Sterling realised how little he knew about his offsider. Her politics, yes. Her course at Birmingham University (the one with its own railway station). How old she was, roughly – 20 or 21. Her friendship with his principal, June Selsdon, and that she lived in Whitstable in vacation time. But did she have parents, siblings? A boyfriend? A girlfriend? Where had she been to school? No doubt he'd find out more in due course.

Leaning against the Perspex at the bus station in front of the 'Triangle' bus bay waiting for her bus to come in, he wondered how much it mattered. She stepped down from the bus towards the end of the procession of travellers, now dressed in a high-waisted polka dot mini-skirt of complicated design – a kind of gathered arrangement with a ruffled hem at the bottom. Her embroidered blouse was a kind of oyster-white with a high ruffled collar, a V-neck and sleeves that stopped and tapered just below the elbow. Sterling didn't generally pay more than a casual attention to fashion, but he noticed that the ruffling at the neck matched the ruffling on the thigh. A small, plain white bag, more purse than actual handbag, and white, low heeled sandals completed the ensemble. The girl was well turned out, and appropriately too, for an evening in a fancy bar. He considered his own attire, grey chinos and what the saleswoman had described as a classic light linen print shirt, and his trusty light brown strap-over shoes, and decided that he'd do – both for the bar and matched to the girl.

He felt a momentary confusion. This was a case, but what they were currently doing was more akin to a date. He sensed confusion in the girl too, in the awkward greeting and turned away gaze. They moved from the bus station into the underpass and out to the other side of the ring road, skirting the cinema house on the corner and into Dover Street. A few yards further on was the queue to The Lotus Blossom. At 9 pm, there was a lull between entry for the early bird and happy hour deals and the crush that would appear later.

Two doormen wearing transparent plastic armbands containing their credentials ran their eyes over the would-be clientele, boredom trumping any lascivious interest in some of the scantily clad women. Sterling experienced a hint of nerves. He reminded himself again that he was much closer to forty than thirty these days, and grey was stealthily infiltrating his dark wavy hair at an alarming rate. This was a youngster's game. Might he suffer the embarrassment of being barred from entry?

'So, to recap,' said Maria, as the pair shuffled closer and closer to the fancy entrance, 'this is another of our "suck it and see" expeditions.'

'Correct. Also known, in Frank Sterling terms, as shaking something and seeing what comes loose. We can have drinks too, of course... on the clock.'

As they got to the front of the queue, they saw that there were three door staff, a young woman tucked into the entrance as well as the two men, all in the same dark jacket and trousers uniform. One of the men was huge – wide as well as tall, with a shaved head attached to his shoulders with a minimum of neck. The hair clippers that had been applied to his scalp revealed an array of bumps and dents.

Maria noticed the top of a paperback stuffed into the large front pocket of his jacket, presumably for a slow time at the end of the night when no one was coming in or out. Her eyes widened very slightly.

Sterling needn't have worried about entry. The serious young woman door supervisor gave him a speedy up and down, checked he wasn't drunk, and paid particular attention to his shoes. She barely bothered to check Maria, and then motioned them in with a tilt of her head. Sterling paid for Maria and himself at the counter – the £30 for wrist stamps causing him to blanch – and then they were walking into the club.

'Did you see what that bouncer was reading, Frank?'

'He didn't seem to be reading at all.'

'You know what I mean. The book sticking out of his pocket.'

'Yeah, I know. And no, I didn't see what he was reading.'

'*The Ragged Trousered Philanthropists*,' she said excitedly. 'The original edition. You couldn't mistake it. You've got to admit that that's a bit surprising.'

Sterling shrugged.

'You've heard of it, right?'

'Of course. No need to patronise. The Socialists' Bible. Did I not tell you, or was it June Selsdon, that my father was of the one true faith? A book with some sense and huge dollops of sentimental treacle. I was force-fed it as a teenager. I don't think I ever finished the damn thing.'

He turned away, distracted, and too busy stoking up his hatred of The Lotus Blossom, which was the exact antithesis of anywhere he'd usually go for a decent night's entertainment, to fuss about a bouncer's reading choices. The loathing started with the music, dominated by an insistent thumping bass. Then he and Maria entered the garish club itself. Sterling was accustomed to pub stone floors, solid wooden tables and benches, the quiet hum of music-free conversation and a calm overall ambience. Now he was assailed by the steel and vinyl décor, the shiny parquet floor, the pink and cardinal-coloured banquettes and booths, and the faux-Japanese wall coverings – lotus blossom (of course), storks, water gardens and the famous wave and Mount Fuji picture in the style he'd seen on greeting cards.

Next to him, Maria was looking around curiously, lacking the antipathy oozing from Sterling, and not entirely out of place. The only thing that was really distinguishing her from the female contingent was that she was showing less flesh.

'Where's the bar?' shouted Sterling.

Maria pointed over to the other side of the pulsating cavernous space, beyond the dance floor. They edged round, between the booths and the dancers, until Sterling found a space in the ruck and Maria hovered at the side. He was so used to the easy pace of the Cinq Ports he'd forgotten how to be pushy at the counter, how to use his elbows, squeeze into narrow spaces and catch the bartender's eye. Finally, more by luck than timing, everything fell into place at the same time.

A young man with shoulder-length brown hair, artfully cut in a kind of floppy, shaggy look and a full sleeve tattoo emerging from the top of his T-shirt down to his wrist, strode over. 'Yes, mate?'

'A Singapore Sling, and… what beer have you got on tap? Anything decent? Something local? Gadds? I can't see anything along here.'

The young man looked at him. It might have been pity. 'We've only got bottles, and only Japanese. Asahi and Sapporo. I'll do the cocktail and come back.' A minute or two later he did come back with Maria's cocktail. He waited, hands splayed on the bar on either side of the drink. The luxurious sleeve looked as if it had a Viking theme, bearded faces, horned helmets and square-rigged galleys.

'Asahi,' said Sterling. It was a toss-up. He'd barely heard of either.

'Jesus,' he said to Maria as they scoured the room for seats, 'the prices are making my eyes water.' All the booths were occupied. Eventually, they found a space at the end of a banquette occupied by a flamboyant bevy of young women in skimpy mini-dresses whose table was crowded with cocktail glasses and a couple of jugs. Thoroughly relaxed by the booze, they wriggled merrily along the bench to make room, a glittery caterpillar. One or two cast a crafty eye over Sterling and an appraising one over Maria. Women liked Sterling, he knew. He didn't know why, just that he couldn't hang on to them. These ones finished their assessment and switched their attention. Too old, Sterling reckoned about himself. He and Maria perched precariously and looked out onto the dance floor.

Neither spoke for ten minutes. They watched the bobbing, sky-pointing and swaying of the dancers and the manic movements of the DJ. Sterling felt the beginnings of a headache and a twinge of longing for the pubs of Sandley. An effort of rapprochement with Angela, Mike and Becky might be a good idea, sooner rather than later before the estrangement solidified. He hated eating humble pie but wanted to be comfortable in the pub again. He'd pay off the tab with some of the earnings from this case. And he might need their practical help at some point.

He turned to Maria. 'I didn't have you down for a cocktail drinker. I didn't think socialists drank cocktails. Singapore Sling. Classy.'

'Blending in, Frank. Waiting for the shaking-things-loose strategy to work. I don't think it's going to at this rate.'

'Early days.'

As he spoke, a slender young man with carroty hair and a narrow face, turned out in jeans and quilted powder blue jacket passed by the booth on the way to the bar. As he passed Sterling and Maria's perch, his glance caught Sterling's. Each man's brow furrowed in ephemeral recognition, and then the man moved on.

A few moments later (no waiting at the bar for him) he returned with drinks the way he came, and while Sterling was engrossed in conversation with Maria, had another discreet look before going on his way.

'Cheers, Mac,' said the girl to the carroty-haired man as she sipped her Sidecar. He'd got her from Jack Hankinson's CanterburySugar website – £150 per night for escorting, extra if there was... extra. Which, with him, wouldn't take long anyway. She was dark and sultry, and not that keen on her date, although he was keen enough on her to keep coming back. It wasn't his narrow face, red hair and pale, blotchy skin but his personality – self-absorbed, insensitive, and without a sentence of decent conversation.

'Wait here,' he said. 'I've got to go upstairs and see Charlotte Hankinson.'

Not 'Can you excuse me for a second, Abi? So sorry,' thought the girl. *What an arsehole.* She sipped her cocktail. *Still, this is good.* She was a medievalist at the university in the city. She looked up at him. 'Off to pay homage then. Do a bit of swearing fealty?'

'What are you talking about?' said Mac. His formal education had to all intents and purposes ended at fourteen and a half, when he stopped attending a Wythenshawe comprehensive in Manchester.

'Nothing.' She looked back to her drink.

He stared down at the parting in her black hair. He knew he'd been taunted but not how.

He weaved his way around the dance floor towards the stairs up to the first floor. He'd intended to stay downstairs out of Charlotte Hankinson's way after his clumsy and ill-judged attempt at a challenge that afternoon, but as he'd set the girl's drink down, enlightenment had come to him. The bloke in the booth was the snoop who'd royally messed up all the scams at the college on the coast, where Mac had been a gardener, with some drug-dealing and *'security'* on the side. What a fuck-up that business had been after all the promise. Still, he hadn't done badly out of it. Some cash. Opportunities here in Canterbury. But that snoop – what was his name? Sterling – was dangerous. If it hadn't been for him…

Downstairs at The Lotus Blossom was ukiyo-e. Upstairs was manga, cartoons and animations covering the walls, with the same Japanese script at the top and centre of each wall. At the stairs, Mac didn't even need to look around. Charlotte Hankinson was in her usual place in one of the exclusive booths just to the left of the upstairs bar, a solitary half-full flute of champagne directly in front of her. If Mac had any shred of sympathetic feeling, he might have believed that she seemed lonely among the throbbing noise and heaving throng. He walked over, feeling exposed as she spotted him and fixed him with a cold stare.

'You've got a nerve,' she said, 'after this afternoon.'

'Why? I was just trying to get a handle on the new arrangements.'

'"The new arrangements",' she mimicked, her face twisted in an ugly sneer. 'Seeing if you could take over, more like. You'd better watch your back, Mac, until you can show you're still reliable. I could line up one or two people to take over what you do.'

'No one's indispensable, Charlotte, not even you. You might be running things now, but you'll soon find out who your friends are if things start to go wrong.' In a quick insight, he realised that now he knew what little Abi downstairs was talking about, what those words meant. In his rough Manchester upbringing, he understood more about dogs. But she was wrong. He hadn't come up here to grovel. This was alpha dog business.

Hankinson sipped her champagne and said nothing. She hadn't invited him to sit down. It suited her to keep him standing there.

'Since you're... still in charge then,' said Mac, irony unmistakeably evident in his tone, 'there's another thing. There's a private investigator downstairs, with a girl.'

'So? He paid to get in. They've got drinks presumably. All sorts come here, as you well know.'

'Yes, but when I was over in Earlsey, before I came to Canterbury, there was a big racket at the college. I did one or two... extra things while I was working there – security and stuff. The college got this snoop in and basically, the whole thing collapsed. There was mayhem, and he was at the bottom of it. You must have read about it. It was all over the *Gazette*. As he's here, he could well be sniffing around.'

'Of course I read about it.' (She had known about it too, though there was no profit in telling that to Mac. There had even been talk of a link-up, and it was fortunate that nothing had come of Jack's overtures when the balloon had gone up). 'Leave it with me,' she said. She turned away, looking out into the dance floor.

Mac fumed. He was a naughty boy who had been dismissed.

When he'd disappeared back down the stairs to the ground floor, she reached into her handbag for her phone.

'Get Fridge up here,' she said. 'Straight away.'

Chapter 15

The clubbers upstairs parted like the Red Sea for the Israelites as the Fridge lumbered along the shortest possible route from the stairs to the booth. He stood in front of the woman with his hands clasped across his midriff.

'There's a couple here – a slightly older man, late thirties – and a girl, probably early twenties, sitting in the same booth as me but downstairs. I want you to check with Mac that they are the ones he's just talked to me about, get a few good still pictures of them from off the CCTV, and then give them to Jimmy. Tell Jimmy to get to see if they're the same couple his man saw in the Martyrs Field Memorial Garden earlier today and get back to me. Got it?'

The big man nodded and moved off in his curious, unique mixture of lope and shamble. Hankinson drained her drink and only had to wait a second or two before the bartender, a clone of the one serving downstairs, looked over. *Another*, said her eyebrow and slightly raised flute. After that, it would be time to do her rounds, make sure everyone was having a good time and, more importantly, spending money. It would also be time to check out the PI and the girl, and assess if they were threats.

After ten minutes, she stood up, surreptitiously running her hands down her thighs, ensuring that the short dress covered her as it should, and at the same time giving herself a shot of confidence in front of the punters, knowing that her figure was perfect. Tonight, she'd re-plaited her chestnut hair in a single braid down her back, accentuating her smooth, oval face. She'd been careful with the champagne so that there was no hint of a wobble as she set off on her silver stilettos. The dress, of a sophisticated, sequinned material with long sleeves and a plunging neckline that made every other one in the venue look cheap and tawdry, shimmered as she moved to the stairs, smiling and nodding to individuals and couples as she went, occasionally exchanging a word. But the silvery outfit, the smile that did not extend to her eyes and the willowy sway on sharply tapered heels, created the uncanny effect of a tall ice queen gliding through her domain.

Don't stumble on these damned heels, she muttered. *Keep your back straight. You're not vulnerable. You're not lonely. Keep people at a distance and keep them guessing. And don't let that idiot Mac's threats affect you.*

Downstairs, she paused and surveyed the room from banquettes and booths to dance floor and back again. She saw Mac with that dark little trollop again, wondering what he saw in her, and made brief eye contact. Then she spotted the PI and the girl. It wasn't difficult because the girl, although stylishly turned out, perched prim and aloof on her seat while the PI looked just plain disgruntled. He was older than the usual crowd too. Working the room, she gradually made her way over to their booth.

'Alright, girls?' she half-shouted to the group with the cocktail jug who had made space for Sterling and Maria at the end.

'Great, thanks, Charlotte.' They raised their glasses and gave out a ragged, giggly cheer.

She loomed over Sterling, a dark, glimmering presence with the disco lights and flashing strobes obscuring her face and establishing control of the exchange, exactly as she intended. 'Are you having a good time? I haven't seen you here before.' Her voice remained loud but was more focused. The cocktail girls returned to their chatter.

'Haven't been before,' said Sterling, squinting upwards.

'Well, it's my place. Charlotte Hankinson.'

'Charlotte Ha– Wasn't it your husb–?'

'Yes. Gutting. But if I don't keep busy, I'm going to go mad.'

Sterling stood up and moved to the side so that the woman was not framed by the light. Her perfect face, unlined throat and glittering dress came into clearer, breath-taking focus. She was still half a head taller but the crick in Sterling's neck disappeared and he felt less at a disadvantage. He put his hands in his pockets, not knowing what else to do with them. He did not recognise her scent but knew it was expensive, in contrast to the Tommy Girl, or similar, wafting from the booth. Maria had suddenly been excised from the exchange.

He paused. 'It must be a difficult time.'

'Of course. If you don't mind, I'd prefer not to talk about it. I wasn't really expecting anyone to raise it in here. Generally, people are more concerned with having a good time. More interesting for me is why you're here.

If you don't mind my saying so, you're a fish out of water, and I could tell that from the other side of the floor.'

'Yes, well, the pub is more my natural habitat, but Maria, my niece, is doing some research for uni on student behaviour, so I said I'd fund this evening for her birthday.'

Charlotte Hankinson looked coolly down at the girl and then back to Sterling. 'I see,' she smiled. Her face was amused and mocking, and Sterling was glad of the ambience to hide his blush.

'Right, well, Uncle Frank,' said Maria – her face too was a mixture of amused and mocking – 'I'm off to powder my nose and do a bit of participant observation in the Ladies. You can have my seat if you want, Mrs Hankinson.'

Sterling and Charlotte Hankinson watched Maria weave her way across the dance floor. 'I hope your niece is really going to powder her nose and not... powder her nose, as it were. This club's clean and drug-free, and I certainly want to keep it like that.'

'She's a good girl, Mrs Hankinson. No worries on that score. She's offered you her seat. Shall we?'

'Good idea. To be honest, I'm fond of these heels but they're killing me.' As they sat down, Charlotte Hankinson smoothed down her dress and let a slender thigh touch Sterling's knee. He looked at his bottle. There was a mouthful left at the bottom. He drained it.

'Drink, Mrs Hankinson? I'm getting another beer.'

'*Charlotte*, please. Champagne for me. May I call you "Frank"? I noticed that's what your niece called you.'

'Sure.'

'And, Frank, it's all on the house. Just tell the barman it's for me.'

*

Maria didn't go to the Ladies. Instead, she negotiated the stairs and the heaving downstairs dance floor, against the general flow of the human traffic, and made for the exit. Outside, she had no trouble spotting the person she'd come to track down. He was leaning on the nightclub wall away from the queue, one leg bent and the sole of his boot flat on the brickwork, clearly having a break. In one giant hand, between thumb and forefinger, was a roll-up. In the other was the battered and dog-eared book Maria had spotted earlier, thumb between two open pages. A floodlight over the entrance provided enough light for reading.

'How are you finding it?' said Maria.

'What?' said the giant, looking up and only then seeming to realise where he was.

'How are you finding it – the book?'

The man's eyes looked back down at it in his hand, as if it had been magicked there. 'Yeah, it's alright. It makes sense.' He glanced at Maria. His experience of girls was that they spoke to him only when they wanted some advantage he might be able to supply. He was used to the false charm and flirting, and his petty position of power didn't affect him. For the girls, he was generally nothing more than a gatekeeper, and he knew it. This was different.

'Where have you got to?'

'Rushton's being an arseh… being a bastard, trying to catch the blokes slacking. The blokes are laughing at Owen's ideas.'

'Well, that happens more than once,' laughed Maria, 'but I get the picture. I'm Maria Goodburn.' She held out her hand.

The big man looked down on it. What was going on? A girl was talking to him about a book she'd clearly read, on a Saturday night outside the club.

She propelled her hand forward and nodded at it.

'Fridge,' he muttered. The girl's hand was cool and preposterously tiny in his huge paw.

'Nice to meet you, Mr Fridge.'

'No, that's my nickname. My real name's Smith.'

'Mr Smith, then.'

'Jason,' he said gruffly. Nobody had called him that for a long time.

With the ice broken, the unlikely duo conversed until the Fridge's break was over. They swapped phone numbers. Maria had hinted at her assignment.

'I'll let you know if I hear anything,' the big man had said, surprised at his openness, surprised at the whole turn of events.

'We'll continue our conversation soon,' said Maria, 'when I'm not so busy. I'll be in touch.' She looked around her dismissively – taking in the jostling queue, the lights flashing from the nightclub windows, the bass notes beating out, the mixture of scents and cruder smells. 'There's more to life than this.'

*

It was still warm when Sterling and Maria left the club just short of 10.30. The last bus to Sandley had gone two hours ago, but there was a 10.50 Triangle bus to Whitstable. After he'd seen Maria onto that, Sterling was going to take a taxi home – ‘On the clock,’ he said, to pre-empt a comment from the girl.

The street was busy. People came in and out of the twenty-four-hour supermarket on the other side. A homeless man in an anorak and beanie despite the warm summer, with a large holdall strapped over his shoulder and a long black umbrella, wandered towards the centre. Sterling had seen him before, often, when he’d had business in the city. Had it not been for Sterling’s own parlous finances, he’d have found him a note.

Groups of young men in T-shirts milled about outside the cinema and the Subway place, one or two breaking away to chat to girls also leaving The Lotus Blossom. Sterling watched a slender, good-looking boy with rich, gold-blond curly hair, a youthful Art Garfunkel, cadge a cigarette from a girl, flirting good-humouredly and making her laugh.

A police van cruised slowly by, its wire drop-down shield raised over the roof. Tonight there wasn’t even a simmer, but Sterling from experience knew things could boil up rapidly.

‘Where did you get to when I was talking to Charlotte Hankinson, Maria? I was drowning in there.’

‘Drowning? It didn’t look like it to me. It looked as though you were suddenly having a great time after all the moaning earlier. An intimate tête-à-tête with the club owner.’

‘Fraternisation is part of the job, Maria. One of the techniques for shaking things loose.’

The girl nodded. ‘Yeah, yeah. And that mini-dress and those long, slender legs in micro-fine tights, and those 12” long stilettos made no difference, I don’t suppose.’

Sterling bridled. 'You're getting too big for your boots. I don't need it.' But she was right. He was flattered. He was like almost all men. If an attractive woman showed an interest, he stopped thinking with his head. 'She implied that she wasn't that close to her husband anymore and that they were leading separate lives. She didn't seem to like him much, to be honest. Interesting, considering he's been bumped off. And she wasn't the cold fish you'd expect when we started talking. But enough about Charlotte Hankinson. What about my question? Where did you get to?'

'I went outside. I was really struggling in there – the noise, the pointlessness. I had a chat with Fridge.'

'Fridge? Who's Fridge?'

'The bouncer. The big bloke on the door who was reading *The Ragged Trousered Philanthropists*. We got on well. He's not as far along on his political journey as me, but I think he might join the Party. I got his phone number, and I'll send him an application form.'

'The politico never rests, eh? In the nineteenth century, you'd have been a missionary.'

'Never. Religion is the opium of the masses.'

They were through the underpass and rounded the corner into the bus station, passing the boarded-up Lost Lamb coffee kiosk standing just as forlorn as the sculpture three metres away. Maria joined the queue for her bus.

'You were right, Maria,' said Sterling. 'We're on a case. We – I – shouldn't be diverted, especially by the wife of the victim we're looking into. It takes another woman to point out a problem like that. She might have got more from me than the other way round. It wasn't an accident that she came over or my amazing charisma.

We were spotted, or I was. There was a bloke there who I had dealings with in another case, a very dodgy character. We looked at each other soon after you and I came in, and it took me a while to place him. I noticed him exchange glances with Charlotte Hankinson as she came down the stairs. So we might have shaken something loose.'

It was Maria's turn to board. She smiled, almost a beam. 'I'm glad I was helpful – Uncle Frank.'

*

Upstairs at The Lotus Blossom, Charlotte Hankinson sat alone in her booth, an invisible cold force field around her as people kept their distance. She ran a finger around the edge of her flute. She was pretty sure that Jimmy Jarvis's man at Martyrs Field would confirm that it was Sterling and the girl he'd seen talking to the Wray woman, when he saw the photos. *That guff about the girl being his niece and doing field work in a disco. He stuck to it, even though he knew I knew it was rubbish. At least he'd admitted that he was a private investigator. What about the girl? Maybe I'll have someone do some research on her. What was it Jack used to say – something out of The Godfather – 'Keep your friends close but your enemies closer.' Good advice. The trouble is I liked old Uncle Frank. He was good company in a grumpy kind of way. He could see something of the real me, beyond the façade, beyond the reputation. Like sly old Jimmy. Probably like that police sergeant earlier. Interesting. And certainly not like the idiots I mostly mix with. The thing is – what could he be – friend or enemy?*

Chapter 16

DCI Nolan's eyes were red through lack of sleep. Ants crawled across his scalp in an unceasing, relentless march the medication seemed to be doing nothing to alleviate. Now, on Sunday morning, one of the reasons for his discomfort – Detective Chief Superintendent Joe Peabody – was emerging from his Jaguar in the car park below.

From his window on the first floor, Nolan watched the stocky, solid, bullet-headed bruiser make his way to the back entrance of the station. He was fumbling in his pocket for his warrant card as he went. Nolan regretted the temporary withdrawal of Mamujee as Officer in Overall Command of the investigation, since he was supportive as well as demanding. Peabody, Mamujee's replacement, was a desk-thumper and thrived on discord.

Nolan turned away from the window and pinched the bridge of his nose. His left eye was itching, along with his scalp. He wouldn't swear to it, but it looked as though he was also going to have to attend to a burst of rosacea on his cheeks.

'CS Peabody is here, guv,' said Murphy with his head in its customary position in this kind of circumstance, halfway up between door and jamb.

'Yes, I saw.' Nolan sat behind his desk. At least it was tidy. There might be no progress, but it was properly organised no progress.

Peabody was courteous enough to knock before he entered. He offered a stubby hand as Nolan rose to his feet. 'Andy,' he said.

'Guv,' replied Nolan.

Peabody wasn't going to waste time. Perhaps he was going on after this meeting for a round of golf over at North Foreland after driving down from Maidstone.

'ACC Mamujee updated me yesterday evening. You've still got nothing as of this morning?'

'Some promising lines of enquiry, sir–'

'Don't bullshit me. I can't be doing with it. Let's see now. Mamujee was generous with what he authorised. So far you've got a team of twenty, beavering away on this and that, round the clock presumably. And, to emphasise the point again, you've still got nothing. Am I right?'

Nolan was good at police politics, but sometimes his patience frayed. 'Twenty-two, sir, in the team. That's including the canteen manager, who's doing some overtime for us. And we've got off to a good start.'

Peabody had come up the hard way from pounding the beat in Gravesend and Gillingham – no fast-track graduate entry for him. He was an effective, shrewd and profane officer who lacked subtlety himself and could not sense it in others. His eyes narrowed. 'Are you winding me up?

'Of course not, guv,' said Nolan. *Of course I am*, he thought.

'So the canteen manager is doing overtime,' said Peabody. 'God give me strength. Right, listen up,

Detective Chief Inspector Nolan. I want a daily summary from you, progress or not, and I'll damn well move you out and get someone else in if you don't crack on. This isn't some itinerant vagrant bumped off in a drunken quarrel over a six-pack. It's high profile. The force's credibility is crucial. And it's a city councillor for Chrissake.'

'All noted, sir. I and my team are putting in our very best efforts.'

'You've got three days. Then I… review.'

After the meeting, Nolan watched from his window as the chief superintendent got back into his car. The officer in overall command looked up, as Nolan had expected, as he opened the car door and manoeuvred himself to get behind the wheel. Nolan put up his right hand in acknowledgement, but his gesture was not returned. He knew Peabody was ruthless – 'my way or the highway'; 'shape up or ship out' – and he wasn't one to make idle threats.

Nolan went back to his desk, painfully aware of another layer of pressure. He scratched his itchy scalp. The trouble was, Peabody was right. All those resources and so far, so little reward. He was wrong about the victim though. It wouldn't have mattered if it had been a homeless person and not a councillor. He would still have needed a full investigation and justice.

Nolan went to the door and stuck his head out. 'Is there any chance of a cup of coffee, Sophie?'

He and his team were all doing the right things, and surely they'd catch a break soon. There was something crucial about the location of the murder – something that everyone was missing. It was worth another mental review. *We know how Hankinson got there, but what about the offender? And presumably the offender blended into all the other foot traffic on the path after the deed. Perhaps he (or less likely she) chose the rendezvous because he lived in the student village – but wasn't that too close and risky? It's clear that Hankinson was lured and ambushed there rather than choosing the spot himself. If there was an ambush, then there was planning, which made the site less random, or not random at all.*

There was no eureka moment.

He put his head around the door again. 'Bill, have you got a moment?'

'Alright, guv?' said Murphy as he closed the door and sat down. 'Was the Peanut his usual truculent self?' The nickname was inevitable, given the CS's surname and shaven, smooth, wonky shaped head.

'I expect you heard, mate.' Nolan smiled thinly. 'Mamujee would have been much better if he'd carried on. Still, we all have our crosses to bear. Moving on, how are you progressing with our, ahem, Covert Human Intelligence Sources?'

'The narks squad,' said Murphy. 'Pfft.' His lip curled. 'The short answer is "not very much". It's gone very quiet out there. It's like our house-to-house lad said, out there in the community is… fear. I'll keep liaising, of course. The trouble is that what with staff cuts and so many fewer of us, we've lost our connection with the populace, and the problem is then magnified in a case like this.'

'Very glass half-empty, mate, and not really what I want to hear.'

'Sorry again, guv. Something will happen. We'll get a breakthrough. It always happens at some stage.' The words were upbeat, but the tone forced. 'I'll get back to it then.'

Nolan rocked back in his chair and waved as his deputy mooched out. His interview with the Peanut and then Murphy's poorly concealed pessimism had made him gloomy. But something else, interestingly, if he reflected on it, was bothering him more. He'd described and discussed his row with Frank Sterling with his wife Jane the night before. As usual, she'd been surprisingly protective of Frank while supporting her husband. 'You know he's a hothead, Andy. You know his flaws. You know his problems with women, poor bloke. But his heart's in the right place. I know you're doing everything right on this case, but a discreet little link-up on the side to a small guerrilla operation, aka Frank, might be helpful. An irregular, as it were, can do things you and your team can't. And he's your pal, *our* pal. A rift would be a pity.' She had smiled – a sly, knowing look. 'And he's got a decent success rate, I'd say.'

He clicked back to the present. The friendship was important, too important to jettison, and Frank did have the knack of making things happen. But there was a downside, a big one. Nolan was thinking of bulls and china shops.

Chapter 17

This time, Maria was waiting for Sterling at the Sandley bus bay at the bus station. It was a balmy evening, and Sterling had enjoyed the ride over. He and Maria strolled down the wide alley between the shops of the Whitefriars centre, turned right and then round to the left into the high street. Being Monday evening, the city centre was relatively quiet, and being warm and light, there were homeless people here who had not yet packed up, including a small group outside McDonald's. Office and shop workers, hanging on after work for a leisurely drink or coffee, were now moving off to the car parks, the bus station or to the trains. A young woman was speaking intensely into a mobile, pacing up and down a short imaginary line.

Maria was in black skinny jeans for the meeting, having abandoned her usual mini-skirt, and a white T-shirt with the slogan 'The Diggers or True Levellers' atop a picture of men and women dressed in the puritan style scurrying around in a rural scene – all in red. A faded blue denim jacket was slung casually over her shoulder, her finger in the tab.

'How are you getting on with Logan Seymour?' said Sterling.

'I had a long search yesterday, but I've found nothing yet on social media – Facebook, Instagram and so on – nothing that fits anyway. The trouble is, the name is quite common. Nothing in Directory Enquiries… I'll keep trying, but he's a man of mystery. What about that bloke you said you saw at The Lotus Blossom – the one from an earlier case?'

'Same as you, a dead end. It didn't help that I could only remember that he was called Mac. I don't think I ever knew any more than that. And that he was dodgy. I'll do some more asking around.'

'I'll keep looking too. About tonight… Do you want to see the agenda?' said Maria, offering her phone.

'Not really,' said Sterling. He felt resentment towards June Selsdon. He hated meetings and now he was going to a Labour Party one. What was it? All Members? What did that mean? He didn't care. Of course, there'd be business to conduct in the pub afterwards, but this peculiar condition of engagement – membership of and involvement in the Labour Party, no matter how temporary – irked him. It might be useful for the case, but probably only marginally so. He'd certainly be putting attendance, travel time, travel cost, drinks cost, everything in fact, on his makeshift timesheet. If he was going to be tortured, he might as well get paid for it.

It occurred to him how the situation highlighted the differences between him and his father, who thrived on discourse and could have been out every evening of the week. It was peculiar how role and age were reversed between the two of them. Sterling, the youngster, was the one who was sceptical of politics and pessimistic, or more accurately indifferent, about the possibility of radical change, whereas his father, older, highly experienced, was the optimistic idealist. Maria would have got on well with him, Sterling thought morosely.

Something else was odd. He often thought about his dead father and their life together, but since this latest enterprise had started, he'd also been thinking about his mother. He knew nothing about her, and up till now, out of respect for the parent who had put in the full shift of raising him, he'd trained himself to avoid the subject. If she was still alive, and if she'd wanted to, she'd have tracked him down and made contact by now. She wouldn't be that old. If she had another family, and he decided to contact her, she might not appreciate it. It was best all round to let sleeping dogs lie, and it wasn't as if it was an issue that gnawed at him.

'OK,' said Maria. 'No agenda, and no progress.'

'No.' Sterling was still preoccupied, thinking about his parents, and then suddenly about the ordeal ahead.

'So... what's–'

'What's the plan, what's the plan, what's the bleeding plan? I don't know, Maria. Sometimes nothing is obvious and nothing shakes loose. We'll go to the pub afterwards, and I'll ask around about Hankinson.'

'Good to know, Frank,' said Maria coolly, 'but actually, I wasn't going to ask about the plan. We've been together a few days. I've got an idea about how you work – how *randomly* you work. I was going to ask about the meeting.'

'What about it?' Sterling vowed to himself not to say sorry, in line with current practice. He hadn't wanted the girl around in the first place.

'Doesn't matter. Wasn't important.'

Sterling shrugged. They turned right into Mercery Lane, walking adjacent to the long Debenhams storefront down the quaint, narrow alley into the Butter Market. Directly in front of them were the cathedral gates, gargoyles on the stone ledge above scowling down at all they surveyed, including the war memorial on the right. Even at this time and on this day of the week, tourists milled around taking selfies and clogging the thoroughfare.

On the corner of Sun Street, Sterling and Maria passed between The Moon under Water pub and the hippy shop on the other side of the road. A group of men in the pub were lined up on bar stools, looking out. Catching the leering gaze of a wiry, compact man much smaller than the men around him, but still unmistakably the pack leader, Maria, the bold feminist, stared back. The man's ogling didn't waver. Uneasy, and unused to such brazenness, Maria was saved by her natural progress out of his eyeline.

With the Marlowe Theatre bathing the whole scene in mellow neon blue, orange and green light, she guided Sterling to the right and into the grounds of the Friends Meeting House, situated just before the small bridge over one of the Stour's tributaries winding through the city to meet the others downstream.

This was a long way from Party and Trades Council meetings at the dingy Thanet East Labour Club in Ramsgate High Street, where Sterling had drunk lemonade, topped up with a splash of lager accompanied by a nod and wink from Felix the volunteer barman. Sitting at the back and doing his homework when his father couldn't get a babysitter was just about par for the course, whichever of the Kent coastal towns they happened to be living in at the time.

He and Maria joined the queue at the door, Maria with her red membership card in her hand. She was nodding and saying 'hello' to legions of people, knowing all and known by them. She was popular, Sterling could tell, and the goodwill around her transferred partly to him. The young man with a curly mop of hair, gentle eyes and gangly hands recording numbers at the little folding table smiled warmly when he looked up. 'Hi, Maria. Alright? Good to see you.'

'Hi, Mark. This is Frank Sterling. He's just joined so he's not got a membership card. He's an observer really, for this meeting, till the card comes through.'

'Noted,' said the young man. 'Welcome, Frank. Make sure you don't vote when the motions come up,' he said jokily.

'Nothing would be further from my mind,' said Sterling.

'He means it,' smiled Maria.

The two of them passed from the lobby into the main meeting room. Having settled Sterling midway to the back and to the left of the officers' table, Maria told him to make sure to save her seat and said she needed to talk to some people.

Sterling looked around the room. The attendance profile was more middle class and less rough-edged than the meetings and rallies he remembered from the coast, where blokes (and it was predominantly blokes) smoked roll-ups and drank Guinness. There was no dense blue fug in this meeting either. The reek of cigarette smoke on his clothes when he was a kid used to last right into school the next day. He supposed that here many attendees had connections with the universities, colleges and schools, or had had them in the past. There were other things. Although there were plenty of youngsters and students like Maria in clusters around the room, they were outnumbered by the oldsters and retirees.

And where were the BAME members? This was a predominantly white British meeting.

Still, none of this was Sterling's business. When Maria came back to take her seat, he leaned into her and whispered, 'Who should I be talking to about Hankinson?'

'I've already thought about that. It's what I was fixing just now. The leader of the Labour Group on the City Council is one. That man standing over there, Mick Masters.' She pointed with her head. 'And there's another man near the table at the front, Tom Spring, who hasn't got an official role but knows virtually everyone in the Party and all the goings-on. He does most of the campaigning stuff. I'll give you a little nudge when he gets up to speak so you know who he is. He's on the agenda. They'll be in the pub afterwards and ready to talk. There are others as well, and after a few drinks tongues will loosen.'

Sterling nodded. 'You're getting the hang of this PI business more and more, Maria.'

She smiled again and then turned to the front, where the constituency chair was bringing the meeting to order. It was just after 7.30.

At Ramsgate Labour Club, or equivalent venues in Deal and Dover, when Sterling had finished his homework, or what he was prepared to finish on any particular evening, he switched to listening in to the business. No one seemed to mind, and no one ever warned him about keeping his lip buttoned about confidential business. Here the pattern was the same: procedural wrangles, obscure motions, feuds.

At last, an hour and three-quarters later, the torment was over except for people jostling with dates for the diary and obscure bits of other business, each of which its advocate believed was the most important part of the meeting.

'Let's get going, Maria. As usual, I'm gagging for a pint,' said Sterling as he made for the door, ignoring the communitarian spirit that had attendees stacking and packing away their own chairs. He reckoned he'd earned exemption after the ordeal. He still couldn't fathom why June Selsdon had inflicted Labour Party membership on him.

People went in gaggles through the silent streets to the pub, the same one Sterling and Maria had been in on the way to the murder scene a few days previously.

As Sterling got in the drinks for himself and Maria, she assembled the councillor and the campaigns organiser at a small table overlooking the garden and the river. The pub's wide, low windows and warm lighting made the whole scene cheerful, a subtly different atmosphere from lunchtime but just as pleasant. Sterling turned from the bar as the barmaid ducked down to fetch a bottle for Maria's wine. 'Drinks for you gents?' he called.

'That's very kind,' said the campaigns man. 'A glass of red for me.'

'A pint of Spitfire, please,' said the councillor. 'Thanks.'

Sterling turned back to the bar and grimaced. *Spitfire. Yuk. Still, if it loosens a tongue.*

Maria did the introductions, and the four Labour Party members toasted at their small table. 'Victory,' said the councillor as they clinked. 'Victory,' everyone echoed.

Around them and at the bar, there was an increasing influx of people from the meeting. Two other servers appeared, obviously summoned to help with the sudden surge of business. Labour Party members spilled into the pub front and back, gathering at tables and in groups.

'Maria says you want to talk about Jack Hankinson then, Frank. There was plenty of chat about him before the meeting tonight, and I expect there'll be even more going on in here, but I guess this is as good a starting point as any.' Mick Masters took another pull of his beer. He was an open-faced, tall and slender man with a violinist's fingers clutching his pint.

The campaigns man, Tom Spring, who had a grey widow's peak, a goatee and a ruddy complexion, had already disposed of half his large glass of red. 'He was a shit,' he interjected vehemently. 'An absolute shit.'

'Well,' said Masters, 'I was trying to be a bit more diplomatic–'

'Fair play, Mick,' said Spring, 'but he's dead now so it doesn't matter. He was a shit, a turncoat who tossed the Labour Party aside and joined the enemy for personal gain. He could see he wasn't getting anything out of us, so he jumped ship. Next he's a Tory councillor for one of the village wards.'

'Personal gain?' said Sterling.

The two other men looked at each other. 'There was talk,' said Masters, backed up by council voting patterns, particularly the planning committee, which he made sure he served on. There are some big private housing developments around the city at the moment. With planning permission, the land earmarked became worth an absolute fortune. The Labour Group can't prove it, but we think that Hankinson was greasing deals, getting other councillors onside, fixing votes. And then getting kickbacks from the landowners, and kickbacks from the developers.'

'Not just that, either,' added Spring. 'Like any city, Canterbury has various thriving criminal enterprises. Unusually, Canterbury's are, or were till last Wednesday, probably controlled by a city councillor. I'm talking about drugs, maybe a brothel, protection. There's a pub not far from here called The Moon under Water. A group of blokes in there are said to be involved. Have you heard of "sugaring"?'

'Yep. We've talked to someone about it locally too. We know it's not just sugaring *per se*.'

'Add escorting, blackmail and extortion to the list. The police are hopeless,' said Spring. 'Mind you, since austerity started in 2010, they haven't had the numbers. They've lost it, actually. They have less idea than ever about what's going on here.'

'It wasn't just Hankinson, Tom,' said Masters. 'What about his wife? Some people say it was she who wore the trousers. I expect she's definitely wearing them now.'

It couldn't be an improvement on last night, thought Sterling. 'We met her yesterday when we were poking around at her club. I was wondering about her.' He ignored Maria's look. *Wondering,* it said, *but not about her criminal proclivities*. 'So who do you reckon bumped him off?'

Both men shrugged. 'There are loads of candidates,' said Spring. 'As I said, he was a shit.'

Sterling paused, but he couldn't find a subtle way to say it. 'Anyone from the Labour Party?'

Masters laughed. He looked around the pub and the knots of people standing and seated. 'There are words and there are deeds, Frank. Which do you think this lot are good at? Everyone in the constituency party was fed up when Hankinson crossed. People waxed lyrical about the wickedness of it. But that's all they did. I reckon you need to look elsewhere – in the criminal enterprises.'

Spring nodded his agreement. 'I wouldn't recommend The Moon under Water though. If you went asking around in there, it could well turn nasty. I know a young man who works for Deliveroo – an asylum seeker from Cameroon – my wife and I support him through one of the asylum charities – Sunday dinners and suchlike. He might know something or someone because he gets about on his bike and works, shall we say, at the sharp end of the local economy. He's a good lad, well brought up, decent set of principles. Trained as an engineer in fact. He could at least point you in the right direction. You'd need to be careful though – for yourself, but for him as well. Not only is there an atmosphere around the city, but his residency status is delicate, shall we say.'

'I'll set you up with one of the Tories as well if you like,' said Masters. 'They're not all bad. I've got someone in mind – One Nation Tory – one of the few left – Jerry French. He'd probably open up. Unusually for that lot, he hates corruption. Going back a bit – interesting that you met Charlotte Hankinson. It sounds as though you've been busy.' A beat went by. 'How did you find her?'

There was a commotion at the entrance to the pub.

'Billy,' people were calling out.

'Good to see you, mate.'

'Alright?'

There was a common movement among the groups and gaggles, a kind of leaning, like flowers straining up towards the sun and light. At Sterling's table, Maria sprang up, her delicate, squashed-up face transformed by a wide smile that Sterling had never seen before. The girl had a sense of humour and was bright, but there was always that sense of her holding back. Now she was animated and excited.

'Jenkins!' she called. 'Where the hell have you been?'

A tall and slender youth hove into view, glad-handing and nodding and smiling and back-patting as he went, like the most grizzled of politicians on the stump. Cheaply but stylishly dressed in skinny blue jeans and a fine flower-patterned cotton shirt, by the look of it from Top Shop, and sockless white and blue striped canvas yachting pumps, his tanned skin glowed, highlighting translucent blue eyes. His thick blond hair was unfashionably long, latter-day Keanu Reeves or Brad Pitt and sun-bleached, but the charisma that oozed from him rendered that irrelevant. In fact, he probably set trends rather than followed them.

'Goodburn! I could say exactly the same to you. It's the summer holidays, and you're nowhere near Whitstable beach.' He took both her hands in his, and they pressed cheeks. 'Mick, Tom,' he said, shaking each man's hand in turn and receiving their smiles. 'Sorry I couldn't get to the meeting. Work finished too late.' The young man seemed to make the whole atmosphere cheerful.

Sterling looked on with a complicated melange of emotions.

'Billy, this is Frank Sterling. He's the reason why I haven't been around the last couple of days.'

'Mr Sterling, good to meet you.' The young man hit exactly the right note of friendliness and formality. 'I expect Maria will tell me why in due course.'

He looked away to thank someone for the drink pressed into his hand – *Guinness, of course,* thought Sterling – and then back. He seemed to have another knack, making the person he was interacting with the most important in the whole world. 'I'd be glad to catch up later, but right now I'd better circulate.'

'I'll join you,' said Maria. She looked around the table. 'If that's not a problem, comrades?'

The three men made no protest, and she waltzed, yes, waltzed, merrily away. The hubbub increased as she and Billy Jenkins penetrated further towards the other end of the pub.

'Rising stars,' murmured Spring. 'We need the young ones to carry the torch. If they stay enthusiastic, they'll go far.' He took his gaze from the youngsters' regal progress and turned his attention back to Sterling. 'So you've joined the Party as well as investigating Hankinson. Quite a late decision – normally people do it between fifteen and twenty-five. What did you think of the meeting?'

While they had been talking, someone had replenished their drinks. Sterling had opted for an extra-strong pilsner of genuine Czech origin called Holy Mountain Three Fates. He felt the alcohol's strongly intoxicating and relaxing power, amplified by the cosy, comfortable pub and the agreeable company. At the same time he was unsettled, not so much because of the case but more because of the cumulative effect of various undercurrents that festered under the surface – rifts and fallings out. Something out of kilter in his interview with June Selsdon still lingered.

'It was a curate's egg,' he said. 'Mostly bad if I'm honest. Debates about the camping rights of travellers and legal rights of sex workers. And what was it – open selection of MPs versus jobs for life, subject to re-election by the actual electorate, of course. I mean, talk about how many angels can dance on the head of a pin. I'm not saying these issues are not important – they are, I guess – but the country and the world are going through vast, big changes and you were going down little cul-de-sacs.

'Most of the talking was done by old white blokes like you so the patriarchy is still going strong. I got the distinct impression more than once that a meeting had already taken place before that one. But not everyone was invited. There was a load of people clapping some speakers and stony silence for others. I don't get it. You're all on the same side. Why do you hate each other?'

Sterling looked into his clear, golden drink. Some people were mellow when they'd had one or two. He wasn't one of them. The pub had grown quieter, with a subtle change in atmosphere. People looked thoughtful, reflecting on what the outsider had said.

'Well, I asked,' said Spring ruefully.

'And got it right between the eyes,' laughed Masters.

'I said "curate's egg", didn't I?' said Sterling. 'There were good bits. The debate on housing for instance. The Green New Deal. That's the way to go, I expect. Anyway, what I think doesn't matter very much, and it won't make much difference.'

'It might. You make some good points. I'd just say with some of the more obscure things, we're in the vanguard, and they're symbolic of the need for a wider change of attitudes.'

Sterling pursed his lips and went quiet. He'd said his piece. He suspected that the cause of the outburst came not from the meeting but from the undercurrents. Then there was the heroic appearance of this Billy Jenkins. He was many things Sterling was not, including young and popular, and extremely pally with Maria. He shook his head at the irony. He hadn't wanted an assistant, but now his assistant had temporarily gone off, he'd become proprietorial.

He tipped down the rest of his pilsner. 'Gents,' he said, 'thanks for meeting me. I hope you won't take my rant too seriously.' He pointed to his glass. 'The drink talking.'

'Don't worry, mate,' said the councillor. 'A thick skin is essential in this party.'

'Good,' nodded Sterling. 'So, Tom, you'll put me in touch with that Cameroonian lad, and Mick, you'll do the same with that Tory councillor.'

The two men raised their glasses – goodbye and no hard feelings – and Sterling stood up. 'Right then, I'm off. I'll just catch up with Maria before I go.'

He wove his way through the press of Labour Party souls to find the girl. He couldn't see her, but he knew where she'd be so he headed towards the sun-bleached mane of hair. Billy Jenkins was telling a story, in which Billy himself seemed to be the butt of the joke. His large audience was rapt. Sterling touched Maria's shoulder. 'Maria, I'm off. Do you want me to walk you up to the bus station, or…?'

Maria dragged her eyes from the storyteller, unwilling to be distracted. 'You're off?' she echoed.

'Yes, do you want…'

'No, I've got a lift, thanks, Frank.'

'I thought you would have. Right, well, I'll see you.'

'See you, Frank.' She turned back to the group.

Dismissed, thought Sterling.

As Sterling made to leave, Billy Jenkins, consummate politician, met his eye and gestured a silent farewell, gaze and nod, without a pause in the anecdote. A swell of laughter followed Sterling out of the pub, the punchline delivered.

On the way to the cab rank, he cursed. He'd forgotten to ask for a receipt for the drinks.

Chapter 18

Charlotte Hankinson started. The telephone echoed tinnily through from the small decorative table of the large house. If it had been one of the burners, or her usual mobile telephone playing *Dancing on my own*, she wouldn't have blinked. But the landline… she wouldn't even be able to recite the number.

She walked through from the yellow-and-grey front room where she had received the two policeman – *what were their names again? Nolan and Murphy,* she thought absent-mindedly – and picked up.

'Hello?' she said tentatively, her natural caution accentuated by the current circumstances.

'Mrs Hankinson? Mrs Charlotte Hankinson?' The voice was soft and muffled, and Hankinson couldn't even tell if it was male or female. There was an odd, hard-to-recognise quality to the sound at the other end.

'Yes.' She felt the hairs prickle on the nape of her neck. She'd been expecting something, one way or the other. Here it was.

'Are you free to speak confidentially, Mrs Hankinson,' said the voice.

'Yes,' said the ice queen. She sensed danger, and it gave her voice a distant, detached quality. But her mind was racing, trying to pick up every nuance of the voice, its inflexions, and accent and where it was coming from.

'Good. Something has come unexpectedly into my possession that will be of great interest to you. A flash drive. Amazingly, not even password-protected.'

'Did you kill my Jack?'

'I'm thinking that we can come to a mutually beneficial arrangement,' said the voice. The speaker was cool and confident. 'Involving cash for goods.'

'My Jack. Was it you?' Charlotte Hankinson tried again but had never been an actor – her school reports had suggested coolness, detachment and, her mother reading between the lines, more than a hint of woodenness. She wondered if she'd managed to convey any plaintiveness or upset.

Clearly not. The voice continued imperturbably. 'If we can't, it would be very serious for your operation if the information I've come upon were to fall into... official hands.'

Hankinson dropped the pointless pretence. 'How can I trust you?'

'Well, it's going to be an effort, obviously, but I don't think you have much choice. But trust goes both ways. Let's start off with a kind of trial run.' As the voice spoke, there was a sudden 'pip, pip, pip' interruption and a clanking. Hankinson realised that the speaker was using a payphone and was putting in another coin. She hadn't received a call from one of these for years. '£10,000 in cash in a black plastic bag. Put it underneath the top, city-side bench in Greyfriars Garden in Canterbury the day after tomorrow. That's Wednesday evening at 20.45. Go in on the path off St Peter's Grove so you know you're in the right bit. You'll find a flash drive in a small black plastic bag under the bench. No one else will pick it up' – there was a short chuckle – 'it looks like the bags they use for dog shit. You only have a few minutes because the garden closes at 21.00. Just you, mind. We don't want any unpleasantness. As I say, a trial run. You won't get everything – just a sample to prove my good faith before we sort out what next.'

Hankinson was quiet, but in the end she knew there was no choice but to agree. She couldn't even plead that getting the cash so quickly would be difficult. The missing flash drive indicated exactly the opposite. There was silence at the other end of the line as Hankinson let everything sink in. 'Alright,' she said eventually. 'I've got all that.'

'Good,' said the voice, and then all Hankinson was left with was the dialling tone. She returned the phone to its cradle and went back to the sitting room, cocooning herself in the armchair and wrapping her arms around herself. She had to keep calm. Breathe. Think things through. Jack had been the gung-ho one, the risk-taker, insouciant in the face of threats and difficulties. The time he'd shoplifted in Marks and Spencer, just for a cheap couple of shirts, laughing in the street afterwards about her prissy attitude, as he'd called it. And that was only the first and most minor escapade. There had been a part of him, she knew, that hadn't really cared whether his criminal activities caught up with him or not. The thrills often seemed more important than the cash and comfortable lifestyle. She was the cautious one, the one who had been scared of getting a parking ticket in the early days, and now facing disgrace and prison.

This latest thing had to be nipped firmly in the bud.

She reached for a pen and notepad from the coffee table. *Think. Breathe.* Was this Jack's killer? Possibly.

Probably – unlikely that he, or even she – was a go-between. She wrote down the details of the transaction. £10,000 (she probably had that amount in the house). The garden. The time. The other arrangements. But it was weird. It felt old-fashioned. These days, gangs and scammers got up to their tricks on the internet – sextortion via indecent images and rash sex acts – and the kind of things that led on from Jack's Sugar website (she knew what Jack got up to without ever being interested in the details). Cash was old-fashioned. Even the means of communication, the pay phone, was old-fashioned. Wouldn't it be easier, and safer, for the blackmailer to do things via an online account and send the flash drive in the post?

Maybe not though – the bank transfer, anyway, would be problematic. She'd go online to her account, opt to 'pay someone new', enter account number and sort code, and then there'd be the name of the payee. If that wasn't correctly described, then she wouldn't be able to make the payment, while being warned at every stage about scams. If everything was correct, she'd be able to engage someone to track down the account holder's identity and other details.

Perhaps this old-fashioned way involving cash was better. Cash is anonymous. Perhaps the blackmailer didn't have a bank account or even a mobile, given that he'd used a payphone. So this was the best approach for him. Which gave her openings and possibilities. She reached for a burner phone down the side of the armchair. She waited for pick-up. 'Jimmy, I've got another job for you.'

After she'd explained, her enforcer replied, 'All noted. We'll be ready. And I've got some information for you. I showed that photo to my bloke, the one who was at the Martyrs keeping an eye on Janice Wray, and he's confirmed that it was the two you saw in the club. You've got their names. What do you want me to do? A bit of frightening maybe?'

Charlotte Hankinson, cradling the phone between her shoulder and her ear, went to the cabinet, poured a slugful of Rémy Martin XO and took a pull. 'I'll think about it. Stay ready.' She ended the call and tossed the burner aside, suddenly bone-weary. Too much was happening. It felt as if things were spinning out of control.

Bloody Jack, getting himself topped, probably lured along that river path by a piece of skirt or the promise of one. And no password on the flash drive. God. Things were not going well.

Chapter 19

Things had moved quickly for Sterling after the meeting the previous night. True to their word, the Labour people had put him in touch with the young Cameroonian asylum seeker, Patrick Ngono, and the Conservative city councillor, and he'd organised meetings.

Communication with the Anglophone Cameroonian had been all, 'Dear Mr Sterling... With best wishes, Patrick Ngono' and so 'Dear Mr Ngono... with best regards, Frank Sterling,' and seemed to increase in formality rather than abate as the exchange continued. Sterling deferred to the young man in the selection of rendezvous place and time, reassuring him about what he wanted, and checking that it was acceptable for Maria to be there too. He'd taken Tom Spring's warnings about Patrick's status seriously and knew he could not give him any reason for alarm.

Sterling got off the bus two stops after the university, just beyond the public school. He crossed the road and made his way to the bus stop on the other side, where Maria's bus was due in five minutes. Maria – Ms Reliable – stepped off the bus on the Canterbury side, and she and Frank set off, immediately comfortable in each other's company. Even what they were wearing chimed – a summer rose-patterned frock and sandals in

Maria's case and grey chinos and loose, light-blue linen shirt in Sterling's.

Sterling cocked his head over to the school. 'First to go, come the revolution, eh, Maria?'

She laughed. 'Not biting, Frank. It's a glorious morning and even I need a rest sometimes.' She put up a little parasol decorated with storks and bamboo in a far-eastern style and twirled it as she strolled along. 'If this is PI work, I'm going to have a think about it after I graduate.'

'You're in a good mood,' said Sterling.

'Yep,' she said.

'So…?'

Maria smiled and shrugged.

Just opposite the school entrance, they turned left down a track signposted The Crab and Winkle Way. 'Patrick said along here about 150 yards. Look out for the watching man – whatever he meant by that.'

'There,' said Maria, a few moments later.

'Whoa,' said Sterling. 'That gave me a jump.'

In front of them, on the very edge of the university's grounds to the right, was a building that looked as if it had once been an oast house. A man stood motionless at a window halfway up and to the side. As Sterling and Maria approached, man became dummy, and when they got to the front of the building, in the bottom window was a little notice that read 'Forensic Crime Scene Studies'.

'Someone's little joke,' murmured Maria.

'I'd have got even more of a start if we'd come up at night. Anyway, we're a bit early.'

A cyclist appeared suddenly, emerging from the leafiness beyond the cycle track and pulling up just short of Sterling and Maria. He was tall and slender, in loose-fitting blue jeans, red T-shirt, and battered green and white trainers, as if he'd picked the ill-matching ensemble blindfold from the racks of a charity shop. The bike was battered – an old tourer with drop handlebars in black and faded white, and no mudguards.

'Midday on Tuesday. The man in the window. You must be Patrick Ngono,' said Sterling.

The young man unhooked himself awkwardly from the large box-like contraption strapped to his back and dumped it on the ground beside him. His dark skin seemed to glow in the sunshine, either from his riding exertions or as a natural condition. He smiled, a small and shy effort perhaps at least partly explained by a badly chipped canine in an otherwise even, white set of teeth, and held out his hand. 'Yes. Mr Sterling and Ms Goodburn?'

'I think we can dispense with the formalities,' said Maria, unusually taking the lead. 'It's Frank and Maria.'

'OK... Frank and Maria. And, of course, I'm Patrick. I chose this spot because I come up here with pizza to Park Wood' – he indicated the low-rise student residences in the leafiness behind him – 'every Tuesday lunch time for a group of students in one of the residences. As you said you were coming by bus, I thought it would be good from that point of view too. Follow me. You probably saw that you passed the entrance to the community garden. We can go in there where it's quiet.'

Sterling picked up the large square food bag, waving away the Cameroonian's efforts to carry it himself as well as push the bike. In the garden, Patrick propped his bike against a post and flopped down on the only bench. 'Excuse me,' he said. 'It's been very busy this morning.'

'That's OK,' said Sterling. 'It's good of you to find the time. Obviously, you know that Tom Spring put us in touch with you.'

'Yes, Tom and Marjorie. Good people. Kind. I was in a very bad state when Room for Refugees set me up with them. Now I've got my own place. Not perfect but OK, and I still go round to them for dinner sometimes.'

'How come you're here in England, Patrick?' said Maria.

Sterling fell silent.

Patrick looked across at her. 'Well, as you can hear, English is my first language. I'm from a town called Kumbo in an English-speaking part of Cameroon in the central and western part of Africa. There are two mainly English-speaking regions – the Northwest and the Southwest. Everywhere else, the main language is French... Wait a moment, you're not here about my story. I think it's enough to say that it became dangerous for me in Cameroon because of the political situation, so my family urged me to leave to find a better life, and that's what I've tried to do.'

He smiled as he stole another sideways glance at Maria. 'You were lucky. I almost got going. We... displaced persons think a lot about our predicaments. We often have plenty of time to do it. And when we have an audience, it all pours out.'

Maria looked at Sterling. He sat quietly staring in front of him, concentrating. She could see no sign of impatience. 'We'd be very interested in your story, Patrick,' she said gravely.

'Well, there's plenty of it, but perhaps another time. Tom said you wanted to talk about the man who was murdered, Jack Hankinson, and that I might know something.'

'What can you tell us?'

'This is confidential? I couldn't say anything to Tom and Marjorie. My status here is fragile and saying something might cause difficulties. Tom knows a bit but not a quarter of it.'

'Yes,' said Sterling. 'Strictly confidential, as I said in my texts. We're not the police. It's a private investigation for someone in Whitstable. Anything you say is just between you, me and Maria. You and your name stay out of it, absolutely.'

Patrick nodded, reassured. 'Well, I see a lot on this job, delivering pizzas. This is rare – that I'm delivering during the day. Most of the time it's at night, and often very late at night.' He smiled wryly. 'People get very hungry after they've got... bladdered, I think you say, after a night of drinking. Not just drinking either. You know, there is terrible corruption in Cameroon. The government set up various bureaux to address it, but nothing has worked. I came here because of the language, but also because of England's reputation for honesty, freedom, democracy and human safety. So I've been amazed at the criminal goings-on here in the heart of the Church of England. Sorry, here I go again... Anyway, to get a little extra cash, but not by choice, I must deliver drugs with the pizzas. And I deliver not only to ordinary homes but to a brothel. I know also that the pizza shop I work for has to pay money not to be burnt down or vandalised. Protection money, I think you call it.

'I have a friend at the brothel – the one who usually comes to the door to collect what I bring – Lucija. We have had coffee in town when she is allowed out.'

'Allowed out?' said Maria. Her face darkened.

'The brothel-keeper allows the girls out in pairs once a week for shopping. They go to Ann Summers and Primark. A man called Fridge keeps an eye on them to stop them running off, but I think there is a soft heart somewhere in that big body. He lets them be themselves for a little while.'

Sterling and Maria exchanged more looks.

'Lucija knew Mr Hankinson very well. He went there to collect money, have a girl... look for blackmail opportunities. His favourite was Lucija's friend Nina. There was pillow talk. Nina is a clever girl and Mr Hankinson was proud and boastful, and reckless. There was talk of a record, on a memory stick, of all Mr Hankinson's business affairs, all the illegal ones. The girls up there in Westgate Close think that that is why he was murdered, for that information. Unfortunately, there is no shortage of... candidates who might have done it – people being blackmailed, people accepting bribes, people running drugs, people paying protection, people in competition...'

'Did the girls have anyone particular in mind?' asked Sterling.

'No. They just know some of the activities. You must understand, they have a very limited kind of life.'

'What about you?'

'You mean, did I do it?' Patrick's face was blank, and then he broke into a smile.

Sterling put his hand to his heart and mirrored the smile. 'Any theories?'

'Yes, I do have one or two. It could be Mac, or at least someone working for him. Mac's the one who manages the drugs. We don't see him very often. He's further up the ladder. But he's ambitious, because since the murder he's been trying to expand the drugs into other areas, and a takeaway pizza place had its window smashed. The rumour going around the riders is that he organised that. And then there's Jimmy Jarvis. He keeps us chickens in the coop. If there's any trouble or disagreement, he's there, with his thugs. Poor Lucija. She's his favourite.' Patrick looked around nervously. 'We riders always avoid The Moon under Water. But it's less likely to be Jimmy, because why? For him, everything was perfect just the way it was. He likes bashing and threatening. He doesn't want to run things.'

Sterling had a hunch. 'Does this Mac have red hair, like a carrot, and very pale skin? Thin. Sharp nose, narrow face?'

'And is Jimmy Jarvis a small wiry man with big-framed black glasses?' asked Maria.

'You are both magicians!' exclaimed Patrick, laughing now.

'Not really,' smiled Maria. 'We saw the man Mac on Saturday night in The Lotus Blossom. He and Frank recognised each other from one of Frank's earlier cases. A bit unfortunate. And we passed The Moon under Water on the way to a meeting yesterday evening. Jarvis – I'm sure it must have been him, you mentioning that pub – leered at me through the window. Shameless.'

'I didn't know that,' said Sterling.

Maria pursed her lips. 'You weren't paying attention. I didn't mention it because it happens too often to make anything of.'

Conversation died away from the odd trio. A warm breeze drifted through the garden. Patrick closed his eyes and lifted his face up towards the sun. Sterling stretched his legs out and looked out over the unruly layout and vegetation. He'd seen plenty of gardens like these, where progress occurred in fits and starts as new volunteers with new visions and hard work came in and then disappeared, in this case students graduating and moving away, he imagined. Allotments were the same. People often came with ambitions not matched by commitment. Now this garden was at the bottom of the development cycle, the vegetable section overgrown, the netting over the berry patch faded and torn, the little orchard in need of a good pruning, tendrils of brambles encroaching over the fence. But Patrick was right. It was calm and peaceful here.

Patrick opened his eyes. 'I've got to get going. I hope I've been of some help. Get back in touch if you need to.' But he lingered. 'Those girls, me – we're trapped. I'm not sure what's going to happen.'

Maria was about to speak, but Sterling put a hand on her arm. 'We'll have a think, Patrick. Thank you for your help. We really appreciate it.'

Patrick strapped on his big, square bag and wheeled his bike off. There was a slight buckle in the back wheel and the chain cranked as he disappeared out of sight and back to the city.

'We don't start making promises and commitments, Maria.'

'What makes you think I was going to do that?' she said hotly.

'Well, you were, weren't you? A bit of rescuing.'

Maria flushed. 'There's so much that's wrong. Why can't we try and do a bit of good where we can? You can be such a cold-hearted bastard, Frank.'

'I'm on a job. I can't get diverted. I've got a mortgage to pay. Bills. I can't afford to dilettante around in my summer holidays, kept by the bank of Mum and Dad.'

'Not fair, Frank. Not accurate either.'

Sterling shrugged. 'Next on the agenda is the Tory councillor. Are you coming or what?'

Chapter 20

Maria fell silently into step as she and Sterling walked back to the bus stop. Sterling had said his piece, a dribble of resentment oozing out of his consciousness. He couldn't tell if Maria was seething, sulky, or resentful in turn. She might even have accepted the rebuke. The girl was often hard to read, like a poker pro. They were silent at the bus stop and on the short bus journey. Conveniently, the councillor lived on the London Road near the church in St Dunstan's, on the same bus route back into the city.

Ten minutes after parting from Patrick Ngono, they were looking up at a large, gracious Georgian terraced house, its front door guarded by two small bonsai trees in pots.

'Pays to be a Tory,' murmured Sterling, as they tramped up the steps.

The bell pull transmitted a rolling, trilling tinkle through the house. Moments later, a short man kitted out in fawn slacks, open-necked white and mustard-yellow paisley cravat, appeared at the door.

'Frank Sterling? Maria Goodburn? Good. You know me, obviously, or you wouldn't be here.' He shook hands briskly and ushered them through the airy hallway into the bay-fronted room on the left. 'I call this the library. A bit of conceit at my age does no harm in my view.'

The bay window faced to the northwest, so there wouldn't be any sunshine until later on in the afternoon, but light still streamed into the room, and the volumes on the shelves all around, mostly dark, could not overcome the light ambience. There was an old rich-red chaise longue under one of the walls of shelves and Jerry French ushered the investigators to it, while he took a matching high-backed armchair.

'I lie on that to think, now that I've retired,' he said, 'and pretend I'm making progress with the novel I'm meant to be writing. This' – he pointed downwards – 'is the reality chair where I make myself recognise that I'm not getting very far. I'm prattling…'

Sterling put his hand up. 'It's fine. It's a nice room to… dream in.' He'd glanced at the shelves, recognising that he'd lighted on the economics section – Adam Smith and David Ricardo through to the more modern economists – Keynes and Friedman, and then philosophy – Plato, Aristotle, Locke, Kant and again through to the more moderns. The chaise longue was surprisingly comfortable, and he'd got the end with a bit of support to it. Jerry French's easy, welcoming manner relaxed him, but in the lair of a mortal enemy – a Tory – Maria sat straight-backed, awkward and stiff a foot away.

'Mick Masters said you wanted to talk to me about Jack Hankinson.'

'Yes, we've got a commission to investigate his death, and I guess this is part of the process of getting background.'

'Well, Mick vouched for you – decent chap for a Red – so I'll help as far as I can.'

Sterling sensed Maria bristling from the other end of the chaise longue and ignored it. 'I haven't really got any set questions. Just tell us what you know, and I might come back with something when you've finished. Do you mind if Maria takes notes?'

'Not at all. Do you need a pen or paper, young lady?'

Sterling put his hand over his mouth, leaned forward and looked at the highly patterned Persian rug at his feet – flowers and whorls in intricate patterns within a rectangular border, the background the same shade as the chaise longue and the chair. The main questions exercising him at that moment was whether French knew exactly what he was doing to rile Maria or was completely unaware, or even, improbably, if it was somewhere in between. He decided that French knew.

Maria reached into her bag. 'I'm fine, thank you, Mr French,' she said as she pulled out a notepad and a biro. The words were enunciated precisely and in themselves almost exaggeratedly polite. Sterling almost shivered as an even chillier atmosphere descended. There was something else. He felt a sense of masculine ganging up, akin to the female solidarity he'd been excluded from in the company of women, including Maria. Mingled with and reinforcing that was something hard to identify - he was sheepish. No, that was too weak. Ashamed. More feelings jostled. It felt good. It was payback.

Jerry French steepled his hands together, fingertips under his chin, elbows on the chair arms. Perhaps he was oblivious to the atmosphere he'd created. Sterling could not find confirmation for his original read.

'He started out a Red,' started French, '– sorry, that's pejorative I imagine – he started off *Labour*, but it became clear in full council and on the committees we both attended that he didn't have much in the way of political beliefs. He'd got in originally in Westgate, one of the city wards, but only by the skin of his teeth – about twenty-five votes. He switched to us and next election time got nominated and elected in one of the village wards, which have never been anything but Conservative, so he was onto a winner. From the start, he was much more interested in… business opportunities. We served together on the planning committee. Jack was a real glad-hander – what you'd call a networker these days I suppose. He knew everybody – both on the committee and anyone who came before it. He was always the life and soul of the proceedings, and they always went a particular way – his way.

'You know that there is a massive push for housebuilding in this area – on the hundreds of acres to the south of the city, on the plot around the hospital, in the area abutting Thanington Without. I believe in decent housing, and there is a great need for it, but not in an indiscriminate, loosely regulated way. But those planning meetings were always going the developers' way, and there was always a sense that the key decisions to grant permission had been sorted out before the council meeting took place. I'll never be able to prove it, but I'm pretty sure that Hankinson was getting cash from developers, and from landowners trying to get planning permission, and using it to influence decisions. I won't repeat it outside this room but I'm convinced he had councillors of all stripes on board. There's so much at stake. Farmland worth £50,000 at most could sell for £5 million with planning permission. Without him, maybe – fingers crossed – probity will return.'

'Mick Masters said something similar,' said Sterling. 'Hankinson never got you on board, then.'

French laughed. 'He never even tried. I suppose I've got a sort of reputation myself but in the opposite direction. The fact that I've had a successful business career insulated me from grubbiness.'

'So, any theories about who might have done the deed?'

'One or two. If you think about it, in those council and planning and developing circles, most people would have wanted to keep him alive. He was the one getting difficult decisions to go his and his allies' ways, undermining the council planning officers, nullifying protests and objections. But not everyone.'

Maria looked up, a sweetly innocent smile on her face. 'So, as one of those who objected to all that, you'd be quite a good candidate, wouldn't you, Mr French?'

'Touché, Miss Goodburn.' French laughed again, and Sterling couldn't resist a smile either. 'But I don't think my motive would be strong enough, and' – he looked around the room and out of the window – 'I've got too much to lose. Jack Hankinson was a cancer on the council, and he spread his poison. He was a dishonest, unpleasant man, beneath the façade. God knows why we let him into the Conservative Party. A switcher is always dubious in the best of circumstances. I expect all the political parties agree on that. But murder, well, no one quite deserves that.

'But I do have two candidates for you. One is a developer whose planning application was turned down for an even larger one. Mark Prideaux. He and Hankinson were...' – French smiled wryly – 'thick as thieves up to that point, and then there was a public and acrimonious falling out. Prideaux is a hothead with a nasty streak. I've seen him in action browbeating and bullying.

'The other is a smallholder, Fred Hume, caught in the crossfire in that larger application for houses over the orchard fields towards Bridge. His land is right across the only possible access to those fields. Hankinson and his associates were putting him and his family under huge pressure to sell up, but Hume made some pretty inflammatory statements at public meetings along the lines of "I'll kill you all" and similar. Now that Hankinson has gone, everything is in abeyance. If you give me a sheet of paper, Miss Goodburn, I'll write the details down.'

Business more or less transacted, French turned to other matters. 'As I was referred to you by Mick, I take it that you're both of the socialist persuasion.' The tone had a sceptical tinge as if such a position were too outlandish to be credible.

'Too right,' said Maria, her chin jutting out.

Sterling shrugged. 'Maybe a bit of that bent. I don't really think about it.' He winced. It was true when it came down to it, but his poor, dead father. The cock would crow.

Maria's reaction was enough. Jerry French was off. 'Interesting. I can never really understand it. It feels like the politics of envy. You seem to want to spend other people's money, via taxes that go up and up when Labour is in power, on things that are inefficient and costly, like nationalisation. Your too-generous welfare provisions create a dependency culture. I'm–'

'I think we'd love to have a bit of ding-dong about politics, Mr French,' broke in Sterling, 'especially Maria, but sadly we're on the clock.'

French put his hands up in surrender. 'Of course, of course.' He seemed very small in his large living room. It occurred to Sterling that for all the comfort and opulence of his home, the man was lonely.

Maria had already stood up and was casting her eyes over the serried shelves of books. 'Fantastic library, Mr French. It's got something in every area as far as I can see. Much better than our public one in Whitstable – after ten years of austerity,' she said. The look over her shoulder was a mixture of knowing and sardonic. 'The economics section is particularly strong. One or two omissions, though, in my opinion. I can't see any Karl Marx. Or even, for a centrist like you, Thomas Piketty. Surely, whatever your views, you need to know what the opposition's thinking or at least have some balance.'

*

At the bus stop a few minutes later, Sterling was chuckling. 'One or two barbs there, Maria.'

The girl allowed herself to join in, her face just slightly flushed. 'He was just getting going. I would have come back with both barrels if it wasn't for the case.'

'Yeah, the case,' said Sterling. 'Eyes on the prize. All in all, an interesting afternoon before we do our report back to June Selsdon. We've got three more possible suspects, in addition to that Logan Seymour. Patrick's given us Mac the drug trade manager, who I knew already and who was in The Lotus Blossom on Saturday night. Jerry French has suggested this developer, Mark Prideaux, and the smallholder, Fred Hume. And the flash drive is intriguing. That throws up a completely different possible motive. Yep, a very decent afternoon's work. I'll tell you what though – early days and a small, probably biased sample – everyone we've spoken to has been utterly consistent about one thing.'

Maria raised an eyebrow.

'Hankinson was an utter bastard. I haven't heard one single good thing about him since I first started this case.'

'I don't think you're going to, either,' said the girl.

Chapter 21

Charlotte Hankinson stuck carefully to her instructions. She started with a walk down St Peter's Grove, a narrow street with the Methodist primary school squeezed in at the top and terraced cottages on each side. The extortionist wouldn't have known it, but the school was where her education started. How well she knew the path from the street into Greyfriars Garden, the backyard fences of the houses on either side engendering the long-familiar claustrophobic feeling. She noted with distaste that the graffitists' tags might have changed over the years but they still disfigured the wooden panels.

The garden seemed an oddly chosen place for picking up a ransom payment. Apart from the entrance via St Peter's Grove, there was only one other way of getting in – through the path off Stour Street at the other end, which went over two narrow little footbridges across channels of the river. To the north, the garden was separated from the back of the school by a dauntingly high metal fence topped by wicked spikes and an ancient, high masonry wall that segregated the garden from a private space behind it.

She sat on the bench specified by her tormentor. As expected, she saw the small black plastic sack under it, ends neatly knotted, just as the extortionist had said, and indeed just like the bags dog walkers used for dog shit. She reached down and paused for a second, her nose wrinkling. Suppose he was toying with her, and instead of containing a flash drive, it really did contain... Overcoming her qualms, she picked up the wrinkled bag and felt the small hard plastic-metal rectangular shape. In the same place, she put her own black bag. She smiled wryly and spontaneously. Suppose she *had* been left excrement to pick up and had left a sample of her own in exchange – a kind of shitty double-cross – she wondered if the extortionist would have seen the funny side as she had. Probably, based on that small exchange on the phone.

She had arrived early so she had a few minutes and decided to linger, her mood reflective in the familiar surroundings and warm evening. She should have stuck to one of her early boyfriends. If it hadn't been for Jack, surely she would have been making a decent living with the estate agents business and a husband who was an accountant or solicitor in the city. Two decent incomes – enough for the house up there in south Canterbury. Perhaps kids, though she'd never been that keen, and Jack had been positively hostile. She felt tired suddenly, tired of the stress and dishonesty, tired of having to do with criminals like Jarvis and Mac, tired of the front she was putting on, the front that was becoming the only way she presented herself to the world.

And all this for such a... parochial, Heath Robinson criminal enterprise. Jack had talked of 'going big'. He'd gone away a few times, destination unspecified, and there had been talks of links with drug kingpins in Liverpool, Manchester... Nothing had come of it. Canterbury was too small for the big boys to bother with, and Jack was always much keener on being the big fish in the little pond. It was all too late now. She was in too deep, and in the short term extracting herself unscathed would be virtually impossible.

Only the road she was already on seemed viable – containment, maintenance of secrecy and then a review, and, with luck, exit in the long term. If you had become dishonest, could you then become honest again, with the punishment bit in the middle missed out completely, or were you always tainted? Too philosophical. She glanced at her watch. It was just before nine o'clock. There had been no instructions about which way to leave the garden after the dead drop, so she strolled off across the two little bridges and into Stour Street. ABode, on the corner of Stour Street and the High Street, was the classiest hotel in the city, the very place for local *glitterati* like herself, and she could do with a brandy, but she turned left towards the Westgate Towers. The problem with ABode would have been her companion.

*

The slender figure in the bushes watched Hankinson from when she arrived until she moved off to the Stour Street exit. He glanced around and then emerged, clad in grey trainers, leg-hugging black tracksuit bottoms and a dark green T-shirt. Incongruously for the time of year, a beanie was pulled over his head, covering his ears and almost his eyes. Quickly he placed a Joker mask over his face and then padded over to the bench. Rummaging in the bag, he flicked through the notes. By denomination and wad thickness, he reckoned that all the cash was there.

Out of the corner of his eye, he saw two shadows appear at the St Peter's Grove exit. On the Stour Street side, as his glance flicked that way, four other shapes emerged, one huge, completely blocking out the first small bridge, black against the dark cerulean sky. He slipped the cash into a tiny rucksack and settled it on his back. The huge shape stayed at thc bridge while his three companions fanned out and stepped forward. One of the men at the other end, wiry and narrow-faced, produced a baseball bat whose barbed-wire spikes glittered from light at the back windows of the cottages. He swung the bat loose-wristedly in an arc just above the surface of the grass. Time stopped.

Then the wiry man sprang silently forward, his companion remaining to guard that exit. The Joker edged backwards, his body hunching as if he were fearful and as if making himself smaller would somehow mitigate the threat. Jarvis smiled knowingly, anticipating fun and retribution. The other three joined him in a loose semi-circle, relaxed and alert, while Fridge lolled against the railings of the inner bridge, looking on apparently dispassionately. Few people came into the garden at this time of night, but if they had, they would have been turned away at either end. At St Peter's Grove, words might have been exchanged with the sentry there, but no one would ever have considered arguing with the Fridge, and certainly not offering a physical challenge.

Jarvis was savouring the moment. He enjoyed intimidation, but actual violence and torture were much more appealing. He'd rip that stupid mask off the bloke's face. There was no escape. The high masonry wall was the diameter to the gang's semi-circle. He stepped forward, and that was the cue for the others.

Calmly and smoothly, the Joker turned around, and with the lithe effortlessness of a big cat propelled himself in rapid, short strides at the wall. Having created momentum, he leapt a good three feet high at the masonry. His hands and feet found immediate purchase, aided by the wall's slight cant away from his body. After the initial grip, other, higher hand and footholds presented themselves regularly as he scuttled upwards.

His would-be assailants were mesmerised for a long moment. Jarvis was first to leap forward, swinging the bat one-handed and hissing with rage. He reached the wall just as the Joker's right hand grasped the top. In triumph, Jarvis felt a spike catch and grip something soft. He jumped with his left foot at the wall, using it as leverage so that he could pull down on the bat. A second later he landed two footed back on the grass, the Joker's left trainer affixed by the heel to the spike. A smear of red gradually spread in a stain through the lightweight material.

From the top of the wall, comfortably out of reach but in an overwhelmingly advantageous position to repel boarders if anyone were thinking of an attempt, the Joker looked down from where he'd scrambled. An onlooker would have sworn that the expression on the mask's face was malevolent and gleeful. There was a rustle and a scrape, and the figure was gone. Jarvis smashed the baseball bat on the grass and did a jig of rage. His companions shuffled awkwardly. At the bridge, Fridge shifted from one foot to the other.

'Don't just fucking stand there, you idiots,' screamed Jarvis through gritted teeth – aware that more commotion might attract attention from the flats south of the garden. 'The bastard can't have got far. Split up, go out through both exits and beat along towards the high street. A couple of you get into that area next door where he went. He's got one shoe and he might be limping. I'll be in The Cricketers. Report back to me there.'

The thugs trotted off.

Jarvis packed Barbie away and kicked the bloody trainer. 'What are you waiting for, Fridge?'

The big man shrugged. Strenuous exercise was not his forte. Even Jarvis was loth to pick a fight. He shook his head disgustedly as Fridge shuffled behind him, followed two of his gang over the two bridges and into Stour Street, and headed to the pub. He feared little, but plenty could make him uncomfortable. The forthcoming meeting with Charlotte Hankinson was shaping up that way. When he looked round, the Fridge had stopped at the corner of the street. Jarvis ploughed on.

*

Two minutes later, a face appeared at the top of the Greyfriars wall and did a swift reconnaissance. Then the figure clambered lightly down, landing exactly in the place he'd escaped from minutes earlier. He slipped on the trainer and strode with a slight limp towards the St Peter's Grove exit. Hyper-alert, he paused for a moment and looked back. Fridge had reappeared at the Stour Street end. The bruiser and the young man gazed at each other across the wide expanse of garden. Fridge nodded, as if acknowledging the boldness of the bluff, but barely visible as the light was failing completely. The young man looked away and padded off.

At the gate, the night warden was just putting the key in the lock. 'You're just in time.' Normally, he would have added 'mate', but something held him back. 'I would have locked you in.'

'I could think of worse things,' said the figure. 'Much worse.' He turned left, away from the city, and disappeared quickly from view, into the maze of cottages beyond the gardens.

*

The patrons in The Cricketers were scruffy. Hankinson had dressed down as best she could for the garden rendezvous and then the meeting with Jimmy Jarvis, but her estimation of casual, in her Versace blue jeans and rose-themed white T-shirt, was still like wearing a tux to a barbecue, and not helped by her customary ice-cool demeanour. The bartender, a young man with blond highlights in his dark hair and grubby bitten-down fingernails, had raised his eyebrows when she'd insisted on a cleaner glass for the brandy whose brand she hadn't been remotely able to recognise, and which tasted as cheap as the label on the bottle looked. She retreated to a corner table with her back to the wall and the scarred wooden partition that separated the booth from the one next door. She didn't have to wait long.

Jarvis entered the pub as if he owned it, his usual approach, and probably his writ did run large here, as in many of the watering holes in the city. He paused in the doorway, searching for Hankinson, and in the bar there was a perceptible change in atmosphere from listless relaxation to edginess. Their eyes met, and he nodded and strode over. 'Mine's a...' – he cast his eyes over to the selection of beers at the bar – '... a Peroni. Pint.'

Charlotte Hankinson looked at him. She took a sip of her drink and winced.

Jarvis stared back and then shrugged and looked away. He went up to the bar and shouted out, 'Oi!' to the barman.

'I'm next,' said a skinny young man in baggy jeans and T-shirt.

'No. You're not,' said Jarvis. 'Unless you want to make something of it.'

The young man opened and closed his mouth. 'Nah, it's alright, mate. No hurry. Be my guest.'

Back at the corner table, Jarvis took a long pull at his lager. 'We missed him, unless the blokes have come up with something in the last few minutes. Slippery little bastard. We had him trapped against a tall wall, no way out, and he climbed it.' He clicked his fingers. 'Just like that. If I'd had a bit more warning... I can't get results if I don't get the full picture.'

Hankinson closed her eyes. *This poxy little pub, the table scored and scarred by God knows what. The decrepit partitions and booths. The dirty glasses. The punters with their pathetic attempts at nonconformity. The company I have to keep. The incompetence. Why aren't I angry?*

Her mind drifted to a crash she'd been in. A boy racer in a Mini had been coming too fast to the Rhodaus Town roundabout and had gone straight into her. Moments before impact she'd known what was coming and a relaxed fatalism had washed over her body. In the aftermath, having escaped only with bruises, mostly from the air bag, all the urgency had drained from her day. She was alive. She was whole. Nothing else mattered. That's what she was feeling now, exactly, helped by the awful brandy.

She blinked and clicked back to the present. 'Well, the "slippery little bastard" is certainly enterprising. Cocky. A risk-taker. Well-organised.'

'The blokes are still looking for him,' said Jarvis. 'We might still get lucky.'

She shook her head, disbelieving. 'Could it have been Mac?'

Jarvis's leg was quivering. 'The right height but doubtful. He looked too fit, and he was less scrawny. But Mac's got a tight group of blokes. Some of those are gym bunnies and into steroids and the like. It's possible it was one of them, working for Mac. It could have been Stevie from the student village. Mac wants to boss everything though. Why would he be into blackmail?'

'What about one of the others? Prideaux. He was all sweetness and light at the meeting, but he and Jack had had a falling out. Maybe he's behind everything. Or Spedding? She might think that her cut from the brothel isn't enough.'

Jarvis took another swig of his pint. 'The same thing with both of them. Why blackmail? And what's on the stick lands everyone in it, unless some of the content is removed. Something else is bothering me. We keep talking about Ja... your husband's murderer as if it was a bloke. I'm not sure if that person in the garden was a bloke. Most likely was, but maybe not. It was getting dark and the light was playing tricks. Not that I've got any woman in mind,' he added hastily. He could think of one or two candidates, revenge being the likely motive, but if they weren't likely, why bother his boss?

Hankinson pushed the brandy away and drummed her fingers.

'So what now?' said Jarvis. He was the enforcement and executive arm. Strategy and tactics were beyond him.

'I don't know. We wait for another opportunity. We wait for damage and then do damage limitation. I don't believe for a moment that it's over, even with the flash drive I picked up. Why wouldn't he – or she – have made a copy? I'm off home to see what's on it. As for this,' – she looked around the dingy pub – 'the occasional meeting between us is OK, Jimmy, but generally burners are best.'

She glided away, the waft of Chanel No. 5 drifting in her wake.

'You've left your drink,' he called after her. If she'd heard, she gave no evidence of it. He sniffed. 'Brandy,' he muttered. 'Excellent.' He had a chaser. And he hadn't paid for it.

Chapter 22

Trudging with Maria up Northwood Road and into Clare Road from the bus stop at the bottom, Sterling felt the same odd emotions as before. He wasn't usually uneasy when reporting back to a principal. Why was this different?

Soon they were sitting at June Selsdon's table at the back of the kitchen, with welcome cups of freshly percolated coffee and top-of-the-range chocolate digestives on side plates. Sterling was a biscuit dunker by custom. He resisted the dunking urge as June Selsdon scanned the day sheets and summaries.

'You've been busy,' she murmured. 'Can you add some flesh to the bones so I have a fuller picture?'

'Certainly,' said Sterling. He recounted the interview with Janice Wray, the clash with Andy Nolan, the serendipitous visit to the crime scene where he and Maria had met one of his former colleagues, and Saturday night at The Lotus Blossom, including the chat with Charlotte Hankinson and recognising Mac the drugs manager. The Labour Party meeting had been interesting, he supposed, but more useful had been the meeting with Mick Masters and Tom Spring in the pub afterwards, and the contacts they'd given him – Patrick Ngono, the Cameroonian refugee and the Tory Jerry French. Generally, he focused on the activity as it related to the murder victim, but French had been the last port of call, and the sparring with Maria was still fresh in his mind.

'Well done, Maria,' said the older woman, when she'd heard. 'I like Jerry, and he's decent enough, but he always says irritating things, and he's always trying to score points. What about a summary, Frank?'

Sterling noted the familiarity and felt oddly gratified. 'Your main brief was for us to establish that the Labour Party's reputation doesn't take a hit if someone from the Party is involved in the murder, or the murder, and/or the victim, somehow reflects badly on it. We've established that Hankinson is an extremely unsavoury character – everyone has said so – and almost certainly responsible for a web of criminality across Canterbury. At the moment we can't tell if that's anything to do with Labour or any other institution or individual for that matter.

'Essentially, we've got four leads from our contacts and other activities – a shadowy figure called Logan Seymour, probably newly on the scene and somehow involved in the sex trade, a man called Mac, surname at present unknown, who runs the drug distribution arm of Hankinson's alleged enterprise, Mark Prideaux, a property developer, and a smallholder called Fred Hume. We've also had wind of a flash drive possibly stolen from Hankinson's body with incriminating material on it. That could be a strong motive.'

'So how are you going to proceed with these... leads,' said June Selsdon.

'I'm thinking that through,' said Sterling. 'We're not the police, so we can't go and formally interview them, or ask them if they have alibis, or be even more direct – "So, Mr Prideaux, did you, or one of your associates, murder Jack Hankinson?" – it's not viable. We're going to have to go sideways on somehow, except maybe with the smallholder. We've been trying to find out more about Seymour, but no luck so far. We'll carry on working on it. The others, including Mac, we can find.'

June Selsdon looked back down at the day sheets. 'Can you say any more about Mrs Hankinson?'

'She and Frank got on like a house on fire,' laughed Maria.

Sterling scowled. 'She approached me. Nothing untoward in that – she was doing the rounds of her club, as hosts and hostesses do. And nothing untoward during or afterwards. I don't think she much liked her husband anymore, and she certainly knew a dodgy character in the club that I know from an earlier case. Perhaps she was involved in whatever her husband was involved in, perhaps not. She's a cool one. The jury's out on where she fits in.' He sipped his coffee, struggling to make eye contact.

'Plenty of sound and fury, not much substance,' mused June Selsdon, seemingly to herself. The room was silent but for the occasional faint hum of a car passing in the street.

'The web of criminality...,' said Maria. 'Patrick, the refugee, is mixed up in it, June, very much against his wishes. He's got leave to remain, but his status is precarious. He's a very nice man in a difficult situation. He also told us about trafficked girls from Eastern European countries – Slovenia, one of them, if I remember rightly – trapped in a brothel.'

'Maria,' said Sterling. He lifted his eyes and fixed her with a glare.

'I don't think we can just ignore it, Frank. Patrick was so polite he couldn't bring himself to ask for our help, but it would be tragic if he got into trouble. And those poor girls. He can't go to the police. They can't get out of the brothel. They're all trapped.'

'Well, if it's not relevant to the brief June gave me' – Sterling pointedly put emphasis on 'me' – 'it's not something I can be involved with. I'd be wasting her money.'

Selsdon's eyes were shining. 'There's nothing stopping me from extending your brief, is there? It seems to be a worthy cause. I very much trust Maria's judgement. It would probably mean quite a big extension to the time you'd need to spend on the case. How are you fixed in terms of other commitments, Frank?'

Before his eyes, Sterling's Calendar programme on his computer screen came into focus. He scrolled mentally through the months – July, August, September, October – blank, blank, blank, blank. He switched back to the scene in front of him, the expectant looks of the older woman and younger one. 'I can juggle things around, I expect, if I'm clear about what you have in mind.' He should have been angry with Maria but his shaky finances left no room for anger, or wounded pride.

Maria looked relieved. 'Janice Wray,' she said carefully. 'She's doing that degree in sociology and social policy at Corpus Christi right enough. But that's not all she's doing.'

Sterling and June Selsdon waited. So did Maria. She looked out into the scrubby patio and yard beyond it, as if spies might be skulking, and over her shoulder, instinctively now, back down the long length of the house. A switch seemed to flick in her head, a decision taken. 'She won't mind me telling you – I've checked it, and she's run some checks of her own – Janice is station mistress of the Canterbury station in England's Underground Railroad.'

'Station mistress? Underground railroad?' Sterling's face registered puzzlement and incredulity, but Selsdon's eyes were gleaming again.

'I knew it,' she said. 'I knew there'd be something like this. We talked about it so often when I was much younger, but too often we were just dreamers.'

Sterling was shaking his head.

'Harriet Tubman?' said Maria. 'Rescuing runaway slaves from the Confederate states and sheltering them in the North and in Canada before the American Civil War? Maybe I shouldn't be surprised. Any history you did was probably whitewashed. Anyway, Janice and her organisation help people escape from modern-day slavery and similar oppressing circumstances. The girls at the brothel and Patrick will all qualify.'

'And you know about this how?' said Sterling.

'I'm not just in the Labour Party or a feminist group within the Party. There are networks in the universities. We link up. When we're home on holiday, we firm up contacts. People get to know each other. Word of mouth. Believe me, we didn't get to this point off the cuff. There's been plenty of stuff going on behind the scenes.'

'I'm just a pawn in all this,' said Sterling. The all-women vibe had started again, far more powerful than the opposite one he and Jerry French had been able to generate, and far more focused.

'No, Frank, honestly. The Railroad is passive at the sharp end. It doesn't do anything to identify people who need rescuing, and it doesn't get involved in the first stages. You can look at it as just whisking people away once they've been received into the process. Our job would be – will be – now that June is backing it, getting the rescuees, as it were, to a safe house or area for onward despatch. All stages are kept completely apart from each other.'

'What if June hadn't come aboard? What if I can't fit this into my schedule after all? What about the leads we've got to deal with? What about' – he felt a twinge fuelled by selfishness and opportunism – 'danger money?'

'I didn't expect anything, Frank. It was all ifs and buts. I still don't if you're having second thoughts. Either we'd have to let the situation with Patrick and his friends continue, or find a way without you, after the Hankinson murder is sorted out. But Janice looked at your other cases… you've been in plenty of scrapes, and you've always got out of them. You're just the person for this sort of operation – dubious but legal, if you get my thinking.'

'The danger money, Frank,' said June Selsdon softly. 'We can factor that in.'

Sterling blushed. 'As and when,' he muttered. 'So, to clarify. In the case of Hankinson's murder, principally protect the reputation of the Labour Party if we identify – or someone else identifies – the murderer, and secondly, rescue a refugee and two sex workers from part of Hankinson's criminal enterprise. Just the two, mind. We haven't the resources for a whole harem. Hmm, I don't think I've had an assignment with these kinds of twists and turns before.'

'I expect there'll be some more before it's over,' said Selsdon cryptically. 'It's not as though they are different cases. You've already demonstrated how joined-up everything in this sorry business is – all originating in one dreadful man.'

'It'll be part of our "shaking things loose strategy",' said Maria.

'More like stirring up a hornet's nest,' said Sterling. Still, it was guaranteed extra income, and he was beginning to come around to the idea that it might indeed be useful to the main case. There hadn't been much progress so far. It would be a provocation that might take things up to the next level. 'Right, I'll have a think and consider the best way to proceed. I guess it falls into the "important but not urgent" category. I don't think there's anything else for the moment, June, so I'm going to head off for my bus.'

The older woman nodded. She'd become thoughtful, her gaze drifting beyond her visitors. 'Mention of danger money is making me anxious. You'll both take care, won't you?'

'I've been in lots of rucks, June, from my time on the job. Kent sea fronts on weekend nights were the perfect apprenticeship. And so long as Maria can run fast...' He smiled.

The briefing over, Sterling glanced back at June Selsdon as he and Maria walked off down the road, acknowledging her wave with a nod.

In Northwood Road, Maria broke the silence. 'I didn't mean to... outmanoeuvre you, Frank. I'd taken on board what you'd said about not getting involved beyond what we were meant to be doing. It's just that

June and I talk a lot about injustice and oppression, and I suppose I got a bit… over-exercised.'

Sterling looked down at the cracked pavement. 'I'm not that fussed now I've got used to the idea, Maria,' he conceded. 'You're right that it might open things up, and at the moment my business is precar–' He fell silent.

Maria chose not to notice the half-shared confidence. 'We've finished for the day, right, apart from ongoing desk research on Seymour and the like? If so, I'm going to see BJ. He only lives a couple of streets from here.'

'BJ?'

'Billy Jenkins. Why don't you come? He's always good entertainment value.'

'No, count me out of this one.' BJ was a wonder boy too far at this time of day. 'After all, I've got leads to follow and abductions to plan.'

'Yes, right, Frank. Of course you have. Shall I contact Janice Wray?'

'Hold back a bit, until things are firmed up.'

Now they were at the bus stop in front of the faded little parade perched above them, a down-at-heel retail border post between Whitstable and Tankerton – the chippy, the laundrette, the wool shop, the newsagent-cum-bottle shop.

The bus swung around the corner. They'd parted like this before.

'One last thing, before our next get-together,' said Maria. 'It'll probably be useful at some stage.'

Sterling had his ticket punched by the bus driver and then turned back. 'Yep?'

'I think the Fridge – Jason – has become – what do you call it? – I think he's become my snitch.'

The doors closed and the bus bore Sterling away. He clambered up to the top deck. Having a snitch was promising. Once again, the girl had done well. But something else was preoccupying him. It had nothing to do with Jack Hankinson's murder, or the brothel rescue, or all the other murky goings-on in Canterbury. It nagged at him every time he took the bus to Whitstable, every time he plodded up Clare Road and met June Selsdon in her house, every time they spoke on the phone. Something other than the case was going on, and he couldn't work out what. It made him delve into his past, but without enlightenment. Should he worry at it, or simply wait for something to come to the surface? The feeling was getting stronger. This was more than a policeman's instinct. He was reminded of a word that had come up doing a recent crossword with Angela at the Cinq Port Arms. It fitted perfectly. Visceral.

Chapter 23

The police investigation was still going nowhere, a week and a day after Jack Hankinson's murder – a team of twenty doing this and that, busy as ants, without a clue. Murphy, as deputy senior investigating officer, was on his way to interview a confidential informant with Sophie Stephens, the office manager. He was glad to be out of the office, and, although he liked and was comfortable with Nolan, Stephens was a welcome change.

The young woman was muttering mild curses as they drove up and down Wincheap's narrow streets and terraces looking for a parking spot. 'We could have walked this in fifteen minutes, sir,' she said.

'Hindsight,' murmured Murphy. 'There. Someone is just coming out.' He looked at the map on his phone. This was Claremont Terrace. The nark – the confidential informant – lived in the parallel terrace, Grove Terrace.

Wincheap was an enclave, divided from the city centre by the inner ring road and the London to Dover railway line. The cottages here were late Victorian and had survived world wars and corporate planning vandalism. There was still a corner pub, and corner shops dotted around, picking up the trade between the weekly big shops at the supermarkets.

The two detectives left their car and walked around the corner to Grove Terrace, approaching the front door of number seven. Murphy noted the cottage's bedraggled look, especially compared to most of the others in the street, which had been lovingly restored and upgraded. At number seven, the letter flap hung forlornly off one hinge. The brickwork needed a thorough re-pointing. Greenery was growing in the top gutter, including a dandelion providing a hint of yellow, and Murphy became aware of sparrows darting into a nest in that upper area. The cottage had what looked like its original sash windows, but probably not for much longer. The paint was peeling from the frames that wet rot had already penetrated. Stephens wrinkled her nose and rolled her eyes slightly as she rapped on the glass-panelled front door.

The door opened straight out onto the pavement. Stephens was about to knock again when a blurry figure loomed behind the frosted glass. A crack appeared between door and jamb, filled with rheumy eyes and a nose reddened and purpled by hard drinking. A grey head protruded, and the eyes flicked up and down the street. No act to allay neighbourly or other suspicions could have done more to arouse them, if anyone had been watching. *We could have been door-to-door double glazing salespeople, God-botherers, pollsters,* thought Murphy. *Now we are 100% the police.*

Apparently satisfied with his quick reconnaissance, the man gestured his visitors inside with a tilt of the head. The entrance gave straight into a dingy front room. Stephens and Murphy stood just inside.

'Go on then. Sit.' There was a truculent, disgruntled note in the man's voice.

Murphy went for the speckly brown two-seater settee, covered in a greasy kind of acrylic material, which was part of a three-piece suite with two armchairs arranged at each side. A television by the central wall completed the rectangular pattern. In the middle was a glass coffee table, circa 1960, with a full ashtray that provided the interior's stale, smoky smell and foggy, blue-tinged atmosphere. Overlapping coffee and beer mug rings dominated the glass. Murphy found that the settee was surprisingly well sprung and comfortable. Stephens didn't immediately sit. She did what offsiders always seemed to do, moseying around the room looking and poking about. The nark, Ken Todman according to Murphy's notes, followed her with resentful eyes.

'Vettriano,' said Stephens, gesturing towards the only prints on the walls. 'Two of my favourites. The dinner party and the picnic on the beach. I can't remember their names. They suit the room.'

Todman wasn't biting. 'My wife left them when she went.' He shrugged. 'Better than an empty fucking space.'

'She had good taste.' Stephens wasn't giving up easily.

'She was a bitch.'

Stephens finished her poking about and took the less lived-in armchair. 'This is comfy.' She settled back and rolled her shoulders.

Todman looked over at Murphy and then back to Stephens. Murphy braced himself. The man would say something disparaging and seek solidarity – *is she always so bloody cheerful. Does it not wear you out?* Instead he produced a smile, albeit a pinched one. 'Full marks for keeping going, detective. How can I resist?'

Stephens laughed, showing her white throat. 'Vettriano really is a favourite.'

Murphy smiled. The atmosphere lightened. 'Thanks for agreeing to see us, Mr Todman, and of course for being in after we initially phoned.'

Todman nodded.

'You're on our list as a registered confidential informant. We're here today about the murder of Jack Hankinson. Anything that you can privately tell us from your contacts in the city will help us apprehend the killer or killers. I'm sure your input will be very valuable.' Murphy wondered why his words had become so stilted.

Todman hmphed and folded his arms.

'We will of course make it worth your while according to the guidelines.'

'There'll be a drink in it, if it's good,' translated Stephens. Murphy looked at her without resentment. *Mind-reader.*

Todman scratched a hairy ear. 'Hankinson ran stuff in the city. He had a finger in all sorts of pies. He chased skirt too. He put up a lot of backs, one way or the other. There is plenty of talk in the pubs. Some people are saying that one of the big developers wanting to build out over the fields towards Bridge had him done. Hankinson double-crossed him. Took his cash but didn't come up with his side of the bargain, which was planning permission in the Council. Some people say there's been a takeover of 'operations' here – the big boys have moved in on the drugs, via county lines – and Hankinson was kicking up a fuss about it and making threats about going to you lot, or doing reprisals in some way. There's even talk that Charlotte H got fed up with his womanising, and got Jimmy Jarvis to top him. It's unlikely that it would have been Jimmy – murder's beyond his paygrade, and anyway, he and Hankinson were close – but perhaps she got someone else in.'

Stephens had her notebook out and was scribbling furiously. 'Jimmy Jarvis?'

'Jesus, where have you been? You plods have really lost it. Don't you talk to each other? Or anyone around and about? It must be austerity,' he said slyly. 'Hardly any of you left. Jimmy was Hankinson's gopher if you like. His... problem-solver.' He winked.

'Stephens is new,' said Murphy. 'I know Jarvis.' There was a defensive note in his voice. He did know him, and the kind of low-level activity he got up to, but not about the connection to Hankinson.

'Anyway, from what I'm hearing, it's probably not one of those things.'

Murphy leaned forward.

'Who in this place would want Jack Hankinson dead? Nobody, that's who. Everyone knew which side their bread was buttered. The bent councillors got a bung now again, especially those on the planning committee. The developers got their applications through. The big boys doing the drugs from London and Manc and that were happy to use him as a distributor, and to make sure things ran smoothly. Charlotte H lives up there near the hospital in that big fancy house with the big fancy Merc and all the trimmings. Why would she do him in? They got on all right, even if rumours had it that they'd gone their separate ways. Things were much quieter and calmer with Hankinson pulling the strings.

'So it's something else. Hankinson tried a bit of blackmail too far, or upset a bloke by screwing his wife, and that was the trigger. But there's a twist. The murder is personal, but the doer of the deed saw an opportunity. There was no wallet on the body, right? No car keys, credit cards, personal stuff.'

'How did you know that?' said Stephens. 'It wasn't mentioned in the press conferences.'

Todman tapped the side of his bulbous nose. 'Hankinson was careful when he was alive, but when he was dead - careless. You won't find any evidence of dodgy dealings on his computer or in his office or anywhere like that, or on – what do you call it? – the cloud. Everything was on a flash drive he kept on a chain around his neck. Easy to get from a body.'

'Names, Ken,' said Murphy.

The nark flared up. 'Haven't you been listening? If Hankinson was done in because it was personal, I'm not likely to know anything, am I? If you don't agree that it's personal, go off and talk to the developers and the councillors and the druggies. Strewth.'

'Back up a moment,' interjected Stephens. 'What about Charlotte Hankinson? You mentioned she might have a motive because of the womanising. Was she involved in her husband's criminal enterprises?'

'"Criminal enterprises",' imitated Todman. 'Oooh.' Then he shrugged. 'Nobody knows what went on between those two. It's possible. Anyway, you now know what I know. So…'

Murphy stood up, dug his hand into his pocket, peeled off notes from a wad and passed them over. He'd do the paperwork later.

'Don't mind if I do,' said the informant, as he trousered them, his mood palpably uplifted.

*

As she and Murphy were opening their car doors in the next street, Stephens spoke across the roof. 'He wasn't your usual snitch, was he, sir?'

'How do you mean?'

'From the way he was talking, he's got a bit of education.'

'According to the file, he was a technician at Canterbury College, but he went bad. The drink probably. And that's where he ended up. He'll be in the pubs tonight. He's not a lone drinker type. He likes the company.'

*

Back in Grove Terrace, Todman picked up the phone and dialled.

'What?' said Jimmy Jarvis.

'Just to let you know... The Bill have just been round to talk to me about Hankinson. I got the strong impression they're getting nowhere.'

'What did you tell them?'

'Nothing. No names. Vague rumours. But you're on their radar.'

'You told them about me?'

'Of course I didn't,' lied the nark. 'They mentioned you. I didn't.' He kept quiet about the flash drive. There was no need for... complications.

'Right, so I can expect a visit.'

'I imagine so.'

'And you're still keeping an eye on that Wray woman?'

'Yes.'

The connection ended. Jarvis didn't do 'thanks'.

Fuck him, thought Todman. *And fuck the busies.* That was the point about playing both ends against the middle. Why should you care about anyone and anything except yourself and the booze money in your pocket?

Chapter 24

The call came as Nolan was driving out of Canterbury towards Sandley. Immediately he activated the hands-free. 'Nolan,' he said.

'DCI Nolan, Mamujee.'

'Sir.' Nolan hadn't been able to check caller ID. He sat up straighter in his seat and concentrated on the road.

'How is the investigation going?'

'Not too well, sir. I can't fault my team, and we're following various promising lines of investigation, but we're not getting anywhere.'

'No possibility of a breakthrough?'

Nolan paused. The honest answer was plain. 'No,' he said. I'm afraid not, sir. We're going to need more time.'

'Right. Well, I have a small update for you. Chief Superintendent Peabody will no longer be overseeing the investigation, with immediate effect. There's nothing significant in this – he's been seconded to a counter-terrorist task force with the Met. So I'll be resuming oversight. In that light, is there anything I can practically contribute at this point?'

Nolan punched the air with a short jab. 'Yes!' he mouthed. The only bit of good news since the murder last Wednesday. 'No, sir. We've just got to plug away.

As you know, all investigations are different. This one is more challenging and complex than usual but something will emerge, and we're being as active as possible.'

'Noted. Let's leave it for a few days, and then I'll come down for a complete update and strategic review.'

'Fine, sir. Thank you.'

Good news at last. Some people did their best work with supervisors breathing down their necks, and thrived on hostility and conflict. Nolan wasn't one of them. If he and Mamujee trusted each other, that would benefit the investigation. His mood had gone from sombre to cheerful instantly, bolstered by the fact that he was taking a temporary break from the office and heading in the opposite direction to all his burdensome responsibilities. The empty passenger seat was good too. He liked and worked well with Bill Murphy, but Murphy had a pessimistic side that had emerged more strongly as the investigation got bogged down.

His phone trilled again. 'Bill.'

'Guv. I thought I'd report back straight away, as there might be a bit of a glimmer.'

'Go on.'

'Soph... Detective Constable Stephens and I have just got back from seeing that nark... the confidential informant on our list. Several things came up.'

'Can you summarise, Bill? You can give me the full report when I get back to the office.'

Fifteen minutes later, fully briefed, Nolan had passed the white mill on the edge of Sandley and was weaving through the medieval street layout to Sterling's office.

Just before midday, there was plenty of parking space in Market Street, and Nolan found a slot just beyond the library entrance. As he was entering the library, at the bottom of the stairs leading up to Sterling's office, he caught a glimpse of Angela Wilson. He looked at his watch. He had a couple of minutes. 'Angela,' he called.

'Andy,' said Angela. They met by the helpdesk. 'How are you getting on? Panjit mentioned that you're leading the investigation into that murder in Canterbury.'

'Yes, I spoke to him on the way over. He's taken back overall supervision from one of the Maidstone superintendents.' Nolan and Angela had both been involved, in various ways and to various degrees, in some of Sterling's previous cases. 'To be honest, it's a stroke of luck for me. Your chap is demanding in his way, but he's fair and lets me get on with it without micro-managing and interfering.' Even if it were virtually certain that Angela would say nothing to Mamujee, the politician in Nolan was never far away.

'So, as you're in Sandley, presumably you're going up to see Frank.'

'Correct. Some fence-mending.'

Angela tipped her head, suddenly more alert. 'Oh?'

'I don't know what else to say until I've seen him, except that we had a falling out last week.'

'Interesting. We did too, Panjit and I. We were coming back from the theatre one evening and he was in a very funny mood, outside his house. I'm expecting a kiss-and-make-up some time, but I'm not instigating it, since we're the injured party. You know Frank. He comes round eventually.'

'Here's hoping,' said Nolan. 'Anyway, I'm just a bit late. See you again soon, Angie.'

Upstairs, Sterling had seen Nolan arriving and parking. He wondered why he was only just hearing the footfall and creaks on the stairs. Surely Andy wasn't changing a library book. There was a rap on the door.

'Come in,' Sterling called out.

'Frank,' said Nolan. He stopped in the doorway, his stance awkward and tentative.

'Andy,' replied Sterling, half-rising from the chair behind his desk.

'I'm a bit late. I just bumped into Angela downstairs. We had a bit of a catch-up.'

'Right.'

'It's weird, because her bloke, Mamujee, is supervising my investigation. It puts a different spin on things. Alright if I sit?'

'Of course.'

'Jane sends her love.'

'Thanks. Send mine back.'

Nolan eased himself into the client's chair on the other side of the desk. He noted a fine patina of dust on the surface nearest to him. Into the room's uneasy silence, noises from the street filtered through from the open sash window – the short beep of a car horn, someone calling a greeting across the road, the whine of a small-engined motor bike. The room's furnishings hadn't changed since Sterling was starting out. Nolan felt a pang for his friend and his hand-to-mouth existence, but he kept his feelings to himself. Sterling wasn't one to welcome pity or concern or any emotion on that spectrum.

'I'm–'

'So wh–'

Both men had broken the silence at the same time. Sterling leaned back in his fancy chair and gestured with his hand.

'I'm sorry we got off on the wrong foot the other day, Frank.'

'Got off on the wrong foot… Hmm, I didn't think we were on any foot to begin with.'

Nolan shrugged. 'You know what I mean. It was an awkward moment, and I was taken by surprise. I wasn't expecting a parallel private investigation by my best friend. These are reasons, not excuses. As I said, I'm sorry.'

Sterling kept a poker face, but his mind was working rapidly, processing. The senior investigation officer of a major murder investigation was taking a couple of hours off at the peak of said investigation to drive over to Sandley – to his office – to apologise. Andy was being characteristically generous. But he was a politician and always was, even back in the day when they were starting out.

'Good of you, Andy. I appreciate it. I probably shouldn't have just dropped in, and at such a crucial point. I hope you apologised on my behalf to your office manager.'

'I did. She's had much worse so she wasn't overly fussed.'

'That's what I said to Maria afterwards. Still. Out of order… So anyway, you came all this way to say sorry for the other day.'

Nolan laughed and raised his hands in a 'you've-got-me' gesture. 'Of course not. That was the most important bit though. It was bugging me that we'd had a run-in. If you don't deal with rifts they fester. But no.'

Sterling smiled.

Nolan scratched an eyebrow, one of his tells from the old days. 'I've got a big team working on Jack

Hankinson's murder, but... but we're not getting anywhere. In fact, we've hit a wall of silence. The forensics aren't revealing much. Only a couple of leads Bill Murphy reported this morning look promising.'

'So you're thinking that I may be able to contribute on the basis of my own investigation.'

'Yes. Jane pointed out that your success record is excellent, and that you've probably got to places an official police investigation couldn't. She didn't like the fact we'd argued either, and obviously I agreed with her. She thought it would be handy to link up with an irregular.'

'That's me, is it?' said Sterling. 'I suppose that's accurate. Well, you could say that we're in the "shaking things loose" phase at this end.'

'Ah,' smiled Nolan. 'That one. The one before the "all hell breaking loose" phase.'

'Hopefully. And hopefully, you'll be around for that one.'

Over a cup of tea, the two men continued to discuss the case, but like boxers in the early stages of a bout – probing, shadow-punching, getting a feel for things.

'For me, a few things stand out, in no particular order,' said Sterling. 'One is that most people regarded Hankinson as a complete shit. Even Charlo... even his wife no longer liked him. Another is that he was running a number of rackets in Canterbury. Combine those two things and you've got plenty of motives in terms of grudges, turf disputes, rivalries and so on. The missing flash drive, which we've both heard about through two different sources – my leave-to-remainer and your snitch – is an interesting element. And the theory that the murder could be personal, not business, is plausible.'

'I agree, Frank. Interesting that you got on so well with Charlotte Hankinson.' Nolan let the comment hang in the air. 'Right, I'd better get back and catch up properly with Bill Murphy. I expect we'll be in touch again soon, discreetly. It was good to see you, mate. I'm glad we were able to mend our fences.'

The two men shook hands, and Nolan pattered down the stairs. To Sterling's ear, his tread seemed lighter than when he'd arrived, but the mind could play tricks.

Sterling went to the window and looked down. Freddie Henderson, in his pebble-thick glasses, was engaged in banter next to his boxes of outside fruit and vegetables with an elderly hippy woman in her Woodstock smock and skirt. A painter and decorator in his paint-smeared whites and peaked cap was getting cash from the ATM. Wanda at *Magic Gifts* lingered outside her shop for her midday smoke. Sterling watched Nolan get into his car and pull away.

He went back to his desk. What had he learnt from Andy? Not very much, but there were a couple of nuggets – the angle that Hankinson's murder was personal, and corroboration about a flash drive.

For now, there were two outstanding tasks. First he'd go downstairs and make his peace with Angela, since reconciliation was the order of the day. Apologising was going against the grain, but he had to face up to it. There was calculation in his thinking. At some stage, he'd need her help. Second was planning the rescue of Patrick and the trafficked girls. Andy hadn't needed to know about that either, or its disruptive implications. Being back on good terms didn't mean full disclosure or anything near it. Anyway, being the politician he was, Andy would be holding something back himself.

*

Driving back to Canterbury, Nolan was also reflecting. The fence-mending had lightened his mood, but he sensed that he'd given more to his friend than the other way round. Frank was definitely holding something back. No change in that department. If things followed the usual pattern, he'd find out what Frank was up to sooner or later, and it would involve fireworks.

*

Perched on a barstool in The Moon under Water, Jimmy Jarvis stared at his pint of San Miguel. The barman kept to himself at the other end, occasionally cursing and chuntering at his phone, seemingly in a downward spiral of losing bets. Jarvis's crew were elsewhere – not working – they were all on the social – but even Jarvis knew that his was not exactly company to seek out and savour.

Since Jack Hankinson's murder, Jarvis had been bored – a worse boredom than when he'd been a squaddie, especially in Afghanistan. At least there, long spells of nothing had been interspersed with short bursts of extreme danger and excitement. It wasn't just boredom. He was unsettled about the current leadership. He'd had dealings with Charlotte Hankinson before, because Jack involved everyone in his schemes and scams, but did she have the guts to take it over? The jury was out. For the moment, it was in his interest to keep on side, but when someone started blabbing, or the cops got too close, or something else happened to shake things up... It wouldn't take much for things to slip completely out of control. Then it would be time to strike out on his own, jump ship while he had the chance. As for who'd topped Jack, Jarvis, despite energetic searching via his networks, still didn't have a clue.

'Oi,' he shouted. He waggled his empty glass at the barman.

*

On the coast at Whitstable, it was cooler as a sea breeze spilled its bounty through the town. Maria was in Billy Jenkinson's garage, the place attached to his parents' house that he called home. Billy had gone into the garden to fill the kettle from the outside tap on the kitchen wall. She sat in one of the striped, foldable garden chairs and waited in a reverie.

'What?' Billy had returned with the kettle and noticed her faraway smile.

'Nothing. I was just thinking... "a place for everything and everything in its place".' She waved her hand around. 'It applies perfectly to your... eco-gaff.'

Billy grunted. 'No alternative. It would be chaos if I let things go. How do you want your tea? The usual?'

'Of course.'

'How's the sleuthing going?'

'Alright. We're doing plenty of stuff, but I can't say we're making much progress. The famous Sterling strategy of shaking things up and seeing what comes loose doesn't seem to be working this time, though we're developing another bit of that.'

'Yeah?'

'We've been in contact with an asylum seeker, who in turn has told us about some girls trafficked to a brothel in Canterbury. June Selsdon's widened our brief to rescuing them, so that's the next step.' Maria shrugged in a kind of reflex movement. She considered telling Billy to keep it to himself but he'd do that automatically.

Sensing the mood, Billy glossed over it himself. 'Sterling. He was alright when we met in the pub. The kind of bloke you can have a pint and a chat with.' Billy handed Maria the chipped mug, 'Red till I die' etched (in red) around it.

They drank their tea. The silence was companionable, as always. But nothing would be quite right till she could get back to normal. Whatever that now was, she hoped it would be soon.

*

In the considerably more luxurious ambience of her south Canterbury pile, Charlotte Hankinson was also thinking. The freshly percolated coffee was helping to clarify things, assisted by the air circulating gently through the tops and bottoms of the large, sash windows of the yellow-and-grey front room. She was gripped by a kind of remorse. The more she reflected, the more she was beginning to believe that her entire choice of direction since Jack's death was misconceived. Up to that point, she'd just been the bookkeeper. What on earth had motivated her to be meeting with Jack's awful crew of criminals and fraudsters, and establish (for now) her leadership? What was she doing meeting with the odious Jimmy Jarvis and directing his menace and violence? Why was she trying to deal with her husband's murderer, and now her blackmailer? Anyone thinking straight would know that it could almost certainly only end one way – in disgrace and ultimately, prison. Was she in too far to change? Did she stick or twist? She'd been thinking along these lines before, but now everything was coming into a sharper focus. It wasn't just remorse. The ice queen was melting, and in her place was a scared, out-of-her-depth little girl.

*

There were no fancy sash windows in the Fridge's bedsit over the hairdresser's, whose pungent upward-drifting peroxide smells only abated in the evenings when the shop closed. Almost certainly, Jimmy Jarvis would be in The Moon under Water, and that's why the Fridge was staying where he was. He finished the last lines of *The Ragged Trousered Philanthropists* and set it down almost reverently on the small, wobbly, spindle-legged table next to his tatty armchair.

Things had been confusing lately. The book had given him a different perspective, and so had Maria Goodburn in their conversation outside the club. He didn't want to go on like this, a thirty-five-year-old nobody working as a bouncer and criminal enforcer, exploited, he reckoned, by everybody. He picked up the Canterbury College prospectus. Maria had been right – there were art courses he could do, politics, social sciences (whatever they were). Perhaps he could make something of himself. He thought of his art teacher at secondary school, Mr Le Mare, the only one who'd encouraged him, praising his extraordinary watercolour landscapes – 'So delicate, Jason. So precise.' He should have listened a bit more to him – and to his mother, bringing him and his brothers and sisters up single-handed on the Sturry Road estate.

He'd have another chat with Maria. She'd mentioned careers advice he could get. Careers. Not a word he'd ever thought applied to him. She'd mentioned her Labour Party membership. Other books. He'd look into it all. And he'd help her with her current... assignment.

The Fridge had started on a new path.

Chapter 25

Sterling knew about brothels in Kent, and raiding them, from his time in the job. It was always a tricky business, creating as many problems as it solved. It didn't necessarily mean freedom for many of the victims, who were often illegally trafficked and, but for the brothels, homeless. It made sense for there to be a secret network geared to victims rather than law enforcement to whisk young women away and take them somewhere safe so that they could make their own decisions about their futures. And what he was planning had a good feel to it because it was specific – specific targets for rescue, specific focus on rescue. Janice Wray and her organisation would do the rest – the messy stuff of resettlement and support.

He'd spent time on the phone organising a meeting of the key people for the evening – Maria, Patrick and Janice – now there was no more putting off the next task. At least Andy Nolan had shown him how to do it.

Angela's second-in-command, Kerry was at the desk in the library when he went down.

'Is Angie about, Kerry?'

She tipped her head towards the office. 'She's responding to another management consultation, so...'

'Thanks.' From frequent previous experience, Angela might well not be in the best of moods, but he'd psyched himself up. Postponement wasn't something he could contemplate. He knocked on the glass of the door to Angela's cubicle opposite the loans desk, and waited, looking at the floor. Unless Angela had the blinds down, she could see out into most corners of the library, and Sterling thought it best to let her see who was calling without him being pushy.

'Yes, Frank,' she called.

'Got a moment?'

She indicated to the chair opposite her desk. Her expression was neutral.

'I've been an ars... an idiot. I'm sorry.' There it was. Humble pie. This was the moment that Angela could rub it in.

'You've got a lot on your plate,' she said. 'Things haven't been easy lately.'

'It makes no difference. I shouldn't have treated you like that. And Mamujee. And I shouldn't have waited so long to tell you.'

'Well, I'm pleased you did. I don't like rifts. I haven't heard you going up to the office lately, Frank. Are you busy?'

'Yes, a decent case. I had an advance payment too. I'm going down to the Cinq Ports this evening to settle my slate with Becky and Mike. There are fences to mend there as well.'

'I did hear something,' murmured Angela.

'I wonder if you're going down. Usual time. I've missed the crossword. The drink would be on me. And then I'll be having a confab with some of my... associates.'

'Intriguing. I could be persuaded. Panjit's preoccupied with that murder in Canterbury, among other things.'

'Right. Good.'

Angela smiled. 'I've got to get on. Another blessed consultation. See you later.'

*

In the pub at 7 o'clock, Sterling was wondering why apologising was getting easier. It had something to do with practice. When he had been in the force, it had been virtually a matter of honour for him not to, but now he didn't have the luxury to do as he pleased. Mike and Becky were as gracious as Angela. Settling his slate sparked further exchanges along the lines of him saying he wouldn't let it get out of hand again, and the publicans denying that it had ever been an issue.

'It always comes right in the end,' said Becky. 'This time is no exception.'

At 7.30 pm, Maria arrived with Patrick Ngono and Janice Wray. Maria looked around at the neat décor, which combined an old-fashioned cosiness with obvious modern efficiency. The grey stone-flagged floor – an original feature retrieved from beneath the worn carpet and underlay of a previous regime – gleamed, along with the solid-oak tables and chairs. Where there were banquettes against the walls, the dark red upholstery had been refurbished, and the upholstery studs glinted in the late evening light through lattice windows, the leaded diamond panes adding to the olde worlde ambience. Although winter was far off, logs and kindling were stacked in an alcove next to the large, scrubbed, open grate in the middle of the old public bar. Behind the bar, a neat blonde woman in a ponytail made immediate eye contact and smiled. Maria smiled too, and not just in polite response. No doubt about it, compared to The Lotus Blossom, this was Frank Sterling country. And there he was, through in the snug, entirely at home in his own milieu, head bent over a newspaper next to a highly striking woman of colour.

'Frank,' she called. 'We're here.'

Sterling looked up, said something to the woman and walked over. The woman bent her head back over the newspaper.

'Right, drinks everyone. Maria? Janice? Patrick?'

Patrick shifted from one foot to the other. He wasn't used to the places in England that the indigenous folk took for granted, and there was always the possibility of rejection and abuse.

'Take your time,' said Becky softly from behind the bar. 'There's no hurry.'

'Perhaps you could try half a pint of bitter to start off, Patrick,' said Sterling.

'OK.'

'Bitter shandy for me,' said Janice. 'More lemonade than bitter, please. Designated driver…'

'I think I'll have a vodka and coke, Frank,' said Maria. 'I may need fortifying.'

'And another Red Top for me, Becky.' He motioned to a banquette and matching low table. 'Why don't we assemble over there?'

The huddle in the corner lasted an hour. As Patrick participated and contributed, he relaxed. After he'd switched to the guest IPA – Viceroy – without any apparent awareness of irony, he thought he'd manage a pint. If his family in Kumbo could see him…

Janice Wray was generally quiet, chewing at her nails and making her shandy last. She wasn't entirely new to this kind of activity, and when she did contribute, it was to emphasise that there might be danger.

At the end, Sterling asked Maria to summarise.

'Right, so it's going to be tomorrow night at 9 pm, when Patrick always delivers pizza and Lucija always takes it at the door and pays. Patrick has already alerted Lucija and Nina that they're going to be rescued and taken to a safe place to recover and rebuild their lives. Nina will find a way of being with her, or near her, when the pizza comes. We're making the strong assumption that the girls will be having a break at that time, before the night shift, as they always seem to do. Patrick will be leaving as well so that he can make a new start in a new locality and get out of the drugs trade. Patrick, you'll be saying goodbye to all of us tomorrow, but you'll be with good people at the next stage. We'll be in an Underground Railroad people-carrier with one of their drivers. Frank will join you at the front door of the brothel just before nine in case there's a problem.

'According to the map and Google Street View here, there's plenty of room to park in Westgate Close. When Patrick and Frank have got the girls, they'll walk them quickly from the… premises to the van. Janice will wait with the driver in the van as she might be known from her local activism to people associated with the brothel, and I'll wait with her. Everyone will all pile into the van. The driver will drop Janice, Frank and me off in Castle Street before taking Patrick and the girls off. It should be over in no more than twenty minutes.'

'Problems, issues?' said Sterling. He was finding chairing the meeting surprisingly straightforward for someone who'd never been a team person.

'We're sure about the girls, Patrick?' said Janice. 'We often come up against Stockholm Syndrome with young women in this situation, or something like it.'

'Stockholm Syndrome?' said Patrick.

'When people who are prisoners develop a kind of loyalty to the people who are holding them,' said Maria.

'Lucija and Nina are desperate to get away, Lucija especially.' Patrick looked at Sterling and Maria. 'I told you that she is Jimmy Jarvis's favourite. She really doesn't like him at all.'

'OK,' said Janice. 'But there'll be a security detail in the brothel, a thug, maybe more. I'm wondering if you and Patrick will be enough to deal with any trouble from that quarter. They're not just going to airily wave you through the door.'

It had been a long meeting. The Red Top was relaxing. Sterling's thoughts drifted.

'Frank...?' said Maria.

'Sorry. Well, I can handle myself, but why should Patrick have to, even if he'd had some training? I can get backup.'

'Trustworthy?' said Janice. 'We need to keep it all tight.'

'Absolutely. They've literally saved my life.' Metaphorically, he crossed his fingers. He'd need to talk to Becky and Mike. He'd only just paid off his slate, and only just said his sorry. He didn't want it to look as if he'd done all that just to get some professional backup. There was Angela of course, but the same problem applied, and anyway, her partner was an assistant chief constable. 'I'll keep you posted on that.'

At nine o'clock, Janice Wray, Maria and Patrick made for the door. Maria would be back in Canterbury just in time for the last bus home to Whitstable.

Patrick looked around the pub, the drinkers paying him no attention, the smiling landlady, the bar and beer-pulls behind the tempting labels, the banquettes and windows, a quintessentially English scene.

Maria glanced at him. 'There'll be other pubs, Patrick, and other welcomes, at your next stop.'

'I hope so. It's a funny country, England. This, the feeling of belonging you all gave me tonight… and then the other things. You know, there's name-calling even from people I deliver pizzas to – not to my face, but when I cycle off.'

Sterling joined Angela and Mike in the snug with a third pint and a gin and tonic. The crossword had long been finished and the paper tossed aside.

'We were speculating about your little meeting, Frank,' said Angela.

'Surprise, surprise.'

'We can help,' said Mike bluntly.

'Why do you think we might need help, Mike?' Sterling tried to keep his face impassive. Perhaps getting backup was going to be easier than he expected. For the moment, he was interested in Mike's analysis. When Mike could be persuaded to open up, there were always plenty of instructive insights.

'You couldn't get four more different people. The girl was at ease, in the pub and with you. I suspect you've been working together. The young man was foreign, and not used to pubs. He looked as though he was a refugee or asylum seeker. He was dressed in hand-me-downs from the charity shop. The other woman was nervous and edgy, but also worldly wise. Blue hair. Smoker or ex-smoker. An activist of some kind, likely a feminist. Then there's you.' Mike stopped.

'Yes,' said Angela. She'd leaned forward, now as interested as Sterling.

'Well, it's just that when Frank's got a case, the odds are strong that there's going to be action of one kind or another. Becky and I were talking about it this evening. It's been quiet around here lately. That's why we're offering. And Frank, in case you're worried, we're not connecting the... rapprochement with the case and the timing.'

Thrill junkies. Sterling calculated that he hadn't even needed to apologise, let alone pay off the tab. The first whiff of action, and there they were. Still, it wasn't inconvenient. 'Generous of you both in the circs. As it happens, I may have something. It's an in-and-out job, perfectly legal as far as I can see, but you never know what might turn up on the day.'

'I can help too,' said Angela.

'Really?' said Sterling. *Another thrill junky. They're queuing up*. 'What about Panjit?'

'What about him? You just said it was legal. Anyway, you know I don't dance to Panjit's tune.'

'Right, well, two will be enough. Presumably Becky and Mike will toss for who gets the action and who looks after the pub. This is the plan...'

*

In south Canterbury that same Thursday evening, twenty-four hours after the fiasco in Greyfriars Garden and her earlier crisis of confidence and loss of equanimity, Charlotte Hankinson was rattling around her large house, not particularly focusing on anything, but enjoying the space and freedom it gave her.

She was upstairs when the landline rang, looking with a cool eye into the bedroom Jack had used, working out how she might clear everything out, redecorate and erase his memory. Calmly, she crossed the wide landing, went down the stairs and picked up the phone.

The pips beeped on the payphone, and she waited. 'Charlotte Hankinson.'

'I think you know who this is.'

'I do.' She still could not even tell the gender of the heavily disguised voice.

'Last night was foolish. If this is going to work, there has to be trust.'

Hankinson noted the present tense. There didn't seem to be anger either. She grimaced. 'I had to try, don't you think? I reckon you'd have thought less of me if I hadn't.'

'Well, it certainly got the juices going, and your goon almost got my poor foot. I haven't scampered so quickly up a wall since I was a kid.'

'And of course, you're richer by £10,000, while I didn't get a thing. There was nothing on the flash drive.'

'True,' said the voice. 'For me, that was a trial run, to see if you could be trusted. Obviously you can't. I suppose the bad faith is on both sides. But there's going to be a penalty for yours. Your operation is clever. There are no obvious overlaps between the different parts. So this is what's going to happen. The local press is going to receive exclusive material about one of those parts, which is bound to lead to a police investigation. Heads will roll. Inevitably, given the detail. Then you'll know I really mean business.'

At that moment, Charlotte Hankinson experienced an insight more sharply and clearly than she'd ever felt before, Damascene in its certainty and intensity. Afterwards, because she was normally so cautious, she marvelled at her impulsiveness. 'You could do that,' she said, 'and I couldn't really blame you. But you're a likely... individual. You've done well already. To be honest, if it was you who killed my Jack, I'm not as upset as you might think. Frankly, the marriage was over. Maybe I loved him once, but by the time he was gone I didn't even like him. This clinches it. I don't need the hassle of running Jack's dodgy businesses. It needs someone young, someone hungry, someone who's not afraid of getting his hands dirty.'

'I don't underst–'

'I'm offering you the business, lock, stock and barrel. Not selling it – what is there to sell? – giving it, along with the means to run it. Or rather, the rest of the means to run it. You've got plenty of data already, haven't you?' One moment she'd been fretting about the botched ambush and everything related to it. The next she'd seen the solution to all her difficulties – not perfect but some sort of way out.

There was silence except for a very light breathing. Hankinson held her own breath and expected the pips to go.

'Alright,' said the voice.

Lord, that was quick.

'Who's your Number Two?'

'Number T–?' she started to say.

‘The one who looks after things for you. Obviously, from what I can see, none of this happens by magic. I’ll need his, or her, details.’

‘Jimmy Jarvis. He uses burners. This is his latest number.’ She fumbled for it, emotion making her clumsy. ‘So that means no more…’ But only the dialling tone sounded in her ear. She put the phone down, fumbling it onto the cradle. Her whole body started trembling so violently that she had to rest a hand on the table as she leaned against the wall. She gulped for air. Relief coursed through her in torrents.

Chapter 26

The brothel was like many other HMOs. The original three-bedroomed semi had been extended sideways and at the back. The house's garage had been knocked down to accommodate the extra blocks, and access to the back garden down the side had gone forever. The alteration hadn't extended to removing the concrete tracks to the former garage, the shortest road to nowhere, ever. Ivy and another creeping plant that Maria couldn't name were colonising and weakening the fence at the side. The small patch of vegetation at the front – it couldn't be called a garden – was scrubby and unkempt. A railed block of steps, shared with the adjoining house, led to the front door whose varnish had faded, leaving a mottled and discoloured brown shade.

A nondescript house, an area of high churn, anonymity, and, arriving as a sudden afterthought, plenty of on-road parking. *Yes,* Maria concluded. *Perfect for a brothel.*

The people-carrier bearing her and her three companions had come up from the city centre and turned left into Westgate Court Avenue. They'd driven past the cemetery gates, with the cemetery spread out to the north behind, and up the hill before turning right into Westgate Close and along the cemetery's west side.

Here, the road was narrow and the houses bunched and perched together at the very top. A hemmed-in feeling, triggered by the cramped locale and the crowd in the car, jostled with Maria's other thoughts.

Janice Wray sat in the front passenger seat, gnawing her nails. The driver, a large-boned young woman called Em, short for Emmeline, with short red hair and a small tattoo on her wrist of a clenched fist within the circle of the female gender sign, kept her thick fingers on the steering wheel. Sterling completed the company, sitting next to Maria with his eyes, like the other six, firmly fixed on the target.

'Have you been in a brothel, Frank?' said Maria, her face still directed away from him. A casual enquiry into the male psyche.

Sterling dragged his eyes from the house. He frowned. Was this a wind-up? Over the time of his association with Maria, there had been plenty of back and forth, mostly instigated by him, but Maria had quickly become as adept at baiting him as the other way around. The other women had become more alert. The atmosphere in the vehicle, already tense, took on a subtly different character, expectancy added to the mix. Perspiration prickled on Sterling's back and arms. Here he was, discussing his link with brothels in a car-load of militant feminists.

'I've raided a few, with my fellow officers, back in the day.' He picked out his words carefully, like a sapper in a minefield.

'I meant, have you used a brothel. You know, been with a –' Maria's face as she finally turned to him was a picture of blank, sweet, objectively curious innocence.

'Here's Patrick,' Sterling said. Now he wouldn't have to say 'Mind your own business.'

From their vantage point on the opposite side of the road and further down from the brothel, the would-be rescuers watched as the Cameroonian laboured up the steep slope, standing on the pedals, the large square bag bobbing on his back. Sterling couldn't hear it, but he assumed that the wonky back wheel would still be clanking. An unexpected spell of light drizzle had begun to fall, so there would be a stripe of damp up Patrick's back.

His eyes flickered to the people-carrier and then away. He dismounted in front of the brothel, wobbling slightly under the weight of the bag, and rested the bike delicately, almost reverently, against the block of steps.

To Sterling, it seemed curious and futile. The bike was about to be abandoned and Patrick would never see it again, but perhaps it wasn't so strange. Courtesy, decency and conscientiousness seemed to be pillars of the young man's personality. Hitching the bag further up his back, he plodded up the steps to the door.

*

While Sterling and his companions waited in the van for Patrick to ring the doorbell, in The Moon under Water, Jimmy Jarvis, on his fourth pint, was ruminating on his phone call with Todman half an hour earlier. 'Your girl...'

'She's not "my girl", mate.'

'Whatever. Anyway, she's just been picked up by a large black car, so I reckon something's going on. Thought you might be interested.'

'Details? Car registration?'

'What am I, a bleedin' traffic warden? I haven't got a clue. But I haven't seen the car before. I don't know how many people were in it, if any. The back windows were tinted.'

'Alright. Tell me when the bint comes back, and who with.' Jarvis took another pull of his pint. Like his boss in south Canterbury, he had the sense that things were happening beyond his control.

His phone chirruped again. He looked at the screen. Unknown number. 'Hello?' He frowned as he heard the pips. 'Who is this?' Something in what he was hearing made him alert. There were two items, both obviously important, but one important and urgent.

A flash of insight sparked in his cunning brain, linking the two calls. He'd soon find out if the second was kosher. 'Get the van,' he shouted to one of his thugs at the end of the bar. 'Now. We're going up to Westgate Close. Hurry the fuck up. Where's Fridge? He was at that table a minute ago.'

'He's got the runs, he said. Again,' smirked one of his crew. 'He dashed out to the bog.'

'Fuck's sake,' muttered Jarvis. But four of them would be enough. 'Leave him. Come on.'

In the Gents, Fridge's bowels were in satisfactory order, but the synapses of his brain were crackling, like Jarvis's a minute before. Maria had been asking him about the brothel, and now Jimmy and the gang were rushing up there. He got out his phone and speed-dialled.

*

In the people-carrier, Maria's phone chirruped as Patrick knocked on the brothel door. 'Hi Jason,' she said. 'It's Fridge,' she mouthed to Sterling. Suddenly, she was ramrod-straight from her slouching position, listening intently. 'Jesus,' she muttered, the offsider who virtually never swore. 'OK, thanks, Jason.' She ended the call. 'A group of about five blokes are coming up here in a van. Somebody tipped them off about what's happening.'

'For goodness' sake,' said Janice Wray. 'How on earth–?'

'Never mind that for now,' said Sterling. 'We need to concentrate on getting Patrick and the girls away. Maria, did the Fridge say how long they'd be?'

'About ten minutes.'

'I'm going to help Patrick, as per the plan. As far as I remember, this whole area is one big cul-de-sac from just beyond the cemetery gates. Check the map on one of your phones. We need to find a quiet space down one of the side roads to lie low in. If we meet that van coming up, it's curtains. I'll sort out the backup when I get back.'

'Backup?' said Maria, but Sterling was out of the sliding door and gone.

He leapt up the brothel steps two at a time, slipping next to Patrick but out of the range of anyone at the door. Patrick knocked, two heavy thumps and two short raps. Sterling leaned on the brickwork and tried to control his breathing. The adrenaline was flooding through him. He could sense Patrick quivering next to him. There were sounds of bolts unflapping from behind the door. A small white face appeared.

'Pizza,' said Patrick, unhitching the bag. 'Is Nina with you?' he whispered to the face. The girl Lucija nodded. Patrick nodded in turn to Sterling. 'Come on then,' he said. Sterling could see the whites of Patrick's eyes in the gloomy lamplight.

The girls stepped outside, gingerly, doubtfully, in dressing gowns, discarding their stilettos on the doorstep. Patrick gave Lucija his hand as she trotted down the steps.

'Oi. Oi!' came a loud male voice from inside. 'Where the hell do you think you're going?' A large man appeared at the door and stepped out.

Grabbing him by the lapels of his cardigan, Sterling swung him around and delivered a Glasgow kiss. There was a sharp crack. He released his hands at the point of impact, allowing the momentum created by his forehead to whip the man's head back.

The brothel warden howled with pain, the blood that spurted from his newly broken nose spattering Sterling's chin and shirt.

Sterling shooed Nina down the steps after the other two and hurried her to the people-carrier, his arm around her waist, half-lifting her to save her bare feet from prolonged contact with tarmac and pavement. Outside the brothel, the delivery bag lay unzipped on the scrubby frontage, pizza boxes half in and half out. Patrick's touring bike remained neatly stacked against the steps.

The big man sat crumpled at the top of the steps, sleeve against his gushing nose, moaning. Strewn around him, the fuck-me stilettos, each one capsized, signalled bleakness and loss.

In the people-carrier, Sterling didn't know who to ask about the maps amid the flurry and commotion. He fixed on Maria. 'Maria, we're not out of it yet. We must have used up five minutes. Did you pull up the map?'

Maria proffered her phone. 'Up to the junction, right into Westgate Court Avenue, up to the very top and round the corner. Then we can sneak back down the way we came after a few minutes.'

'Got that, Em?'

The young woman nodded and slipped the car into gear. They moved off briskly and smoothly. No need for drama and screeching tyres.

Through the tinted glass, Sterling could make out an elegant woman in a flowered, knee-length dress framed in the doorway of the bawdy house and backlit from the warm interior light. Her china-doll face was distinctive, with its high and wide forehead, large round eyes and delicate nose, all tapering down to an o-shaped mouth and tiny chin. She was ignoring the crumpled man, following the people-carrier with her eyes and speaking urgently into her mobile. So far, so unexpected. What unsettled Sterling was how calm she was, how unfazed, as if she knew exactly what she was doing.

*

A few minutes later, a white van sped up Westgate Court Avenue and past the cemetery gates. At the junction of Fisher Road, it pulled sharply to a halt and a heavyset man got out. Someone who knew the area, like Jimmy Jarvis, realised that that was the first place where any vehicle driver had a choice of exit from the Westgate estate.

The van jolted off on its way, turned right fifty yards up into Westgate Close, and drew up outside the brothel. Jarvis rapped on the door. The shoes had gone, and so had the man with the broken nose, but Jarvis saw the dark bloodstains at the top of the steps. The madam, Maddie Spedding with her china-doll painted face, came to the door.

'Talk to me.'

The woman was brisk. In her line of business, there was no other way. 'A dark people-carrier was here at the same time as the pizza man, it being Friday. Instead of collecting the pizza, the girls stepped out with the darkie. Joe followed, and another man came out from the side and nutted him. The girls and the men got in the car and left. That's when I phoned you. Good job you were already on your way. How did you know to come up here?'

'Tip-off,' said Jarvis, without elaborating. 'Who went?'

The madam paused. She had news he wouldn't want to hear. Lucija was his favourite when he wanted a freebie. 'Lucija and Nina.'

Jarvis growled and smacked the brickwork. 'Shit. Shit and buggery.'

'Did a dark people-carrier pass you' – she looked at her watch – 'about a minute and a half ago?'

'No.'

'Well,' – she smiled grimly, lips pursed – 'that's the good news. It means you got up here in time. And you've stationed someone at Fisher Road?'

'Yes. But if that's the good news, what's the bad?'

The madam sighed. 'Think about it, Jimmy. The people who took the girls knew you were coming. They were tipped off. We'll need to get back to that later, but in the meantime, they're still around here somewhere, up one of the roads. Time to get busy. We can retrieve this.'

*

In the people-carrier, the initial euphoria of excitement and escape had worn off. Now rescuers and rescuees sat in anxious dark silence at the top of Westgate Court Avenue and around the corner. The scent of cheap perfume pervaded the atmosphere, along with the occasional whimper from Nina, one of the girls. There was something else that Sterling recognised from long association and countless adventures, unconnected to any of the senses at all. Fear. He turned to his phone, his face wan in its eerie glow.

'Becky? We've got a problem. We've got the girls and Patrick, but we're hemmed in up Westgate Court Avenue. Somehow, those running the brothel got wind of things. They've got a van up here, according to Maria's source. We can't move until we know it won't block us in.' Sterling listened. 'Right,' he muttered. 'OK… OK…' And then the call was over.

'Listen up, everyone. We're going to be alright. There's just going to be a short delay, while our backup sorts out a way we can get out without being stopped or followed. We stay in the car, keep the doors locked, keep quiet and just sit in the dark till I get a call back.' There was another whimper.

Next to him Lucija, pluckier than her friend, whispered, 'I hope you are right because if not, there will be hell to pay, as you English say.'

Sterling called up to Janice Wray. 'Janice, I need to swap with you. I've got to talk to Em.' There followed shuffling and squirming that continued after Sterling had reached the front passenger seat as the liberated girls wrestled out of their bawdy house attire and into the jeans, T-shirts, hoodies and trainers their rescuers supplied.

'Em,' said Sterling softly. He leaned close to the ringed and multi-pierced ear. 'You need to be ready for a bit of rally-driving. It may mean some pavement and grass verge. Someone might try and jump or stand in front of the car to stop us. Don't stop. Gun it. Believe me, if you show you mean business, they'll jump out of the way. I speak from experience. As a copper, I did plenty of holding my hand up to stop vehicles and plenty of diving for cover. Got it?'

'Got it.'

*

Jimmy Jarvis and his crew were a quarter of a mile away. Jarvis barked his orders. It was like the army again, except that he wasn't on the receiving end. This way was much better.

'Sam, take the van and join Barry at Fisher Road. Block the road by stopping next to a parked car, not obviously, but if another car comes along and wants to get past, pretend you're manoeuvring or something and make some space. Then block it again. The rest of you, we're going to go up and down each road off this one and the one at the end, Westgate Court Avenue. We're going to check every nook and cranny for a dark-coloured people-carrier with a coon, a couple of whores and some do-gooding meddlers. Keep your phones at the ready. When we find them, there's gonna be no holding back. Don't be obvious. It's dark and there aren't many people about, but there are always stupid dog walkers and the like.'

As Jarvis and his crew set off, two female figures emerged from the path that abutted the north side of the cemetery. They walked briskly past the brothel and back down Westgate Close. As they approached the men, Jarvis pointed down a side road and one of his crew peeled off to check it. The women broke into a trot, as if they were on a run, had had a brief walking rest and were back jogging again. They passed the men, ignoring them, got to the end of the close and turned left.

When the men reached the junction after them, Jarvis gesticulated down Westgate Court Avenue towards the van. 'You take the next side road, mate,' he said to one of the two remaining men, and pointed. 'And you take the two on the other side,' he said to the other. He set off the other way to the top of Westgate Court Avenue. All the roads were covered. If the raiding party were in the vehicle anywhere in the vicinity, he was confident he and his mates would find it. He started padding up the hill, cursing at his deployments. He should have got one of the others doing this road since it was the longest and steepest.

*

Becky and Angela, the joggers, approached the white van, which was blocking the road, not very subtly. Becky rapped on the driver's window. There was a whirr as the window went down. A greasy, pock-marked face appeared, beady dark eyes looking her up and down. 'You're blocking the road, pal,' said Becky.

'Yeah,' leered the man called Sam. 'What of it?'

'Well, people will want to come past, including our lift. Move it down a few yards, so it's not opposite that car.'

'Can't. We're waiting to pick something up.'

'From where?' said Becky. 'The nearest house is twenty metres away.'

Sam's patience ended. 'Listen, lady, if a car turns up, I'll move. Otherwise, here is where we're staying. If you don't like it, you can f... Hard luck.'

Becky stepped back and nodded slightly as if that reaction was expected – she'd tried and now it was time for something else. The man watched her as she stepped in front of the van and looked to the left and right as if measuring distances. Sam's brow puckered. What was she up to? She ignored him and walked past the van. In the wing mirror, he watched her go through the same process. He'd lost sight of the darkie. He looked over at Barry in the passenger seat and raised his eyebrows. *Women, eh?* said the gesture. A dark green roadside Openreach junction box seemed of particular interest on his right, and a tree with low hanging branches on the left. Still, she wasn't bothering them anymore. She moved out of the scope of the side mirror and got out her phone.

Sterling listened. 'OK. Right.' He turned to Em. 'Time to go. When you see the white van blocking the road, veer to the right, up the kerb and on to the verge. There'll be room between a junction box and the van. Turn right and then left soon after, and then we're away. The van won't be following. And remember, we don't stop. Let's go.'

There was another whimper in the back as Em turned the engine on and slipped it into gear. The people-carrier edged out of the alcove where Westgate Court Avenue had petered out. A few yards along, a figure appeared in the middle of the road. Em, as instructed, gunned the engine and the car began to pick up speed. The small wiry figure set his feet in the middle of the road and got out what appeared to be a baseball bat with wicked-looking embellishments which Sterling, from his experience in the job, knew was barbed wire. Sterling could read the man's body language as plain as day, from aggression ('stop') to cocky defiance ('I dare you to knock me down') to outraged disbelief ('Jesus'), all in three seconds, the performance topped by a fling of the bat and a desperate dive between two parked cars.

'Down with the patriarchy,' muttered Em.

'Jimmy!' gasped Lucija, shuddering. The bat clattered onto the road, and a crack appeared in the windscreen

*

In the van at Fisher Road, the two thugs felt a rocking and sinking, first on one side and then the other. At the same time, Sammy, the driver, saw in the rear-view mirror the people-carrier coming at a brisk pace down the road. His phone was buzzing.

'What the hell is happening?' said Barry from the passenger seat, twisting round to look at the road behind him. He saw the people-carrier bounce over the kerb and onto the verge, squeezing between the junction box and Sammy's side mirror with inches to spare. It screeched right into Fisher Road, and then left and swiftly out of sight. It wasn't that Sam wasn't attempting pursuit. He'd reacted quickly enough to turn on the engine but the van had only gone a few feet before the punctured tyres were ripped to shreds and the vehicle ground painfully to a halt. He and Barry watched the two women jog down the road and disappear through the cemetery gates, too stunned to think of pursuing.

*

Jimmy Jarvis dusted himself down and limped down the hill, blood oozing from grazes to his hands and knees. He reached the junction of Fisher Road and Westgate Court Avenue when all the action and drama had finished. Arms akimbo, Barbie dangling loosely from his hand, he surveyed the sorry scene in front of him, the van disabled and listing, his crew in various states of confusion and disarray, tyre marks on the verge, and the quarry not only gone but for all he knew completely unscathed. Jarvis snarled and ground his teeth. The second time in days that he'd been thwarted. There would be payback, said his face.

*

At the brothel, Maggie Spedding was dealing with the pandemonium. 'Jimmy will be back shortly,' she threatened. She set the girls tasks, those who weren't with customers, having them brew tea or scrub the cry-baby Joe's blood from the outside steps. She herself dabbed distractedly at the big soft man's bloody nose with cotton wool soaked in surgical spirit as he moaned his excuses. The customers in the rooms upstairs, thankfully, had been too preoccupied to realise that anything had even happened.

This was Logan's doing. His fingerprints were all over it. Everywhere she went, when he followed, he brought her trouble. But what was he up to? Jarvis had mentioned a tip-off. Was that Logan? She couldn't imagine him being part of pinching Lucija and Nina – unless it was part of a longer game. She sighed. It was all too complicated. She loved him, but he was a millstone.

Chapter 27

The rescuers chose The White Hart for the debriefing, a traditional pub on the corner of St Mary's Green just within the city walls. It was quiet except for the clack of falling bar skittles and the happy chatter of a group of students playing it – almost certainly – for the first time.

Angie and Becky arrived shortly after the main group.

Sterling got the drinks in and carried the tray out to the garden where everyone had assembled. He slipped the receipt into his pocket to avoid Maria's knowing look. He didn't know why he cared what she thought. Nightfall had long arrived, but the evening was warm and a string of lights stretching down to the back gate bathed the rescue cadre in a benevolent glow. Two teeming flowerbeds framed the tables in between.

'Cheers,' he said, sipping his pint. The beer was Gadds. The pub soared in his estimation. 'Mission accomplished.'

The women lifted their glasses.

'Good job we had backup,' said Maria, nodding her thanks to Becky and Angela.

There was euphoria – after all, everything had worked out well in the end – but it was tinged with something else, most likely sadness. Sterling knew that Maria had respected and become fond of Patrick, and he had liked him as well. They wouldn't be seeing him again, or the girls and plucky Emmeline, strangers as they were. At most, the acquaintance with them had lasted a half-hour from the door of the hostel to Em driving off with them towards the A2 and London. So euphoria and sadness, but casting a pall over proceedings was a far more dangerous matter. How had Jack Hankinson's crew known about the brothel raid? Was there a Judas in the ranks? Had careless talk almost cost lives?

'We need to talk about how it could have gone really badly wrong,' said Sterling. There was no point in beating about the bush. 'Did anyone talk to anyone else outside the group? Maria, what about your snitch, the Fridge?'

'No way, Frank.' Indignation, upset and defiance flushed her face. 'The opposite. The Fr… Jason phoned us up and warned us before it all kicked off. Why would he do that if he was dropping us in it?'

Sterling shrugged. 'I dunno. Mischief? Some other angle we don't know about? Did you talk to anyone else?'

Maria turned away, eyes and cheeks glistening under the uneven lights. 'Why don't you ask the others if they've done any blabbing?' There was bitterness in her voice.

On one of his other cases, there had been a moment when he *had* doubted Becky and Angela after a sequence of dangerous events, but it had later emerged that a tracker had been put on his borrowed car, which Becky herself had recovered, and that had explained everything. He didn't want to risk another rift with them.

'I haven't talked to anyone, and I know Becky hasn't because we discussed the possibility on the way over,' said Angela. She gave Sterling a careful, measured look, pre-empting and dealing with his dilemma. Becky nodded.

Janice Wray leaned over and put her martini on the table. 'We shouldn't fall out about this. I'll just confirm though that I haven't talked to anyone except one person at the Underground Railroad. Even my partner back at home doesn't know. We operate in cells, and we rely on secrecy, discretion and caution. Everything would fall apart if we didn't. I'd never met Emmeline before tonight. She wouldn't have got her assignment until the last minute, and when she drops those girls and Patrick off, it will be somewhere neutral in or near London where they'll be taken on to the next place by another woman who knows no more than she needs to.'

'But maybe' – she swirled her drink absent-mindedly – 'Patrick or one of the girls said something to the wrong person, and it got back to that crew. One or both girls could well have been conflicted – we see it more often than you'd imagine. Their lives in that brothel were dire in almost all respects, especially from our point of view, but you never know all the circumstances, and the madams... well, that one could have been kind. And after all, it's a life they'd become familiar with. A foreign country with no papers and the prospect of returning to what is probably a poverty-stricken home in Eastern Europe? That might not be welcome. Nothing is straightforward. An overheard conversation, last-minute cold feet, a change of heart...'

'One of those kids was Jack Hankinson's go-to girl, according to Patrick,' said Maria, who was recovering her equilibrium after plenty of recent practice. 'And maybe the other was someone else's favourite. They might have had special status.'

'There you are. Another factor,' said Janice Wray. 'It's messy. They want to escape. They want to stay. Stockholm Syndrome, as I said before...'

'Well, we're not planning another stunt like that, but now that we've stirred things up, we need to stay safe and alert.' Sterling looked around the table, noting that everyone had finished their drinks. He drained the last dregs of his. 'Right then, I guess we're all ready to make tracks. Maria, will you be OK for a bus? Janice, how are you getting home?'

The group parted at the car park at Castle Row, Sterling getting a lift with Angela in Becky's car. Janice and Maria reached Dane John's Gardens and the steps up to the pedestrian bridge across the ring road to Canterbury East Station.

At the top, Janice stopped. 'Frank can be blunt.'

'Tell me about it,' said Maria.

'Apart from tonight, how are you getting on with the Hankinson case?'

'A few leads, but not much progress,' said Maria. The two women lingered, not quite ready to part.

Janice Wray nodded. 'It's causing a lot of churn. Things could do with settling down around here for my... constituency. I wish you luck. Well, I'm this way.'

'Goodbye, Janice,' said Maria. The bus station was at the other end of the city wall. The Simmons Memorial where Charlotte Hankinson had met Jimmy Jarvis an eternity ago loomed in the darkness.

Janice Wray crossed the footbridge. At 10.30 pm on Friday evening, the stream of headlight beams on the ever-congested road was abating. In contrast, at Club Chemistry, the nightclub converted from an old warehouse opposite the station, things were warming up, and she could see the faint kaleidoscope of disco colours flashing at the windows to a solid bass beat. In front of the station, she turned right where it was well lit, got to the bottom and turned left under the railway bridge. The rumble of a train mingled with the hum of traffic and Wincheap's bustle at the end of the week. The main road, studded with businesses, was lively and cheerful, especially with a pub on the corner where live music blared out.

Wray walked briskly into the maze of Wincheap side streets. A wave of fatigue swept over her as she turned into Grove Terrace towards her cottage. She wouldn't want anything like tonight's excitement and drama again for a good while. It would be good to get home and relax.

Fatigue and familiarity dulled her senses. She didn't notice the black saloon pull out at the top of the road. Cars didn't interest her and she had no idea which belonged in the area and which were from elsewhere. She might have recognised the white van from earlier but Green Flag, a tow truck and two puzzled operatives were dealing with that on the other side of the city. She was almost home. She had even got out her key to insert into the Yale lock.

The car pulled to a quiet halt in the middle of the road. Two balaclava'd figures emerged. Seizing her, they frogmarched her roughly away. Her arms were pinioned behind her back, the hand of one burly man clamped over her mouth. Not that she would necessarily have screamed – she was too shocked and surprised.

Wray's partner sensed something from behind the window of the living room. She was in time to see Janice's legs and distinctive trainers disappear after the rest of her into the back of the car. Men got in. Doors slammed. The car moved away. Too late and terrified to dash out to intervene, she sprang to her mobile on the sofa. Her fingers trembled as she jabbed for 999.

'Hello, emergency service operator, which service do you require? Fire, police, or ambulance?'

'Police,' said the woman. Back at the window, her eyes darted up and down the street.

'I'll just connect you now.'

'Hello, this is the police. Can you tell me your name, your phone number and where are you calling from? Your town, street, house number, postcode or any other distinctive features around you.'

'Jeez. Miranda Towers, 13 Grove Terrace Canterbury, CT1 3 SZ. 0758 408 1627'

'What is the nature of your emergency?'

'Abduction. Kidnapping. My partner, Janice Wray... bloody hell, we're wasting time.'

'Where is it happening?'

'It's happened. It's over. Janice has gone.'

'Bear with me... Is anyone injured?'

'I don't know. They stuffed her into the back of a car and drove off.'

'Are there any weapons involved?'

'Christ, I haven't got a clue. There's no one here now. I've told you this already.'

'Right, thank you, madam, the police will be with you shortly.'

Four doors down, someone else had seen the drama. Ken Todman jerked together the raggedy, faded flowery curtains. There might be a drink from one source or another based on what he'd just seen. For the moment though, best let sleeping dogs lie.

Chapter 28

Detective Sergeant Murphy was thinking of home and maybe the pub over the field with the dog. A pint in the steep garden out the back looking over the hop fields in the warm evening air, and a million miles from all the crap of the day. But as he passed the control room, he heard the despatcher sending a patrol car to an address in the city. It was like hearing your name across the room at a busy event or party. He waited for the exchange to end before he spoke. 'What was that address again, Amy?'

'17 Grove Terrace, Wincheap, sir.'

'And what's the problem?'

'Possible abduction and kidnapping.'

'Thanks, Amy.' Murphy felt something in his stomach – not butterflies exactly, but that allegedly special gut feeling only the police experienced. He strode purposefully through the Major Incident Room and found DCI Nolan just preparing to leave.

'Guv, something's come in that we might want to look at. I pricked up my ears as I was passing the control room. There was mention of an abduction at Grove Terrace in Wincheap.'

Nolan sighed and put the jacket he'd just picked up back over his chair. 'Grove Terrace? What's special about Grove Terrace?'

‘It’s where the snitch – the CI – lives, the one Sophie and I went to see. I reckon he’ll know something, and given the weird things going on in this city, I’d be surprised if there wasn’t some connection to the murder.’

‘So what are you suggesting we do?’

‘Tell the attending officers that we’ll be joining them shortly. It shouldn’t take long…’

Nolan scratched his scalp. ‘Come on then. Hopefully, this straw we’re clutching might lead to something.’

*

Ten minutes later, Nolan was in Janice Wray’s house in Wincheap. Wray’s partner was enveloped by a large armchair in the front room. Her legs were drawn up and her arms wrapped around her knees, her head resting on them. Her eyes stared out at nothing.

Nolan noted that the attending patrol officers – O’Brian and May – were experienced and calm, and that had transmitted itself into the atmosphere of the room. Surreptitiously, he clocked that it was clean but shabby, with a tapestry depicting a women’s suffragette march hung on one wall above a large maroon sofa matching the chair, multi-coloured rugs on the bare, unvarnished floor and a small television in the corner. Almost opposite the front door was the entry to the kitchen, separated from the living room by a beaded curtain. Light came not from a central ceiling fitting but two floor lamps with intricately patterned shades and faux-lead borders. On the coffee table was a packet of Rizla and a tin of tobacco, but no ashtray, and no stale odour of nicotine. The smoker in this house practised her habit out of doors, and a fat candle dispensed a scent Nolan didn't recognise. He resisted comparisons with an opium den. Instead, he sensed respectability, even if it had a Bohemian slant.

'Ms Towers, I'm DCI Nolan. I'm here because this is clearly a serious matter. Officer May,' – Nolan nodded at the policewoman standing by the front door – 'briefed me before I came in, so I'm up to speed with what's happened. I think the key question is whether you know of anyone who wanted to take your partner. Has Ms Wray got any enemies – anyone she's fallen out with or owes money to – something like that?'

'I don't know,' said the young woman, dragging her attention from some far-off place and focusing on Nolan seated on the sofa.

Nolan sensed a holding back. 'It's difficult to develop a plan without having as full a picture as possible of Janice's life,' he said gently. 'Our patrols are on the lookout, obviously, and we'll set things up so that we're ready if you get a call about her, but…'

'I doubt anyone will be demanding a ransom. Look around, Mr Nolan. Janice and I haven't got anything. We're both students. I'm on the tills at Waitrose on the weekends. She does some hours in a care home. And I'm not trying to hide anything either. We've been together a year, living together here for the last six months. But there are things Janice is involved in that she tells me nothing about. "It's safer for you that way," she always says. So I'm thinking that it's to do with that.'

'Things?' said Nolan. He looked behind him at the tapestry.

The young woman followed his movement. 'I told you. I don't know. But yes, she's a feminist, as am I, and yes, if you do some digging, you'll probably find out that she was' – she gulped – 'a sex worker, in London. But she's turned her back on all that. That's why she was down here doing a degree. She's with me now...'

The exchange petered out. Nolan's long experience indicated that the young woman was telling the truth, and that information about her partner and her activities would have to come from somewhere else. It was a good strategy to keep a colourful and probably at times dangerous past from a partner – until something like this happened. Then secrecy and anonymity backfired.

'What I'm going to do is put out an all-county alert to my colleagues in the force about the car and any suspicious activity. We'll set things up so you can alert us if you receive any phone call about Janice, or, for example, a demand for a ransom. With your permission, we'll borrow her laptop and I'll have an officer look over the house to see if anything relevant turns up. If you think of anything you may have overlooked, phone this number' – he produced a card from his wallet – 'and leave a message for me.'

'Alright. I don't think you'll find anything on her laptop, and there's nothing much around the house.'

'You never know. Is there anyone who can be with you when we leave?'

The woman shrugged. 'I'll be OK.'

Nolan wanted to be upbeat – *in nine cases out of ten, everything in this sort of situation turns out well...* But he had no idea of the statistics, and all the details he'd received didn't fill him with optimism. 'Goodbye for now. We'll review things tomorrow if there's no more news.' As he left, the sobbing started. He exchanged glances with the policewoman May, who moved into the living room and out of sight.

On the pavement, he looked around. Murphy hadn't come into the house with him, simply saying he'd be back in a moment. Where had he gone? Then Nolan remembered – the snitch – four doors down. He approached just as the door opened and Murphy appeared, catching sight of a time- and alcohol-ravaged, embittered face behind him.

'Strewth,' said the man. 'You lot. Can't we have a bit of peace and quiet down here of a Friday night?' The door shut with a slam, and Murphy and Nolan were left standing awkwardly in the street.

'Not much help there,' said Murphy. 'I expect you got the picture. No money changed hands either, which explains the last little scene. Two balaclava'd men bundled the woman into a black car – the same story as you heard I imagine – that's all he knows.'

*

But that wasn't all Ken Todman knew. When he was sure that the detectives had gone, he got out his phone – the same performance as usual. When he got the connection, he gave his message.

'It's me. The filth have been here about the woman. She was snatched outside her front door. If it was you lot, and I'd be amazed if it wasn't, a word to the wise. They're on to it, and they're taking it very seriously. So whatever you do, you need to take that into account.'

'No idea what you're on about,' lied Jimmy Jarvis as he ended the call.

*

Later, when Nolan had finally got home and mercifully his wife was massaging his itching scalp, working in soothing lotion, he recounted the events of the day, including the abduction.

'Do you think it's all connected?' said his wife.

'Yes. And I wouldn't be surprised if Frank Sterling is involved too. I'll contact him again tomorrow.'

Chapter 29

The slight pony-tailed Polish girl approached the Zoar Chapel for the fourth Saturday morning in a row. An hour of cleaning at this funny little place inserted in the city wall – before her busy shift at Costa Coffee in the High Street – suited her very well. The minister, if that's what he was, had been kind and encouraging when she'd gone for the interview. He'd explained that as the only service was on Sunday, Saturday was cleaning day. So reliability, as well as cleaning skills, was essential. The man wasn't a priest, and she wasn't even sure if he was anything else except a kind of elder. Things were much clearer in the Roman Catholic church, comfortingly so. On the second Saturday, the man had met her at the chapel to review her work and the whole arrangement, which they'd both agreed was satisfactory and could continue.

The chapel was separated from the walkway by a well-maintained waist-height brick wall topped by black railings, with a matching metal gate in the middle. As she approached, she knew that something was wrong. The gate was ajar, and worse, the chapel door had been crudely jemmied. Tentatively, she approached the entrance. Supposing the intruder was still inside, rummaging around for money or cash she knew wouldn't be there? Should she simply phone Mr Carter and the police?

She fumbled in her bag for her phone, but as she was about to dial, she heard a low sound from within, in the range between a wail and a moan. Her stomach lurched, just like in the moment on a plane when it's freed from the earth's shackles. It was a woman's voice, she was sure of it, so gingerly she pushed the broken door inwards and crept in. Nothing is plainer than the inside of a Baptist Chapel. In this one was a simple aisle between two sides of varnished brown wooden pews, and a pulpit in the same shade, slightly elevated with a short, spiral series of steps and matching railing.

At first glance, everything was the same as last week, and the girl was encouraged, or at least, not too dismayed. Then she looked more closely at the floor. There were brownish splatters in the middle of the aisle that certainly had not been there last week. The wailing and moaning started again. It wasn't coming from the side room or the kitchen area. Then she realised. At their meeting last week, Mr Carter had worked up the rings slotted neatly into two hinged panels in the middle of the aisle and pulled the panels open, revealing the baptism tank embedded in the concrete under the floor. That was the source of the awful keening.

'I'm coming,' said the girl, as she scrabbled for the rings. It felt as if the desperate voice was becoming firmer in response. Finally she was able to pull each panel open, despite the resistant, squeaky hinges, rarely used. Inside, cowering in a foetal position, bloody, naked, and with a savage, ragged, diagonal gash down her back, was a woman with matted blonde-blue hair.

It being high summer, all the Polish girl was wearing was a simple Costa T-shirt in readiness for her shift, baggy, comfortable black jeans and dark trainers. She knew there would be nothing in the chapel in which to wrap the naked woman. But first things first. She called 999 and gave details clearly and calmly.

Leaning into the immersion space, she felt for Janice Wray's wrist and contented herself that the pulse was firm and steady, cooing and speaking softly in response to Wray's initial flinches.

'It's OK, it's OK. I'm Mariana. I'll make sure you're safe.'

Soon, the terror faded from Wray's eyes and she was able to focus on the girl she knew was her rescuer.

'There's nothing here to cover you up with, so I'm going to go outside to find something. OK?'

Wray gripped the girl by the wrist.

'I won't leave you. I'll be just outside the door getting other help. No one will be able to get in. An ambulance is coming, and so are the police.'

The grip eased and the girl rose quietly and went to the door. It was lucky. A string-bean young man in a black waiter's waist apron was at the door of the restaurant almost opposite, opening up.

'Excuse me!' shouted the girl. 'There's an emergency here.'

At first, the young man was suspicious. He carried on fussing around the glass door.

'Please,' said the girl. 'It's an emergency.'

Reluctantly the man walked over, keeping his distance in front of the chapel railings and gate.

'It's urgent. There's an injured woman in here, with no clothes. I need a tablecloth or a blanket, or a rug. Come on, I'm not messing about. HELP me.'

Finally the young man made the transition from doubt to action. 'OK. I'll be back in a moment.'

'Come into the chapel. I have to get back to the woman.'

Back in the space between the pews, Janice Wray lay numb. It was only when the Polish girl managed to wrap her in a tablecloth, blood seeping in patches into the crisp white linen, the police and ambulance arriving, and passers-by lingering outside in little huddles behind the newly unrolled crime-scene tape, that Wray found her voice.

As she was being lifted onto the trolley, she tried to grab her kind rescuer's wrist and look into her face. 'Frank Sterling,' she whispered, 'or Maria Goodburn... You need to contact them, warn them...' But by then it was too late. The paramedics had already eased the girl away and whisked the trolley to the ambulance outside. Wray's message was delivered into the empty Canterbury sky, then soundlessly into the oxygen mask over her mouth and nose on the way to the hospital, and then to the ceiling of the ICU as a preoccupied nurse triaged her injuries.

On Radio Kent, the events on the city wall around the corner from the high street were judged worthy of a newsflash:

'Early reports are coming in about a serious assault on a young woman in a chapel in Burgate Lane near Canterbury city centre early this morning. The chapel cleaner reported that the door had been jemmied open. She found the naked woman in a distressed condition in the immersion chamber under the floor. The woman is being treated for her injuries at Kent and Canterbury Hospital. The police are appealing for information from anyone in the chapel's vicinity yesterday evening through to early this morning. All details will be treated confidentially. We'll give updates during the day when they arrive.'

*

Across the city from the hospital in St Stephens, DCI Nolan listened to Murphy on his phone while watching through the French doors as his boy and girl had a kick around in the garden.

'Decent news at last, or at least,' said Nolan – recoiling at the news of Janice Wray's injuries – 'not disastrous. Thank goodness she's turned up alive. I assume you've told Ms Towers, and are sorting everything out at the crime scene.'

'Yep, it's all in hand, guv,' said Murphy. 'We can go and see Ms Wray at the hospital, but there's no point yet. They've had to sedate her.'

'Right. I'll be along shortly.' His head was buzzing with theories and possibilities, so much so that any intention of phoning Sterling to ask about Janice Wray and any connection he might have had with her had faded from his mental to-do list.

*

Eastward, in Sandley, Sterling himself had risen late after the night's excitement, and was treating himself to a cup of freshly percolated coffee. He wasn't a radio listener – his father's fondness for *The Archers* had permanently put him off – and Janice's own attempted warnings had gone nowhere. So he had no idea what had happened to her after the pub.

*

In her house, however, a few metres down from the district hospital, Charlotte Hankinson listened intently. If Jack had still been around, she'd have known he'd have had something to do with the incident. In his permanent absence, it had Jimmy Jarvis's boot prints all over it, metaphorically speaking, and, knowing him, perhaps literally – one of the punishments-cum-warnings, in which he specialised.

He hadn't taken the news kindly that she was removing herself from the business, although he'd already heard the night before from his anonymous new boss.

'So you're out, are you, Charlotte?' he'd said. He'd never used her first name before. They were equals now. 'I heard last night. What about the others?'

'You tell them or get your new boss to,' she'd replied.

'Well, someone will. Your job now is to keep your mouth shut.' He no longer answered to her.

She sipped her camomile tea. Keep her mouth shut? Of course she wouldn't. The question was how to go about the next stage of getting out of the fix she was in.

*

A series of phone calls set in train the next series of startling events. They culminated in the one to Maria as she and Billy Jenkins were on their second coffee in one of Whitstable's fancy cafés that had sprung up for the down-from-London contingent.

'You've no idea what a difference the occasional decent cappuccino makes,' said Billy.

Maria laughed. 'Serves you right for your eco-lifestyle.' She rummaged for her phone as it started trilling. 'Hi, Frank. All good after last night?'

'Fine,' said Sterling. 'I can't be certain, but that little caper could finally be shaking things loose. Can you meet me in Canterbury around 6.30 tonight?'

'Sure. What are we doing?'

'Going to a meeting. I won't tell you over the phone but I'll see you at the bus station later.' After last night's shenanigans, Sterling was cautious about leaks, though he didn't say that to Maria. You could only ruffle someone's feathers a certain number of times till you were permanently on their wrong side.

'More detective work?' said Billy, when the call had finished.

'Yep,' said Maria.

Billy waited.

'I dunno. It's hush-hush suddenly. Canterbury, early evening.'

Billy laughed. 'You gumshoes. I sometimes think it's all a game.'

'It wasn't last night, I can assure you.' The first part of the current rendezvous had been her account of the brothel rescue.

'Well, moving on… I've got to get down to the harbour. If I don't take that windsurfing class, I don't get paid. Laters.'

Maria watched Billy make his way to the front of the café, through the door and out of sight. She noted that she wasn't the only one, as he swayed gracefully between the crowded Saturday morning tables. Every girl and woman in the establishment was brazenly or surreptitiously doing the same. The eyes of one or two swivelled back to the table that Billy had left, and thence to Maria. She felt herself flushing as silent questions arrowed invisibly her way.

Chapter 30

That evening, Maria was strolling with Frank Sterling into the back end of Westgate Gardens. 'That was a performance. What was wrong with Route 1? Or even Route 2? That wasn't even Route 4c,' she said.

'What's the problem?' said Sterling. 'We had plenty of time. Nice evening. City wall and riverside walk, following the signposts. Avoided the scrum in the High Street. I'd never been that way before.'

Maria shrugged. 'I hope this isn't going to be a wild goose chase.'

'It won't be. My gut tells me.'

'Oh yeah, the famous policeman's gut.'

They reached the gate dividing the Gardens from the pedestrian and cycleway they'd just come along. Something was bothering Maria but Sterling wasn't inclined to find out what. 'It'll be along here on the left.'

They saw Charlotte Hankinson before she saw them. She was wearing an expensive-looking short floral lace embroidered dress whose predominant colour was powder blue. Her legs were crossed and her hands folded over a small matching purse-cum-handbag. The bench she was occupying the exact middle of was set at right angles to the tall garden wall, with a matching bench directly opposite. Against the wall was an array of tablets and stones in shades of grey and black, including military shields and symbols, and blocks of text. Arranged around the memorial were poppy wreaths and wooden crosses, and at an angle on the ground a framed, three-tiled ceramic rectangle of green, white and red. Two small conifers stood sentinel over the immaculate arrangement.

Although the Gardens were crowded – indeed, the Burma Star Association memorial adjacent was attracting plenty of interest from tourists and locals alike – no one was near the Italy Star Association's. Charlotte Hankinson's people-repulsing magnetic force field seemed to be fully switched on.

'Not her,' said Hankinson as Sterling and Maria drew up in front of her. The seated woman looked away.

The situation was delicate. 'I'll catch up with you shortly, Maria,' murmured Stirling, 'further down…'

'Waste of time me coming,' Maria harrumphed. 'I'll leave you two love birds to it then,' she muttered in a parting shot as she moved off towards the Westgate Towers.

Hankinson didn't react, but merely shifted to her left, closer to the memorial, and Sterling took the space next to her. 'You didn't specify "no offsider",' he said.

'Not your niece then.'

'Well, I reckon you saw through that straight away at the time.'

'Yes, I did actually. And I had you checked shortly afterwards. You have an interesting record.'

Sterling leaned forward and clasped his hand together over his knees. The temptation, in the glorious early evening light, was to do the opposite, stretch out and tilt his head up into the sun's gentle rays, but this was business.

'My grandfather fought in the Italy campaign,' said Hankinson.

'Yeah?'

'The invasions in Sicily, then the Italian mainland. Salerno. The bridgehead at Anzio, with the Americans. Up to the Adriatic front in dreadful conditions. He winced sometimes, on the few occasions he talked about it. Rome and northern Italy, rivers and mountains. Awful conditions, rain and snow. Terrible casualties. I lived with him for a while in one of those cottages across the main road, when my parents were struggling. We came here often. He survived. Hundreds of thousands didn't. He was fond of Italy though. Even during the war, the people were kind and welcoming where that was possible. I'm not sure he'd be very proud of me at the minute.'

Sterling waited.

'So why this meeting? Oddly enough, you're about the only person I think I can trust, based on my research, and having met you. An honest man. That's rare.' Charlotte Hankinson gulped and put a finger up to the lower lid of her left eye to ease away the welling tear. 'I need advice.'

'I'll have to have the full picture before I can offer that,' said Sterling. 'Obviously.' He tried a smile, but it was more a grimace. At the same time he wondered about the honesty bit, given the porkies he'd told her in her club the other Saturday evening. People – women – would say anything to get what they want.

'Obviously. Right, well, Jack... Jack had a whole range of scams, as you've probably already found out: planning, blackmail via the Sugarbabies website, drugs, protection, prostitution... and I was the bookkeeper.

It was tolerable when he was alive. I come from a poor home on the wrong side of the Canterbury tracks and now I'm wealthy. I thought I could take over when he went, but I can't. I can't hack it. I don't want to. At the same time, Jack's enforcer, one Jimmy Jarvis, has gone rogue. He no longer pays any attention to me. To be honest, Frank, I'm scared. I don't just need advice. I need protection.'

Sterling looked at the ground and shook his head. *What a mess.*

'I know,' said Hankinson, appearing to read his thoughts. 'But sadly for me, there's more.'

'There always is, in situations like this.' He couldn't say he cared on Hankinson's behalf – you reap what you sow and all that, and he wasn't, for once, taken in by the intimacy implied by the use of his first name – but a semblance of sympathy was getting him what he wanted.

'I'm being blackmailed – or was until recently – now I'm not sure. Someone, I think Jack's murderer, got hold of a flash drive with all the records on it, the one my idiot husband kept around his neck. That person phoned to negotiate with me. Jimmy Jarvis and I tried to catch him a couple of nights ago when I was meant to hand over the first instalment of hush money in exchange for the drive. I wasn't there when the man turned up, but apparently, he was agile. Jimmy was furious that he and his crew had him surrounded but he hopped over a wall like a mountain goat. Needless to say, the flash drive I picked up was empty.'

'No idea who?' Sterling knew from Patrick Ngono and other sources about Jack Hankinson's treasure trove but said nothing to interrupt the woman's flow.

'None whatsoever. He didn't seem very old, but there was a steel and confidence about him, even just on the phone. In fact, we don't even know that it was a man. Jimmy couldn't be sure in the twilight, and likewise the voice was heavily disguised on the phone.' Hankinson flapped her hand as if waving away a wasp. 'None of that matters now. As I said, I've got to get out, and the route out was to offer him – or her – the business. The murder was personal, I'm sure of it, triggered by something awful that Jack did, but when I made the offer the killer saw a business opportunity.'

'The business?' said Sterling. 'That's one way of putting it, I suppose. I have to say, it's an amazing story.'

'The details are on here.' Hankinson rummaged in her bag for a flash drive and handed it over. 'I've not had a lot of luck with these lately,' she said ruefully. 'It's not Jack's original obviously, but this one is accurate as of last night. I want out, and I'm not sure I care about the consequences.'

'What do I do with it?' said Sterling.

'Well, I guess it goes to the police. You're up to date now. So, what do you advise?'

Sterling thought about Jim Selsey, the Police Federation rep who had looked after him after all his scrapes and indiscretions when he had been in the job. Selsey, as well as complaining that he 'Spent more bloody time sorting you out than all the rest of the hotheads and idiots combined,' was honest and blunt, and Sterling had come to value that.

'Get a good brief. That's the absolute priority. You can afford it. A top criminal defence lawyer. He might well advise you to turn Queen's evidence, and I'd go along with that, unless you're sure that your actual name isn't on any of the stuff you've just handed over. I doubt you've got much loyalty to your husband's criminal associates, nor they to you. Get in first. The police will have forensic accountants and the like crawling through the evidence. It will be a long case but if you were arrested, you'd probably be bailed, subject to surrendering your passport and going down to the nick twice a day.

'If you don't go down that road, denial, via your top criminal defence brief. You're just an innocent bookkeeper. You had no idea what your husband was up to. You just did the spreadsheets and checked the figures. I wouldn't do that. The testimony of your husband's people – the ones you temporarily took over – would be too strong, especially because you would have landed them in it. There's one other possibility...'

Hankinson's eyebrow twitched.

'Disappearance. It would have to be abroad and, better still, somewhere without an extradition treaty with the UK. You'd have to get as much money and as many assets out with you as you could. It would be difficult and lonely, starting all over again. You'd probably lose what you couldn't take with you. Say goodbye to friends and family. Would it be worth it?'

'I'm lonely now,' said Hankinson. 'Someone said that the loneliest place is in a bad marriage. But Canterbury's my home. I can't think of anywhere else I'd want to be, even after prison. And my own businesses – the club and the estate agents – are legal. Someone could run those if I had to... go away. If I got this lawyer, faced the music and got convicted, what kind of sentence could I expect?'

'I don't know, Charlotte. Jesus, some of the stuff – drug supply, blackmail, the brothel, sex trafficking, protection...' As he recounted them, he felt a wave of distaste, worldly as he was. This wasn't some innocent he was dealing with. 'If you're found guilty, it depends on your brief, the judge, the degree of your complicity, the deal you strike with the CPS, your liability under POCA–'

'POCA?' said Hankinson.

'The Proceeds of Crime Act. The maximum prison time would probably be fourteen years. A deal: nine years. Two-thirds off for good behaviour: six years... If it's all concurrent and not consecutive. Maybe less. Maybe you were coerced by your husband. Again, that defence brief would look at all the angles and milk the best of them... Talking of your husband, if you don't mind me saying you seem even less grief-stricken about him than you were in the club.'

'I suppose I loved him once, but a long time ago. Either he changed or I never thought about what I was getting into. At the end, I realised how horrible he was. But when I knew I was on the wrong road, it was too late. What about you, Frank? Are you married?'

There it was again, that sudden switch, that invitation to intimacy from the wife of a crime boss who'd become a crime boss in her own right, and who even now was calculating her best course of action. Sterling felt another wave of distaste. Giving an attractive woman the brush-off would never have been easier. He just didn't get the chance.

Chapter 31

'Frank,' called Maria urgently from the footbridge over the river. She nodded to a point behind him. He and Charlotte Hankinson swivelled around.

The woman's face registered shock and fear. 'Jimmy Jarvis. I didn't know, Frank...'

The wiry, lean man didn't seem to be hurrying, but ominously the handle of a baseball bat was sticking out of the rucksack on his back.

Sterling cast a reproachful look at Hankinson, who kept shaking her head, and then walked swiftly to Maria. 'Come on,' he said, cocking his head in the chosen direction as he set off along the riverside path towards the Westgate Towers. 'Let's mingle with the crowds.'

Jarvis ambled up to Hankinson. 'You silly bint. Did you think you could just walk away? Well, I've got a new boss now, and we've been having you watched. First things first, though,' he said as he leaned into her. 'Those two.' She cringed back, avoiding eye contact, smelling the beer on his breath. 'And then we'll deal with you. Remember, I know exactly where you live and everything else about you.'

Sterling and Maria hurried down the path. The river was on one side and a high brick wall on the other. The railed gate in the wall, the second one down, looked inviting. To plunge through into the road would surely lead to more opportunities to shake off Jarvis – less open; more corners to disappear round. But just as they approached, a figure filled the gap. Only the footbridge towards the crenellated council offices was available.

Now Sterling's breath was quickening. He cursed himself for being so casual about his fitness. Over the footbridge they strode, now aware of two pursuers, Jarvis and one of his crew. Luckily for them, at this end of the Gardens it was much busier.

As a punt moved slowly upstream, its passengers, a Japanese couple lolling in front of the languid puntsman, responded bashfully to waves from the bank. There was a wave of scent from the lovingly planted beds of fuchsias, carnations, pelargoniums and dahlias between the blocks of greensward. Across the river, the steep triangular Mill House garden and then the house itself brought the Gardens to a sharp halt on the northern side. In front of them loomed the Guildhall and then, side-on, the Westgate Towers.

'To the bridge, and then right into the high street,' gasped Sterling, his breathing ragged. Apart from a slight, tell-tale flush about her face, Maria didn't seem to be affected by the pace. She merely nodded and pressed on.

But at the bridge, progress was again blocked. This time there was a man on the corner in front of the Mexican café at the beginning of St Dunstan's, and two more lingering on the pavement by the Guildhall, blocking the way to the city centre. On the bridge, a group of French children off a coach from Pas de Calais, squeaking with excitement, had discovered two underwater sculptures below. There was a flurry of phones.

'Straight on?' asked Maria.

'No choice,' gasped Sterling. He was asking himself why they weren't fronting it out, seeking safety in the crowd, but in his heart he knew the answer. Determined assailants could mount a lightning attack in broad daylight and disappear just as quickly, and people's reactions would be hopelessly slow and confused. Witnesses would give wildly varying accounts, and photos and CCTV were grossly overrated.

They pressed on across the busy road in front of the Towers, provoking an angry beep from a startled van driver as he braked just in time to miss them. Now, still parallel to the river but on the north side again, they moved quickly through a car park. Ahead was a block of cottages with walled gardens abutting the river, and a narrow walkway in between.

Maria turned round. From the various vantage points, starting with Jimmy Jarvis at the back end of Westgate Gardens, he and his crew, four of them, were now coalescing close on their heels. 'They're getting closer, Frank. Correct me if I'm wrong, but it feels as if we're being funnelled.'

Sterling cursed. 'Come on.' He scuttled along the walkway between the walled gardens and the river. He knew Sandley and its alleyways like the back of his hand, and that knowledge had once saved him, but here he was completely disoriented. The walkway led to another footbridge back across the river. He and Maria clattered over it. Without looking back, he could hear the urgent pounding of other feet. Then they were in a narrow four-walled space with a profusion of flowers and plants in a low-railed inner square. Escape through the open gate at the opposite end would have been the only possibility. The trouble was that in front of it was a narrow-faced man wielding a large, chunky carpenter's mallet, and behind him, completely blocking out the light in the doorway, the huge figure of the Fridge.

Sterling and Maria edged back to the corner furthest from either entry. A moment later, their pursuers piled through the river door, for a second more Keystone Cops than bullying Canterbury thugs as they piled into the back of each other and pulled up. Jarvis brought up the rear and weaved his leisurely way to the front, Barbie the bat swinging from his fist.

'Rats in a trap,' he smirked. 'Manoeuvre planned and executed to perfection. Third time lucky. There's a choice of endings. If you tell me how I can get my little Lucy back, you might get the least bad one.'

'Fuck off,' said Maria. She looked scared but defiant, her jaw jutting out.

That's my line, thought Sterling. He appraised the situation. Two people, one a sometime-brawler, one a girl, versus seven bruisers, a barbed-wire baseball bat and a mallet. In a walled garden with both exits blocked. If he and Maria had edged into the corner next to the lower wall with the view over the river, they could have jumped over it and into the water. But that was out of the question now. Overall, the odds were awful.

Jarvis shrugged. 'Suit yourself, girlie.' He did a practice swing of the bat.

Sterling noticed Maria peel off her denim jacket and wrap it around her left arm and hand. As he put his own arm out to usher her behind him, she resisted, edging instead towards Fridge and the man with the mallet. 'Decision time, Jason,' she said softly. 'Fork in the road. Your life changed forever.'

Mallet man sneered but held back. Perhaps Jimmy Jarvis was insisting that he himself dealt the first blow.

'Already decided, Maria,' said Jason. With one movement he twisted the mallet from his associate's hand and tossed it over the garden and into the water, where it landed with a surprisingly muted 'plop'. There was a crack and ex-mallet man fell to his knees with a sharp scream, his arm, ulna and radius, clean snapped, dangling loose and useless.

Sterling gulped. Wasn't this poking a hornet's nest? On the other hand, Maria had in one fell swoop reduced the odds from two versus seven to three versus six. And gratifyingly, the new addition to the Sterling-Goodburn axis, the Fridge, counted as about three people just by himself.

Maria took an alert stance, planting her left foot in front of her right and adopting a slight crouching pose, arms out, palms half-fisted. Having failed to usher her behind him, Sterling manoeuvred himself next to her. It came to him that the terrain was in their favour, the little inner square meaning that their opponents couldn't spread out. He supposed that they could jump over the railings, but the vegetation gave extra hindrance.

Jarvis and another thug advanced first in the narrow space. With a snarl, Jarvis launched himself at Maria, provoked by her defiant stance. The other man went for Sterling.

There was an enormous roar, so loud that everyone, utterly startled, paused in mid-action – all except the Fridge, whose battle cry it was that reverberated over the water. He bowled directly into the group behind Jarvis, literally flinging himself at the loosely formed mass.

Jarvis ignored the melee and swung the bat. By some skilful pivot and twist, Maria caught the blow, the glint of the barbed wire around the bat extinguished as it ripped into the makeshift fabric cover on her left forearm. Pulling on the bat with her hand, she drew Jarvis in and delivered a sharp and powerful kick to his groin, causing him to grunt and double over, releasing his grip on the weapon.

Meanwhile Sterling had slipped into brawler-mode, windmilling with his arms and legs and resisting his opponent's grappling. A bite on the man's arm produced a scream, and in a trice Sterling realised what he could do next. Seizing the man by the throat he pushed him violently against the low riverside wall. His opponent did a clumsy, involuntary single somersault before disappearing into the water.

In the other corner, the Fridge's eighteen stone bulk had knocked two opponents onto the flagstones. His berserker rages, manufactured entirely according to need, were well known among his usual fraternity and around the doors of the various nightspots in the city when he was on duty.

Fear and doubt crept into the eyes of one of Jarvis's crew. His eyes flicked to Jarvis on his knees, and then to his pal moaning with his broken arm at the other gate. He slunk away the way he'd come over the bridge and along the walkway on the other side.

Sterling did a quick survey as he gasped for air. It seemed that the Fridge needed his help at that moment more than Maria as his two opponents gathered their wits. Sterling barrelled into the nearest one, kicking and punching as he went, and receiving some punishment in return. The one he'd chosen to fall on was giving as good as he got. He found himself pinned to the ground, the flagstones cool and hard against his head, his arms fending off blows to his head. And then he wasn't. The Fridge seemed to be a quick learner. Having quickly dispensed with his last adversary, who was sitting dazed and lifeless by the gate, the Fridge took Sterling's opponent by the scruff of his neck and the back of his jeans, and launched him into the river.

Sterling got up and bent over with his hands to his knees, wheezing heavily. Beside him, the Fridge was sucking great gulps of air into his huge frame. As they gathered themselves, they watched Maria deliver her coup de grace to Jarvis, a bash with Barbie to the side of his head, just under his ear. Luck for the erstwhile enforcer was mixed. It was highly unfortunate that he was receiving a blow – a blow, irony upon irony, delivered by a young woman with his own weapon – but on the other hand fortunate that the business end was still wrapped in her jacket.

Over the low wall, Sterling could see two of the former assailants, hangdog, bedraggled and dirty, wading and splashing over to the other side of the river. They edged along with the current until there was a spot to clamber out further down.

'I suppose we'd better get the cops,' said Sterling, 'and paramedics.' He reached for his phone. Maria and the Fridge exchanged grins. On Maria's face, the grin was superseded by an expression of modest triumph, with Canterbury's arch-bully insensible at her feet.

Chapter 32

Within minutes, a police car and ambulance had arrived in Pound Lane, and were both mounted on the narrow pavement next to the landward exit of the walled garden. Sterling had been expecting problems with the police – would it not be easier to assume that the unconscious man and the one with the broken arm were the victims rather than the ones still standing? – but he and his associates, one established and one new, had a large dollop of luck. The lead patrol officer had been the one with Peterson at the original murder scene.

Sterling took him aside. 'We'll give you all our details, officer, but you remember that your Sergeant Peterson and I are former colleagues. Here's a quick summary that will be very easy to verify. The three of us' – Sterling indicated himself, Maria and the Fridge – 'were attacked by these two men and four others. The weapon you see Maria holding belongs to him' – he indicated Jimmy Jarvis. 'You'd do well to put both of them under arrest and under guard at the hospital, or certainly arrest them if they're discharged. That's the first thing. Secondly, I've got vital information for DCI Nolan in relation to the murder enquiry. I need to see him in person. Tell him "Frank Sterling" and that should be enough.'

'I think you need to hang around until we've sorted things out here, Mr Sterling. We'll need statements from all of you.'

'No,' replied Sterling. 'We've had a scare. I personally might even be going into shock. I need a drink to steady me up.' Out of the corner of his vision, he thought he saw Maria rolling her eyes. He turned to the Fridge, but couldn't remember his first name. 'Um, Mr Fridge, where's the nearest pub?'

'Miller's Arms.' (It wasn't, but it was the one he fancied at that moment).

Hell's bells, thought Sterling. *Not again.* 'We'll be in there, officer, having a drink and calming down. Get Andy Nolan and Bill Murphy to join us there. They'll need a laptop. And we can sort out the statements with them.'

Doubt clouded the young officer's eyes but, as Sterling had intended, his familiarity with his friend and his friend's deputy tipped the balance. 'Just give my colleague your names, phone numbers and addresses and' – a smile broke out over his intelligent features – 'don't leave the pub till my colleagues get there.'

'Tough condition,' acknowledged Sterling. 'Right, Mr Fridge, lead the way.'

As they set off down Pound Lane back towards the Westgate Towers, Maria took Sterling's arm. 'It's "Jason", Frank,' she said softly.

'Got it.' He sensed that they were moving in the wrong direction for the pub specified, but almost straight away they turned left between a row of Victorian terraces and into the car park behind. Beyond that, the Fridge ambled along at an easy pace on a complicated route of twists and turns that eventually led into another garden hidden only yards from the teeming centre of the city.

'I never knew Canterbury had so many nooks and crannies, Jason,' said Maria. 'I've never been in here.'

'Me neither,' said Sterling.

'I grew up here,' said the Fridge. 'So obviously I know them all. Some people call this Solly's Orchard. I think it's officially Abbot's Mill Garden. Actually, it's part of Binnewith's Island. We're between two forks of the river. We left one at the Butterfly Garden. The other is over there.'

Maria stole a discreet sideways look at Sterling. For the Fridge, those words were the equivalent of a twenty-four-hour filibuster.

There were two paths across. The Fridge opted for the one that led to the river and then alongside it. His pace had slowed, and he looked like a man at peace with himself. On a whim, he hopped from the path onto the narrow wall. Just like the Westgate Gardens stretch of tributary, this one had also been monetised, this time through a rowing boat service from the Weavers House that stood next to the bridge on the High Street.

As he balanced, arms stretched horizontal each way for balance, a spontaneous ragged cheer arose from the company of tourists in the latest rowing boat making its short way to the locks. The Fridge feigned losing his balance. Sterling could see a tier of mouths forming into o-shapes as he teetered, and heard the clack of numerous camera-phone shutters. The Fridge jumped down on the grass and grinned sheepishly. With a slight, stiff-backed bow to his boat-bound audience, he milked another multilingual cheer.

Beneath the zig-zagging walkway over the two adjacent locks, constructed together in a complexly ornate arrangement, the water frothed and gushed, and then they were out of the garden and into the pub across the road.

'My round,' said Sterling. 'Maria?'

'What would you recommend, Frank, after all that?'

'Brandy. Double. The adrenaline will have tapered off. The sheer danger of the situation will be hitting home. You'll need steadying. That's what I'm having.'

'OK.'

'Jason?'

'Pint of lager, please... Frank.' The Fridge looked gratified. By default, in his recent previous life, he was always the one to get the drinks in.

Sterling nodded. He suspected that the recent excitement was not exactly an abnormal occurrence for the new addition to the team, and that the need for steadying was not an issue. He brought the drinks to a table with empty chairs in readiness for Nolan and Murphy.

'Cheers,' said Sterling. 'I reckon Jason and I are past the introductions stage. 'Course, I didn't really need you two. I would have sorted those blokes out myself.' He made jagged swishing and chopping motions with his hands.

The Fridge gave a quarter-smile, his huge hands entirely enveloping his drink.

Maria practised further eye-rolling. 'Right, Frank.'

'But thanks anyway. Good job. Worth you coming after all, Maria. I learnt my fighting skills against school bullies every time I changed schools – which was a lot – and on Margate seafront when I was on the job. Where did you learn your judo?'

'Mixed martial arts, actually, via women's self-defence classes, and then the uni MMA club. Judo wouldn't have cut it. I was still terrified though. Anyway, we certainly shook things loose there, eh?'

Sterling nodded. 'Yep. The plan worked.' He turned to the Fridge. 'Welcome to the team, mate. I hope you've hopped on the right horse. You won't exactly be popular with your mates.'

The Fridge took a long pull of his drink. Half of it disappeared straight away. He'd soon need it topping up. 'They aren't my mates. They weren't my mates. They were just blokes I fell in with. Idiots and liggers mostly – except for Jimmy, a genuine nutter. I can't remember Jimmy Jarvis ever putting his hand in his pocket and buying me a drink. I was just useful to him. I never actually did much. Hankinson used to call me a "presence", an "incentive, to do the right thing." "Insurance" sometimes. I didn't do much thinking. I often just kind of… loomed.'

'Well, you heard my conversation with that cop back at the Butterfly Garden. We'll have to line up our statements, and I've got a flash drive Charlotte Hankinson gave me to hand over to the police, so when the balloon goes up, we'll need to make sure you're OK. She owes me a favour. Weirdly, I guess she also has a duty of care to a former employee. She can afford a brief for you, if it comes to it. I'll work on that.'

'You'll be OK, Jason,' said Maria. 'And if you're still interested in getting back into education, I've got a friend who's doing a course at college that might suit you. If you want, I can get her to talk to you.' A familiar mischievous look flitted over her features. 'I think it includes criminology. It would start in September – give you time to get yourself right.'

'Just up my street,' said the Fridge, 'if I'm not banged up. Then it would be practical…'

Sterling smiled along with him. 'Another pint, mate?'

'Thanks. It'll help me with my story.'

Sterling noticed that Maria was beginning to tremble. A large sob escaped from her throat. Finally, a reaction. 'Breathe, girl. Deep breaths. Come on.' He pressed the brandy into her hand. 'Another slug of this.' Maria managed to keep down a gulp of the drink and gradually her poise was restored. Sterling took a gulp of his own drink. He felt the beginnings of palpitations himself, as if in sympathy, or as if Maria's distress had transmitted itself to him. *Jesus,* he thought, *it could have been a terrible ending.* Another thought occurred. His indemnity insurance wouldn't have covered injury to Maria. He'd completely overlooked that. He took another sharp pull of his brandy. The Fridge was patting Maria's arm, slightly ill at ease, unused to offering succour but not making a bad job of it.

Once everything had calmed down, the 'lining up' of statements was addressed. It was still taking place as three newcomers joined the trio at their table. For Sterling and Maria, it was relatively straightforward – meeting with Charlotte Hankinson in relation to her husband's murder and then getting corralled into the Garden in an ambush by the erstwhile enforcer and his gang. The Fridge happened to be passing and assisted. It might not stand up for long but it would do. Sterling realised that the Fridge would be just as good a police witness as Charlotte Hankinson for some aspects of the criminal empire that had enveloped Canterbury. That would be a handy bargaining chip.

Sophie Stephens had arrived between Andy Nolan and Bill Murphy. 'The organ grinder's brought the monkey,' she murmured.

Sterling's hackles rose. 'I said I was sorry. Did Andy not convey the message? Do you lot want our help or not?' His mood soured, but a truculent tone might be helpful. He was not the supplicant.

Nolan, slipping into politician mode, put a pacifying hand up. 'Sophie didn't mean anything. Officer Knight has spoken with me. It sounds as if you've had a bit of a time of it.'

The Major Incident Room manager busied herself with the laptop she'd brought, the screen casting a ghostly glow over her oval face.

'What about introductions?' said Nolan. 'Sophie and I have met Ms–'

' – "Maria" will do,' said Maria.

'OK, Maria, thanks, but you haven't met my second-in-command, Bill Murphy. And none of us has met you, Mr–?'

' – Smith. Jason,' said the Fridge.

'One of the team,' said Sterling. 'He's actually the main reason we are able to be sitting here rather than up in A & E. Before we continue, what about another round?'

'This is highly irregular,' grinned Murphy. 'I'll get them in. Wait till I come back before you start, Frank.'

As usual, the drink loosened Sterling's tongue, but not so much that he veered away from the abridged and anodyne version of events that he'd hastily prepared all the way from the Italy Star Association memorial to the pub, with interruptions. Update over, he handed Sophie Stephens the flash drive that Charlotte Hankinson had given him.

'We're on,' said Stephens, having plugged it in. 'One folder entitled "Hankinson", then some files. I'll start with "Overview". It's a spreadsheet.' The small, pink tip of her tongue appeared between her lips as she concentrated, her eyes flicking to points on the screen. Everyone at the table fell silent, and the atmosphere seemed to emanate outwards to the rest of the busy Saturday night pub.

Only Nolan, sitting next to Stephens, could also see the screen. He was an experienced copper, with almost twenty years under his belt, but the commentary he started was incredulous.

'Security, income and outgoings – income from subscriptions, expenditure – wages, travel, equipment – this looks like a protection racket...

'Second page – Website – administrator, technical support, maintenance – income from donations...

'Third page – Planning – consultancy fees – I think these are the names of councillors... donations... these are development companies –

'Fourth page – Services – income per operative, expenditure... salary and wages, electricity, council tax, gas, water – that's a premises somewhere...

'Page five, Trading – expenditure on transport, products (with initials), salaries, one off payments, security, income from sales...

'We'll need to get our forensic accountants in, guv,' said Stephens. 'It's going to take a day or two to actually build a case.'

'Yep, but this material is a perfect foundation. There's obviously a large criminal enterprise in the city. There are plenty of names and plenty of detail. We'll need to get going tonight. Jack Hankinson was obviously running it all. There's no mention of Charlotte Hankinson though, even if you say that she's the bookkeeper, Frank.'

'Well, she wasn't going to make it easy for you, was she? I advised her to cooperate, so she's probably protecting herself to leave room for negotiation about turning Queen's evidence. That aside, I think Maria and I can offer good theories for some of the phrases from our investigations. People we've spoken to mentioned what's called *sugaring*, where wealthy older people, usually blokes, link up with girls and young women for mutual benefits via the website mentioned on that spreadsheet. That leads on to blackmail in particular instances. We helped an asylum seeker who was being forced to deliver drugs on his pizza delivery round so "Trading" is a drugs racket. "Planning" speaks for itself…'

The Fridge shifted on his seat and took a long pull of his third pint. '"Security" is definitely… well… protection,' he muttered.

'The "Services" one with "operatives" sounds like a brothel,' said Maria. She took a gulp of her brandy, her eyes flicking away from contact like the Fridge's.

Nolan caught the undercurrents. 'The brothel one is interesting,' he said neutrally. 'We were called to a serious assault early this morning. The victim was someone involved in women's rights… It looked as though she'd been tortured.'

Sterling and Maria stiffened palpably. 'Janice Wray,' said Maria.

'You know her?' said Stephens.

'Yes,' said Sterling. 'We were involved in a project with her. Is she OK?'

'A project,' said Nolan.

'We've given you enough, Andy, and stuff you'd have struggled to get without us. Yes, a project, in which we did nothing illegal. Now stop messing us about.'

'She's alright except for being battered about. There's a nasty wound down her back. She's recovering at the Kent and Canterbury.'

Maria drained her drink. 'Come on, Frank. We'll get a taxi up there.'

'Sophie, get them a squad car,' said Nolan.

'You go, Maria, and I'll catch up with you. There are a couple more things I've got to sort out with Andy.' Sterling had a sudden thought. The Fridge needed removing from the orbit of the detectives given his obviously dubious status. Murphy hadn't said anything but he probably knew of him. 'Take Jason. After what happened earlier on, we can't be too careful.'

If Nolan, Murphy and Stephens had doubts about the Fridge, his relationship to their new investigation, and, related to that, letting him go, they said nothing. Sterling was right. He'd given them a great deal, and minor details like the Fridge's transgressions mattered little at that stage.

Soon, the big man and Maria had been whisked away, and Murphy and Stephens had gone back to the station to start the new work.

Nolan finished his Guinness and waited.

'We rescued a couple of sex workers and an asylum seeker,' said Sterling. 'Last night. From a brothel near the cemetery. Janice Wray organised some of it.'

'Ah,' said Nolan.

'Someone, somehow, got wind of it and we had a... skirmish with Hankinson's gang. When was Janice attacked?'

'Sometime in the early hours, we think. But her partner reported that she'd been kidnapped just as she was getting home at around 9.30 pm.'

Sterling nodded. 'We'd not long finished. We had a drink together and then split up.'

'We've got a snitch who lives a few doors down from her. Like most snitches, he'll be working both sides of the street. I expect he made a phone call.'

'You need to arrest Jimmy Jarvis, Andy, up at the hospital, and put him under guard. Get him out of the way, and everything else will look after itself. He's the one who'll have attacked Janice, but you've also got me and Maria as witnesses of him attacking us in the Butterfly Garden. Charlotte Hankinson was scared. She said he'd gone rogue.'

'In hand, Frank. I told Bill Murphy just now.'

'Good. And with what I've just given you, maybe another promotion.' Sterling felt a wave of bitterness wash over him. All he was going to get out of it was a couple of weeks' pay from June Selsdon and, as things were going, no publicity.

'I don't know what to say, mate, except thank you,' said Nolan, who'd caught his friend's mood. 'If there had been a reward of any kind, I would have made sure it came your way. I could probably get you a commendation. Mamujee would be onside. I can try and put non-police investigations your way, with my recommendation.'

'Better than nothing, I suppose,' said Sterling. 'Marginally. I'll be reporting back to my principal.

From that flash drive, it looks as though there's no Labour Party involvement among those councillors and the rest of it. She'll be pleased with that.'

Nolan's scalp, miraculously irritation-free as strong evidence to smash a criminal empire emerged, started itching again. 'The trouble is, we've sorted everything out except for the most important thing.'

'Yep. Who killed Jack Hankinson?' Sterling kept quiet about Charlotte Hankinson's blackmailer, the one she'd offered the business to, and the one who likely did the deed. He'd have to find a way to work that to his advantage, especially financially, and especially in the absence of other opportunities.

Chapter 33

The Fridge had slipped away soon after the squad car had left the hospital. He hadn't been involved in Wray's abduction, having opted out that evening, but given how precarious his situation was, he and Maria thought it best if he stayed out of the way.

'So you tried to warn us that someone might be gunning for us, Janice,' said Maria. She and Sterling were at Janice Wray's bedside while her partner was having a break.

Propped up by pillows, her face yellow and puffy, one eye still just a slit, Janice attempted a smile. 'The message didn't get through, though, did it?' she whispered.

'The Battle of the Butterfly Garden, as Maria calls it,' said Sterling. 'It didn't matter in the end, thanks to Maria and the Fridge. None of that matters now. It's just important that you get better. Jimmy Jarvis, the ringleader and the one who attacked you and us, is about to be arrested, and the police are after the rest of his gang, so they're not going to get away with it.'

'I'm sorry. I didn't mean to... land you in it.'

'Janice, I assure you,' said Sterling, 'that if it had been me and not you, I would have told my torturers everything even before they started. You haven't got anything to be sorry about. Anyway, you came off worse, and I really regret that. We should have been more careful.'

'How's your back?' said Maria. She and Sterling had received an update from Janice's partner, including about the long diagonal gouge.

'The morphine's a big help. And for once someone else put the needle in.' The invalid gave another wan smile.

'Jarvis was careless, or reckless,' said Maria. 'The police reckon that it's your blood on his baseball bat, since he never bothered to clean it after he... attacked you, and on my jacket.'

'Good, good...' said Wray as she drifted off.

'We'll wait till her partner comes back, and then we'll go,' said Sterling,

At the bus station twenty minutes later, he and Maria parted. 'Have tomorrow off. We'll review everything we've got on Monday. I'll phone June and probably go over to Whitstable to report back on Tuesday if she's available. Will you be around?'

'Yes. I wouldn't want to miss your summary. See you Monday.'

'And Maria? Good work today. Without you, it would have been very sticky.'

*

The next morning, Sterling eased gingerly off the bus at Canterbury Bus Station. The knocks and bruises coming up after the brawl yesterday meant he had to keep going if he wasn't going to stiffen up. Besides, momentum was still important. He and Maria had shaken things up, but that hadn't got them any closer to Jack Hankinson's killer.

Maria... He'd become used to her company and it was strange to be going solo for the day, but he'd told her to rest. And anyway, old habits died hard. He didn't find it easy to share all his business. He walked over to the cab rank between the bus station and the shops.

The first cab driver tossed her newspaper aside as he approached. She had a cheerful, open face with large-framed red glasses and nails painted the same bold colour.

'Oo-er,' she said as Sterling gave the address of his intended destination.

'Oo-er?' echoed Sterling, as he got in the back seat and put on his seat belt.

'There's been some drama with fares over there. A planning inspector was frogmarched off the track at the side. Journalists looking for a story have been threatened. The planning application has been an exciting saga. The cabbies who've been down there have learnt to be ready for a quick getaway. You don't look like an inspector or a journalist, if you don't mind me saying so.'

'Private investigator.' Sometimes it was useful to pique interest and keep a conversation going.

'Really.' The cabbie's eyes in the mirror held Sterling's for a second and then went back to the road. 'In connection with what?'

'The murder down by the river. I'm looking into it... independently for someone.'

'Right. Well, Jack Hankinson, eh? And you're going to see Fred Hume.' She tipped her head. 'Makes sense, I suppose. That's a pretty... sparky family, if you know what I mean.'

'Any other info, while we're on the subject?'

The woman laughed. 'Well, Canterbury's a surprising sort of place, crime-wise, and I hear plenty of talk and gossip, as you might expect. But on Hankinson, the grapevine's not come up with anything.'

Five minutes later, the taxi turned right at a small crossroads and edged down a narrow lane to the south of Canterbury. 'Here we are,' said the cabbie. 'Or rather, here we are fifty yards short of where you want to go. A bit of discretion is probably handy. I expect you're on expenses,' she added with a shrewd smile. 'Do you want me to wait? I can turn around and be ready for a quick exit.'

'Funny,' said Sterling. 'But yes, please, wait. I shouldn't be more than half an hour.' *Another hit for June Selsdon and no Maria to raise her eyebrows.*

He got out of the car and looked around. Not far away, he could hear the swell and fade of traffic noise from the A2 to Dover. He walked away from it for a few metres and looked down the lane opposite. It was lined with a small settlement of farm cottages with gardens to the back. So far, everything fitted with the research he'd done when he'd got home the previous night. He retraced his steps and walked past the taxi and towards the A2. The cabbie, from over her newspaper, gave him another knowing smile.

Fred Hume's cottage was exactly as it looked on Google Maps, ramshackle and enveloped in ivy. Sterling noted the track-cum-driveway on the left leading up to the twenty acres of prime building land behind the smallholding. The track ran parallel to the farm cottages and their gardens. On the right of the cottage were a jumble of farm buildings, a barn, and a stubbier building. The settlement had a hemmed-in feel to it because of the cottages on one side and the A2 on the other. A scruffy board propped on a wayside stone advertised oven-ready rabbits, wood pigeons, pheasant, chicken and eggs for sale in untidy capital letters.

Sterling walked up the short, scrubby, weed-pitted driveway to the cottage's front door. There he paused, shifting his weight lightly from one foot to the other. From somewhere nearby – probably the barn area – a dog barked frantically, evidently not a chihuahua from its deep-throated, reverberating tone. Sterling's stomach lurched, but he knocked again.

A small, angular female face appeared at the door, notable for a sharp, small nose. The woman said nothing and just looked.

'Is Mr Hume in?' said Sterling.

'In the small barn,' said the woman. She tipped her head to the left and closed the door.

'Thank you so much,' muttered Sterling to himself. He approached the outbuildings and ducked down a short path to the side of the house. The shorter building was less a barn and more a kind of loggia, open all along one side under a tiled roof. The barking, from a large black dog of indeterminate breed, intensified, but luckily for Sterling, the dog was tethered in a corner of the building. There was a smell of flesh, blood and countryside, and all around the loggia were hooks, beams and the paraphernalia of game management, with a line of birds – wood pigeon, pheasant, partridge, chicken – hanging and ready to be plucked.

A short, stocky man with black eyes and a matching rectangular lumberjack-style beard, wearing blood-stained blue overalls, stepped forward from a workbench.

In a corner at the back, Sterling caught a glimpse of another human figure.

'Yep?' said the man.

A dozen eggs, please. No, that wouldn't do at all. 'Mr Hume? I'm Frank Sterling. I'm a private investigator. I've come up here to ask if you murdered Jack Hankinson, the councillor.'

Hume's eyes narrowed. The dog barked in the corner. 'Shut up, Satan.' The dog sank back on its haunches and the barking subsided to a low growl. The dog's teeth were yellowy-white and looked large and strong as it slavered. 'What did you say?'

'I think you heard, Mr Hume. I thought about a different approach, but you look as though you're a man who appreciates directness. And it'll save time.' Sterling straightened his back and held his gaze into the other man's eyes. A smile, achieved with an effort, played around his mouth.

Hume folded his arms and looked Sterling up and down. Then a slight, echoing smile came to his features, crinkling his eyes. 'Well, if I did, I wouldn't bloody well tell you, would I?'

'As opposed to the rest of the world, Mr Hume? I've looked you up. On three occasions you've made threats, all reported in the local rag. Admittedly only one was made directly to Hankinson. "I'll wring your bloody neck" were the exact words. The others, to the council planning committee, were along the lines of "I'll do the lot of you".'

'Alright, so I can fly off the handle. The police spoke to me. But would I be so stupid as to actually kill the bastard?'

'It's an interesting one. This is how I see it from looking at the planning permission. There are twenty or so acres of prime building land at the back of you. You've got cottages up one side and the A2 at the other. At the back, you've got the Cholmondeley estate. So the only viable access is by your track or, if you moved out, knocking this place down and putting an access road in the space. But you don't want to sell, you don't want sixty houses out back and you're hanging on to the track. The developers – Mark Prideaux and others, and councillor Hankinson – were putting the pressure on. Hankinson getting topped solves all your problems.'

'More than pressure. Threats. Dead animals thrown in the drive. Phone calls.'

'Plenty of motive then.'

'We could get hundreds of thousands for this place – it would have been more with the sweeteners Hankinson was offering under the table. Where's the motive in that?'

'It's not about money though, is it, Mr Hume? It's about what you're comfortable with, what sort of life you want, where you've grown up. And not being pushed around by some stuck up businessmen and politicians. I get it. I do. If it was me, I'd be thinking on the same lines.'

'I still didn't do it. I've worked it out. I was here with my wife when Hankinson was done in.'

Sterling nodded. 'Alright.'

There was a movement from the shadowy far corner. A young woman came into Sterling's line of vision. She was slender and small-boned, but her face had the solid, plain squareness of her father's rather than the angularity of her mother's in the house. She approached the bench and drew up next to the smallholder and in front of Sterling. Her face expressionless and her eyes cold, she lay out the body of a rabbit on the benchtop with her left hand. With the cleaver in her right, she chopped down in one lightning stroke, severing the head clean from the body.

'Alice,' growled Hume.

The girl looked up at Sterling and withdrew with the bloody cleaver back into the shadows. The dog grizzled softly.

'I'll walk you out,' said Hume. He had gone quiet. 'Pay no mind to Alice,' he said finally. 'She sticks up for me.'

In the driveway, Sterling offered his hand.

Hume's was rough and callused. 'I've had all sorts up here snooping and poking about. Nobody's been so direct.'

'I was too scared to do anything else.'

Hume grinned, a countryman's sly grin. 'Get out of here before I set the dog on you.'

Rather the dog than the daughter, thought Sterling. 'Just give me a bit of a start,' he said.

Around the corner in front of the first row of cottages, the cabbie was waiting. 'You look as though you survived. Had a bit of a laugh even.'

'Yep. Mission accomplished, I think.'

On the way back into the city, Sterling was quiet, ruminating. Hume could have conned him, but he seemed straight enough. The girl though. There would be mileage in further investigation. That cold, steely glare. The glint of that cleaver. The dull thud as it clumped into the benchtop. The rabbit's head. The wordless withdrawal.

And when it came down to it, Charlotte Hankinson hadn't been able to tell if the voice on the phone of her husband's murderer had been a man or a woman.

Chapter 34

That Sunday, Sterling wasn't the only one freelancing. Maria received a mystery text message from an unknown caller: *The Bishop's Finger, St Dunstan's, Canterbury, 8 pm tonight, Mac and Stevie. You might be interested.*

Three attempts to speak to Sterling went straight to voice mail, and a text stayed unanswered. Maria tutted and then made her decision.

A few minutes later she was knocking on Billy Jenkinson's side door.

'Maria, babes, to what do I owe?'

'It's lucky you're in. I need some help. A bit of snooping. I can't get hold of Frank.'

'Excellent,' said Billy. 'I was really getting bored.'

'It's not a game, Billy. I've had to think this through. I don't want to fall out with Frank by appearing to go behind his back. Not only that, but I've seen one of the blokes referred to in the message in a nightclub the other night, and he might have seen me. He probably won't remember, given the noise and lights, but there's a chance. So it could be dodgy. And I want you to try and take a video recording on my phone, and that could be dodgy as well.'

'Alright. I didn't mean to be flippant. Let's firm things up on the bus over.'

Three hours later, at five to eight, the PI's assistant and the assistant's assistant were entering the St Dunstan's pub, apparently independently. It was Sunday evening, and reasonably busy at the end of the weekend but far from jam-packed. On a TV screen beyond the far end of the long bar, a rugby match was being played. Young supporters, some in white rugby shirts adorned across the chest with a red vee, and some in shirts with cherry and white hoops were watching boisterously, exiles from their home towns. Banter in northern accents drifted across the large room. Maria was wearing dark jeans and T-shirt, with her hair tied back in a ponytail, as different in style and look as she could manage from the evening at The Lotus Blossom. She looked around as if for a friend. She fixed her eyes on two men at a table at the street window. Billy followed her gaze.

As Maria settled on a bar stool with a glass of white wine, Billy took his pint over to a table adjacent to the two men's. As he didn't have a phone of his own, he was holding Maria's to his ear. Maria knew that he wasn't having a conversation, but the performance was perfect, a judicious balance of listening and speaking. Just as perfect was Billy's face turned away from the men, while the phone's lens pointed directly at them.

After ten minutes, Maria watched Billy apparently end his conversation and put the phone down. *Sensible, Billy. Hopefully, you've left the audio still running.*

Another five minutes elapsed, and a new figure came into the pub, a young man in blue jeans and light-blue polo shirt that emphasised both his light tan and his muscled torso. The two barmaids at the other end of the bar, enjoying a lull, rushed at once to serve him. Other female heads at the bar and tables turned surreptitiously.

The young man leaned his elbows on the bar right next to Maria. 'A glass of red, please, love,' he said to the barmaid who'd reached him first, the other one in the race dropping back. 'What about you, love.' He nodded at Maria's glass. 'Top up?'

'I'm not your "love",' said Maria.

The young man put up his arms, palms outward. 'Of course you're not. My bad. But your glass is virtually empty.'

Maria searched for signs of mockery in the tanned face and didn't see any. 'Alright,' she said. She shook her head and suppressed a smile. She'd never – never – let a man do that to her before. The barmaid bustled around carelessly, a dark look settling on her face, clinking the wine bottle against Maria's glass and slopping wine onto the bar.

The young man caught Maria's eye and raised his eyebrows a notch. 'I'm meeting those two blokes over there. When I've finished, perhaps we can have another glass together, starting with proper introductions.'

Maria watched him go over and nodded to Billy, who started another phone call. There was no mirror over the bar, so Maria had to turn back to the window table if she wanted to see what was happening. The meeting was tense. The two men already seated let the other man stand. Mac, the one with the carroty hair, scowled, while the man she assumed was Stevie reluctantly made room for another chair, which the newcomer took from Billy's table. The three men huddled together, while Maria fretted about the quality of audio on her phone.

After twenty minutes, the huddle ended with something that seemed to cause amusement. Maria turned around to see Mac make a sound between a laugh and a guffaw. Stevie's laugh had a knowing, sneering quality in it, and mirrored the sneer in his face. The two tipped back their drinks and left without looking back.

Maria's benefactor was still smiling as he returned to the bar. 'Those blokes…,' he said, shaking his head. 'Anyway, this is much nicer. I'm Logan Seymour. How do you do? And you are?'

'Maria.' She almost choked as she swigged her wine, the glass covering her face.

'Another glass of wine, Maria?'

'I'll get them.'

'I wouldn't dream of it.'

'I'll get them,' said Maria.

'Of course. Of course. So, Maria, I expect you are a student, back here for the holidays.'

'Good guess… Logan. I am. But I don't think you are.'

Logan laughed. 'No, I'd be hopeless. I'm not what you'd call academic. I get by doing this and that.'

The glass of wine later, and Maria was none the wiser about her charming companion. She gave up probing before it became too persistent.

'Right, Logan. I'm off for my bus. Thank you for your company in lieu of the friend who stood me up.'

'It's been delightful, Maria. Perhaps you'd let me have your phone number and we can do it again sometime. And here's mine.' He handed over a gold-embossed card with 'Logan Seymour' on it in a fancy font, complete with a telephone number.

When Maria got to the door, she looked back. On his face was a small, twisted smile.

Shortly afterwards, Billy joined her at the bus stop, and they found a quiet seat on the top deck for the journey back to Whitstable.

Billy handed over the phone. 'Are we going to have a look and a listen?'

'You knew what the deal was when you came over with me, Billy. I don't think Frank will be pleased that I involved you in any capacity.'

'OK, OK. Worth a try. I hope you get something out of it. I only heard snatches of conversation because I was talking to myself – not so easy for ten minutes if you think about it. Anyway, I'm not fussed. I expect I'll get the full story sometime.' He looked away from Maria, out into the dark countryside. 'I suppose I'm more fussed about the third bloke. You looked as though you were getting on with him like a house on fire.'

'That was weird. He was charming all right. I thought he was chatting me up, and making a decent fist of it given what I'm like. He stopped with the "love" and flattery straight away. It was as if he could see right through me, and tailored his conversation on that basis. So easy-going and humorous, not pushy and flirty. So then I thought, he's not chatting me up, he's signing me up. Kind of… recruitment, or possible recruitment.'

'Blimey,' said Billy. 'He's a pimp!'

'Well, I suppose I should be flattered. I looked back when you and I left the pub. He had this horrible, cruel little smile on his face. It ruined all his previous good work. Anyway, Billy, as you well know, you're my type.'

Billy nodded and smiled himself – what Maria called the mysterious, wistful one. 'Good,' he said. And I'm glad to have been of help.'

At Whitstable harbour, just off the bus, they began the walk up to their homes. ‘Do you fancy a nightcap, Maria?’

She knew a nightcap wasn’t on his mind. ‘I’d better not, Billy. I need to look at the footage and see how Frank wants to deal with it.’

‘It’s not that really, is it?’

‘I’m still not ready. I’m doing my best, Billy, but it’s going to take a while. You don’t owe me anything. And you could have anyone.’

‘I don’t want “anyone”. I want you, and I’m prepared to wait.’ He hugged her suddenly and gave her a brief peck on the cheek.

As he strode off – angrily to Maria’s eye – she hoped that he hadn’t noticed her flinch.

Chapter 35

After Sterling and Maria had handed over the flash drive to Nolan and his team, everything moved quickly. Mamujee immediately ordered extra resources for the new development. Overnight, specialist forensic accountants were drafted in to pore over the data, working throughout Sunday. On Monday, striking before there were any leaks or suspicions, police personnel from all over the county carried out their allotted tasks.

Murphy and Stephens personally escorted a surly and intransigent Jimmy Jarvis from his hospital ward down the hill to the cells in the police station on Rheims Way. They'd gained some time to hold him by delaying his arrest until he was able to get out of his bed and walk. Now he was belligerently demanding a solicitor.

'I'm the fucking victim here. Look at my head.' He gave Stephens a sly, lascivious look. 'I've got bruises on my balls.'

The duo didn't respond. Witness accounts – principally from Sterling and Maria – and the expected forensic evidence on the barbed-wire baseball bat meant at least a charge of actual bodily harm, and would probably be enough to upgrade it to 'grievous'. When Janice Wray was ready to give her statement, she might not be able to identify her balaclava'd torturers in the

Zoar Chapel, but she could certainly identify the torture instrument. And all that was just the start.

Members of Jarvis's crew, helpfully detailed by name and payment on the 'Security' page of the flash drive's spreadsheet, were rousted from their haunts and houses, the arresting officers receiving the usual abuse from wives, partners and sundry hangers-on. Only the Fridge avoided arrest, Sterling's influence with Nolan and Mamujee offering protection. Sterling continued to work on getting him a good brief.

In offices and houses across the city and beyond, five councillors and two developers, named on the spreadsheet like all other 'consultants' and 'employees', were invited to 'help the police with their enquiries'. They were taken to police stations around the county once the Canterbury one had reached capacity.

A joint operation between the police and a county social work team dealt with the brothel at Westgate Close, finding seven skimpily dressed Eastern European girls, some middle-aged men in various states of undress and the madam, Maddie Spedding, painting her toenails in reception. DCI Nolan had to get in specialist advice about charges, and the girls were taken to undisclosed places of safety.

Mac – full name Thomas McVey – was tracked down and arrested at his flat in Station Road West. A delivery rider spotted him being bundled into the back of a squad car. Immediately after that, passers-by in the high street noticed a peculiar thing. There was a flurry of activity around the war memorial where riders assembled. In under a minute, the little square had emptied.

On the estates, the university residence blocks and in the student villages dotted around the centre, there would be no drug deliveries that week, and even pizzas, although easy to source, might temporarily be hard to acquire except by direct visit to outlets.

It wasn't the wizardry of police IT technicians navigating a virtual private network that led to a scruffy upstairs flat in the Borough, where two 'CanterburySugar' web administrators were arrested for blackmail, but a specific address supplied by Charlotte Hankinson. Like several others taken into custody, they seemed to be developing a defence based on fear and coercion – that originally they'd simply run the website, but had been forced over the boundary into criminality.

Andy Nolan coordinated the operation. For him, the best moment of the day was the arrival, with an immaculately attired lawyer in a dark silk suit, of an equally immaculate Charlotte Hankinson. The woman was tight-lipped in the last available interview room with Nolan and Mamujee himself, who'd turned out from HQ at Maidstone, but the lawyer's words were magical.

'Mrs Hankinson is more than willing to help you with your enquiries. In fact, with certain guarantees, she is prepared to cooperate fully.' *Queen's evidence,* thought Nolan, *just as Frank advised.*

In the local newsrooms, editors were getting wind of the police operation, and pressing for more information. Reporters were scrambling, using their contacts on the phone and face to face. Mamujee promised them a press release and press conference later in the day, 'When the overall picture is clearer.' Later in the week the headlines, in papers and on the internet, would be lurid: 'City enmeshed in web of corruption', 'Brothel busted on edge of city', 'City protection racket exposed',

'Blackmail scam linked to city-based website', 'Councillors and developers charged after planning bribery exposure', 'City reels from new revelations in corruption scandal', and, mischievously via the reporter who had previously baited Nolan, 'No further leads in murder case linked to corruption enquiry'.

The judicial machinery was cranking along more speedily too. Canterbury magistrates court was gearing up for an influx of hearings, and along with it the private security company responsible for prisoner transport. On the nearby Isle of Sheppey, the Category B prison prepared itself for prisoners remanded in custody, those unfortunates who wouldn't achieve bail. For Jimmy Jarvis, HMP Swaleside, while not home from home, was certainly familiar.

That Monday, it was calmer on the streets. Sergeant Peterson, strolling on foot patrol about the city centre, sensed that the atmosphere was lighter, as if an oppressive dark pall had been removed. The gathering volume of phone-ins and messages to the police call centre offering information or complaining about 'protection' seemed to confirm his instincts.

The street grapevine was rapid and effective. With Jimmy Jarvis and his crew removed from circulation, and associated scams and criminality emerging, no one with a grievance, new or long-standing, was holding back.

The rumour, more and more substantiated as time elapsed, that the vicious Jarvis had been outfought by a girl and that the Fridge had flipped, added both to the lightness of atmosphere and volume of calls. Peterson remembered the phrase he'd used to Frank Sterling at the Hankinson murder scene and bandied about the station over the last week or so – the so-called ‘wall of silence’. Well, there was a big hole in it now, and sound was roaring through.

*

‘We could have done this on Zoom,’ said Maria. It was midday, and she and Sterling were sitting beside each other in a coffee shop at the top of Canterbury high street. They had their backs to the wall and Maria’s laptop open in front of them.

Sterling got out his expenses sheet and made some additions.

‘Alright, I get it.’

‘Face to face is always better,’ said Sterling. ‘Less chance of misunderstandings. So, for example, when I say to you, face to face, that I’m not happy with wonder boy helping with the sleuthing, that’s clear, right?’

‘Get off your high horse. You should have had your phone on, and you should have replied to my text. I couldn’t have got what I got without him. Anyway, he took the footage and only heard some of it. He hasn’t seen it.’

‘Whatever,’ said Sterling. ‘Let’s have a look.’

‘Before we do, have you heard this morning’s news? The police have been doing raids across the city. Loads of people being whisked away “to help the police with their enquiries”.’

‘Yeah, on the back of our efforts. Come on.’

Maria looked around. No one was behind them and the tables on either side were empty. Beyond them was a gaggle of foreign tourists on one side and three mothers and their babies on the other. She pressed ‘Play’. ‘You’re going to like this. I've been saving it up: I've found the mysterious Logan Seymour.'

'Really.' Sterling perked up. Maria did stuff he didn't agree with, but she got results.

The two of them stared intently at the screen, straining to hear the audio. Billy had rotated his head now and again to take in different angles of the two men and then the new arrival. His own conversation with himself, apparently on a district cycleway strategy, made the background exchanges hard to hear, but the pictures of the men were utterly clear. Maria pointed. 'You know Mac. Stevie is the one with him at the start, and the new one is Seymour.'

Towards the end of the recording, the screen showed the ceiling of the pub. Sterling sensed Maria's excitement. 'Billy's put the phone down, but listen…'

'So,' said Logan Seymour in a faraway voice, 'you'll think about my proposal and get back to me, right? I think you'll find it'll be a very big winner for us all. You've got my card.'

'Alright,' said Mac. His voice had its usual truculent tone.

'I reckon you've done well since Hankinson got topped, one of the only ones, I'd say. Did you two do it?'

There was a sound of laughter. Another voice came in, Stevie's. 'Did *you*?' it said, and then more laughter.

'Gold dust, eh?' said Maria.

'Well, it's good, especially finding Seymour,' said Sterling, 'but I wouldn't call it gold dust.'

'Mr Glass Half-Empty.'

'Let me tell you what I did yesterday.' Sterling recounted his visit to the Hume smallholding. 'It was worth it, I guess, but like this recording, where does it actually get us? We've got four people of interest. I don't think Mac would be physically capable of actually doing the deed but Stevie looks fit enough, and those two seem to work closely together. Fancy boy Seymour also looks fit, and from what you've said about him I reckon he's well capable. Charlotte Hankinson said she couldn't tell if the voice of her blackmailer and the probable murderer was male or female. That puts Alice Hume in the frame. I tell you, she might be a long shot, but she could have done it, with knobs on. That rabbit…

'All of them have got good motives. The three blokes, from their conversation, are ambitious. The girl was protecting her way of life. Opportunity wouldn't have been a problem. Then our other lead… We haven't even caught up with that property developer, Mark Prideaux, the one who fell out with Hankinson. He's probably been arrested by now if Andy Nolan has organised raids, so how do we catch up with him? And you never know, even Jimmy Jarvis could have done it for some obscure reason. We both did alright yesterday, and we've done OK in general, Maria, but progress? I'm not sure. We've gone from no leads to four or so suspects but nothing certain.'

'I thought we'd done more than alright.'

'We messed up with Janice, and I feel bad about that. I hope she'll be OK. We got Patrick and the girls out. We've helped Andy and his lot. But none of those things was in our main brief, were they?'

'So what now, Frank?'

'I'm going to check with Andy whether he's arrested anybody from the Labour Party. Then I'm going to get a report together for June. She can see us tomorrow and we'll give a full update. It'll be up to her whether or not she wants us to continue.'

'Your other cases must be piling up,' smiled Maria.

''Course. Bermuda's next. Bank scam.'

At the bus station, Sterling called his assistant back. 'I imagine Mac and Stevie have been detained by now, and clearly Mac didn't recognise you in the pub yesterday. Alice Hume doesn't know you exist. But that Logan Seymour... he's a new kid on the block. He won't be on Charlotte Hankinson's flash drive, or on police radar. I'm with wonder boy. Seymour's nailed on for a pimp. It's not that though. There's something else about him. Somehow, he's familiar. Stay alert, Maria.'

'I'm the one who had a drink with him. I agree. He's dodgy. And I was rash enough to give him my phone number. So yep, I'll be careful. See you tomorrow.'

Chapter 36

Sterling got the call from June Selsdon as the bus was going through Honey Hill, halfway to Whitstable. 'Many, many apologies, Frank, but there's been an emergency. My sister's had a fall. I'm on the way to the hospital with her. Can we postpone the meeting till this afternoon?'

'Sure,' he said. *I'll adjust the timesheets in a coffee shop, and add coffee and a pastry to my expenses.* 'About two?'

'Sorry again. I look forward to the update.'

Sterling phoned Maria on speed-dial. 'June's had an emergency. The time of the meeting's been put back till this afternoon. Can you still make it?'

'Maybe. I'm at Billy's now. If you're on your way over, why don't you come here for a cup of tea?'

'Alright.' Sterling wasn't enthusiastic. Billy Jenkins depressed him – the wonder boy whose presence and popularity reinforced all Sterling's wrong turns, even if they were mostly in his own imagination. Even Billy's foray into sleuthing had been a resounding success. He hadn't got caught and he'd got some decent information.

Sterling followed Maria's directions. Billy's garage door, painted dark green, signalled that he was in the right place a street or two away from June Selsdon's house. He went up the side passage and knocked on the side door. It sprang wide open, and there was Billy himself in all his wonder boy splendour.

'Mr Sterling. Delighted to see you again.' Billy motioned him in with a grand sweep of his arm. 'I'll do another brew. I wouldn't dream of serving stewed tea to my honoured guest.'

The flattery was so brazen that it made Sterling smile. While the young man went off to fill the kettle from the garden tap, Sterling stepped into the garage, staying on the threshold to take in the interior.

He noted the neatly arrayed equipment cleverly attached by hooks and fittings to the walls and compartmentalised according to activity. There was a climbing section, with pitons, crampons, rope and other paraphernalia he didn't recognise, and bright red, lightweight, high-spec weather wear. Then there was the water sports section – wetsuit, snorkel, flippers and paddles – and more unrecognised gear. A sleek red touring bike hung from pulleys in a far corner. Fishing tackle, a rod and nets, covered another area. A 'significant events' section of photos and certificates, of running meetings, football matches and even electioneering, seemed understated. A particular photo with Billy holding a large fish was small and unframed. The fish was larger than anything Sterling had ever caught. Everything seemed to come so easily to BJ, whereas Sterling felt his life was one long struggle.

Maria motioned him to a garden chair next to her. 'Cosy, isn't it?' she said with vicarious pride.

Sterling grunted. Cosy maybe, but in his opinion this was the home of an eco-dilettante. Billy returned and busied himself neatly and economically with water, kettle and teapot. He produced some homemade coconut macaroons.

'He didn't bake them,' said Maria teasingly. 'His mother brings in the luxuries from her kitchen.'

Billy smiled. 'I keep saying I'm not perfect, but at least I try.'

'Of course you do,' said Maria.

'I just don't want to be like everybody else. We all accept climate change, but we still want all the trappings of modern life. That old feminist phrase has always resonated with me: "the personal is political", but applied to the environment and climate change.'

'You're like Darby and Joan, you two.' Sterling sipped his tea and dunked his biscuit. No need for politesse here. It was reasonably comfortable in Billy's garage, and the refreshments were welcome, but he couldn't stretch to another two or so hours here waiting for June Selsdon to get home from sorting out her sister. He might go into the town – he'd seen a Co-op – and do a bit of shopping, have a walk along the sea defences and maybe a quiet pint. He listened to Maria and Billy's cut and thrust, witty riffs and affectionate teasing, and wondered why they weren't an item. Maybe they were, but for a mysterious reason they kept it private.

Maria wasn't a prattler, but she wasn't holding back in going back over events such as the fight in the Butterfly Garden, the meeting in the Miller's Arms with the trio of police officers and Fridge's process of political enlightenment. And Billy. Billy wasn't exactly indulgent but he showed interest, laughed in the right places and asked timely follow-up questions. It was clear that he'd heard some of it before, maybe from a different angle. They shared a laugh about the surveillance on Mac and

Seymour in The Bishop's Finger. Occasionally Sterling was invited to add his contribution, but as he finished his tea, he felt more than ever that he was the odd one out. He waited for an opening. 'So, Maria, will you be on for seeing June at two?'

'I thought you were coming for a spin in the boat this afternoon,' said Billy. 'Charlie's got a blank afternoon and he's letting me borrow it. We were going out to the Maunsell Forts.'

'Do you mind, Frank?' said Maria.

'Not at all. It won't take the two of us to get June up to speed. Right then. The cupboard in my house is bare, what with all the recent excitement and action. Not even a coconut macaroon. So I'm going into town to do a bit of shopping.' He put his mug in Billy's all-purpose bowl and made for the door.

'Let me know how you get on, Frank,' said Maria, 'and if June wants us to continue. Fingers crossed.'

'Sure. I'll give you a ring.' He shook hands with Billy or, rather, Billy shook hands with him. Sterling realised that he and Maria, apart from their initial, cool, fingers only handshake at the outset in June's house, and Maria pressing him back with her arm as she faced Jimmy Jarvis in the Butterfly Garden, had never had any physical contact. He wasn't of the 'mwah, mwah' peck on each cheek persuasion and nor was she.

He started back to the town centre along the usual route. It was at the automatic swishing electric doors of the Co-op that he pulled up. He was well blessed with whatever the magic burst of brain activity was that give sudden insights. If he could train it, exercise it, focus it and conjure it up whenever he needed it, he'd really have it made. He certainly feared losing it.

This time the trigger was on the other side of the street, the unmistakeable person of Logan Seymour was striding purposefully towards the harbour, mobile pressed to his ear. Sterling realised why the man was familiar – the high, wide forehead and o-shaped mouth and small chin surely made him the brothel madam's son. In Sterling's mind, a series of other images, conversations, actions and events led inexorably to one conclusion. He had to get to Maria again – urgently – and he fumbled for his phone.

'Are you going in or out?' said a peevish voice. A harassed middle-aged woman with a shopping trolley was trying to get past him as the doors swished manically to and fro. With his ear to the phone, he stepped wordlessly sideways as she tutted her way past.

'Frank?' said his phone.

'Maria. I need to talk to you – face to face.'

'You've only just seen me. We're just getting the boat ready.'

'Something new has come up. It's important. Where are you? Tell Billy I've got some time. I'll come along for the ride.'

There was a silence, and then Maria's voice came back. 'That's fine, Frank. Plenty of room. We're at the quay just opposite Whitstable Harbour Office.'

Breathless, Sterling hurried down the ramp at the East Harbour five minutes later. Logan Seymour was nowhere in view. Billy had already started the powerboat's engine and tossed Sterling a fluorescent red life jacket. 'If you go in the water, pull the cord and it will inflate.'

He and Maria didn't seem fazed by Sterling's reappearance. Perhaps Maria had explained his habit of going off in sudden changes of direction. The harbour area, even on a Monday at lunchtime, was busy with tourists at the whelk stalls, open-air cafés and bucket-and-spade shops. There was envy on the faces of onlookers as they looked down at the trio – a perfect sunny, warm, cloudless June day, a gentle, cheek-caressing breeze, the sea glittering and the promise of a little maritime adventure.

Deftly, Billy eased the boat from the jetty, his hands expertly coordinated on throttle and wheel. He was skippering the boat as well as he could cycle, climb, swim, fish, play football and glad-hand at political gatherings. They backed out and then spun around, herring and black-headed gulls lifting out of the water and screaming with alarm. Sterling spotted turnstones on the opposite jetty, foraging among the ropes and bollards but, as far as he could see, no Seymour.

As they left the shelter of the coast, Billy opened the throttle and the boat surged forward. Sterling and Maria, sitting at the stern, were pushed back by the exhilarating surge of power. The breeze turned into stiff wind, and the boat juddered and bumped as it danced and skittered over the small waves of the shining sea.

Maria tipped back her head and laughed, her dark blonde hair spinning and fluttering out horizontally behind her.

Billy turned his head and smiled, and then turned his attention back to his duties.

Sterling shifted in his seat and stretched around to look at the rapidly receding coastline, which had been transformed into a straight line between land and sea. He couldn't even make out the harbour entrance. What could be more alluring than a boat trip into the North Sea on a classic English summer afternoon? But he couldn't shake off his unease. He should have been concentrating better beforehand. Thought things through.

Only ten minutes later, Billy closed down the throttle and swept out his arm in front of the Maunsell Forts, as if introducing them. They'd been dots in the distance for a small while but up close, the cluster of rusted, ramshackle structures dominated the panorama. Sterling remembered his father's vinyl, Jeff Wayne's *War of the Worlds*. These were Martian war machines stranded in the sea. The boat bobbed and wobbled on the water, and the wind dropped back down to a breeze.

'I love coming out here,' said Billy. 'You get away from all the crap on land. All the selfish people with their know-nothing lives. Do you know about the Maunsell Forts, Frank?'

Sterling noted that 'Mr Sterling' had been dropped. As far as the forts were concerned, he remembered thinking he'd seen them from the top of the bus going into Whitstable at the beginning of the case, and his father's enthusiasm for them all those years ago. 'Yep. This group is called Red Sands. There are others further out and dotted up the coast. Designed by Guy Maunsell. Manufactured in Chatham around the Second World War on concrete platforms and towed out here on buoyancy tanks. Mounted with Bofors anti-aircraft guns, if I remember correctly, and a searchlight tower, ready for the German bombers coming up the Thames. There are walkways between each structure – there's still one over there.' He pointed. 'There were various radio station ventures back in the day. Radio 390. Maybe Radio Invicta.'

Billy nodded. Sterling thought he saw a kindling of respect in the young man's eyes. 'You're right on all counts. There's one off the coast of Suffolk – Fort Roughs.'

'Yes,' said Sterling. 'Sealand.'

A wistfulness spread over Billy's features. 'The Principality of Sealand, a sovereign micronation started by Paddy Roy Bates. It's issued passports and coins. It's got a written constitution with a coat of arms and everything. There was even an attack on it in 1978 by a German-Sealand dual nationality lawyer who hired German and Dutch mercenaries. The Sealand government captured and held him hostage. The German government sent a diplomat to negotiate his release. Imagine having the nerve and determination to start and defend your own nation, letting no one tell you what to do, being completely independent. Establishing your own government and dynasty.'

There had been no previous indication of eccentricity in this direction in Billy Jenkins, and even Maria looked mildly surprised. Her forehead puckered in a frown.

'Not much chance of anything like that for me now,' said Billy. 'You know, don't you, Frank?'

Shit, thought Sterling. He should have tried to get Maria off the boat back at the harbour, but it had all happened so quickly. Having come along on the ride, he'd banked on them getting back to land before the balloon went up.

Maria's little squashed-up face took on a kind of blank, unseeing look.

'How did you guess?' said Billy. Sleight of hand had produced a small gun from the glove compartment by the throttle, which was now pointed at Sterling. No doubt Billy was a crack shot, to go with all his other talents.

'It wasn't guessing. It was adding things up and drawing the right conclusions, which is what I do.' Sterling swallowed. He struggled to see a good ending, for himself at least. Perhaps if he drew things out… 'It was all the stuff on your walls – water sports and climbing equipment, fishing gear and the fish photo on your table. So you swim. You climb. You've killed things… bludgeoned things in fact. I remembered the senior investigating officer, my friend Andy Nolan, commenting on the murder scene, or maybe one of the cops guarding it, saying that they'd drawn a blank with the forensics. That was the cleverest part.

'I reckon you arrange to meet Hankinson there – lure him there in fact – and arrive in your wetsuit via the river. Maybe you swim up from Barton Mill. It would have been dark. You bash Hankinson and leave the way you came. Maybe you have a hidden little nest down there with a bag and your clothes. More likely downstream than towards the city because it would have been quieter down there. I bet the rock you used is at the bottom of the river where no one will ever distinguish it from all the others. Being eco-minded, I expect you got to Canterbury and back on your bike.'

Billy smiled. 'You've got me bang to rights, mate.' Mockney had crept into his tone.

'I think you killed Hankinson because of something personal but you wanted to make it look as though the motive was robbery. So along with Hankinson's wallet and keys, you stole the flash drive you discovered around his neck. Once you'd opened that, you realised you had a blackmail opportunity as well as your original motive, and a new victim. There's no dishonour winkling money from someone who's already corrupt, is there? You contact Charlotte Hankinson and arrange a swap, cash for the flash drive.

'She and Jimmy Jarvis lay a trap in Greyfriars Garden, but you just hop up the masonry wall and disappear with nothing but a small gouge from Jarvis's barbed-wire bat. That's the climbing part. Using a payphone was another giveaway – Billy Jenkins, the greenie without a mobile. At that stage, Charlotte Hankinson's tired of it all, unsurprisingly in my view, especially as Jarvis is becoming such a loose cannon, so she has the idea of offering you the business. All the talent you've got, Billy, and it doesn't seem to be enough. When you talked about Sealand, a little principality off the coast, it made some more sense. Power and recklessness, they sum you up.'

Sterling held up his hand. If he could keep talking… He glanced sideways at Maria's empty face. 'It wasn't Charlotte Hankinson who phoned Jimmy Jarvis about our brothel raid. She'd already opted out. It was you, protecting your new interests and connecting with Jack Hankinson's valued enforcer. Your brains, his brute force, excellent combo. And how did you know about it? We wondered where the leak came from, and then I listened to Maria in your garage, chatting away, trusting you and telling you stuff about our case. Sunday night in the pub, recording that meeting… that was a clever… red herring. Mac and Stevie probably always met there and at that time. Probably you got that from Jimmy Jarvis. And Logan Seymour's arrival was a bonus. The only thing that's puzzling me is why. Why kill Hankinson? What had he ever done to you?'

'He raped *me*,' Maria broke in tonelessly, 'when he was still in the Labour Party. I went to his house to organise some leafletting and a street stall, and I couldn't... I was so shocked... I froze... Afterwards, he laughed at me... Who'd believe a silly girl?' She choked back a sob. '... Billy and I were getting on brilliantly. We had the holidays in front of us, and then I couldn't... I hated the idea of sex. I was traumatised...'

'That's why you were preoccupied on the way to the police station, after Janice Wray talked about him raping women, back in the Martyrs' Garden.' More solutions slotted into Sterling's crossword grid.

'And I wasn't even one of the "vulnerable" ones. I was meant to be assertive and able to look after myself. Hah.' Bitterness had crept into Maria's voice.

'So there you have it, Mr Private Dick,' said Billy. 'And it was so easy to plan and carry out. The man chased anything in a skirt. Arranging the prospect of a bit of riverside "how's your father?" with a mystery admirer via Tinder was child's play. He fucked Maria's life up. He fucked mine up. He deserved everything he got. And now...'

Maria's face went blank again. Sterling just couldn't get a read. What happened next was neatly done. She simply bent over, wrapped her arms around his legs, and in one smooth movement upended him out of the boat. Sterling entered the water in an upside-down V shape, feet first, and then with his head tilting violently back. Sheer surprise had kept his mouth open, and he gagged on an intake of brine. He'd never been a swimmer. He hated being in the water. He flailed and splashed around ineffectually.

From the boat, Maria and Billy looked at him, dead-eyed and stony-faced.

'No need for another killing, Billy. Let him take his chances,' said the girl. She turned away, and then so did Billy, after a last long look. The engine revved, sending up a plume of blue exhaust, and Sterling was buffeted in the wash. Even while he was fighting to control panic as the boat sped away, a small part of his brain registered that, once again, a woman had let him down.

Chapter 37

At least he was alive. But he was sinking fast. In the shock of Maria's duplicity, and hitting the cold water, he'd forgotten he was wearing a life jacket. He pulled the cord as Billy had casually instructed back at the quayside, and inflation and buoyancy were immediate.

The boat was receding into the distance, now more a speck than a shape. He paddled around and looked at the five red-rusty structures in front of him. The one with a ladder hanging down was the second nearest. He'd make for that, clamber up and then… what?

The relief at being buoyant evaporated. This wasn't an area frequented by much maritime traffic. Tankers wouldn't go near, and he wouldn't be seen anyway. It might be days before engineers came near to service and repair the windmills on the adjacent wind farm. He was already cold, even in high summer. His phone wouldn't work after the dousing, and even if it did, would there be a signal? Only Billy and Maria knew he was out here, and Maria had the nous to concoct a plausible story to fob June Selsdon off if she got in touch. The tourists and bystanders who watched three go out would not be the same as those watching two come back. Still, he began swimming in a clumsy breaststroke.

A sound rolled faintly across the water, a vague elongated 'crack'. It was weird out here – vast, hostile. Things were distorted. He stopped moving forward and manoeuvred around in a circle, trying to see what might have changed. Were there mirages at sea? Was bobbing around among the choppy, sparkling waves playing tricks with his perception? He was sure he was wrong – pessimism overwhelming every other emotion and making him determined to avoid self-delusion – but was the speck becoming a shape again?

He closed his eyes for thirty seconds. When he opened them again, shape had become powerboat. They were coming back. They'd decided it was too risky to leave him. Better to finish him off. After all, only he knew who'd bumped off Jack Hankinson. There was something about the boat. Its course was jagged, and it seemed to be approaching in fits and starts. Perhaps that was a maritime technique for searches. He started paddling frantically for the rusty ladder. If they got to him while he was in the water, he didn't stand a chance.

He soon realised that there was no chance of escape. It was too far to the fort, and the boat was moving too quickly. He trod water and waited, a sense of dread sweeping through him. What a way to go, shot and abandoned in the North Sea, his body floating and bloated, he imagined, for weeks until it was found – if it was found at all.

It looked as though they were going to run him down rather than waste a bullet. He swam furiously and the prow of the boat clipped his shoe as it veered past and then pulled to a stop. Maria's scared face appeared over the side. She'd been frightened at the Butterfly Garden, but determined-frightened. Now her face was ashen.

'I've shot him, Frank,' she blurted.

'Help me in,' he gasped, presenting his arm. She grasped his wrist in her palm and fingers and heaved. The boat rocked violently as he slithered into a heap amidships, rivulets of water pooling at the bottom of the boat.

He felt euphoria and confusion and was overwhelmed with dizziness. Recovering, he focused his eyes on the body sprawled across the stern, a bright red patch blooming across the left shoulder. He stumbled forward, Maria anxiously in his wake. He dredged up his first aid training. Billy's eyes were glazed, but his pulse was beating furiously.

Sterling cast around. 'Get me your jacket and something sharp. Look in the glove compartment thing.'

Maria produced a Stanley knife and Sterling cut and tore the jacket into strips. The wound was at the top of the shoulder in the ball where the arm was attached. At first he thought of a tourniquet, but the wound's location made it impossible. And couldn't tourniquets do more harm than good? Then his memory kicked in some more. He folded a strip of fabric into a thick pad. 'Come here, Maria. What you need to do is press this firmly right on the wound. Keep it firm, and don't move it. The blood will start to clot underneath, and things will stabilise. Give me your phone. Mine's soaked.'

The signal was intermittent, but he managed to get a message through – ambulance and police required at the east quay, Whitstable Harbour, for a gunshot incident on a motorboat. The operator was savvy, and when Sterling stated that DCI Nolan should be notified and asked to attend, she didn't equivocate.

Sterling sat in front of the steering wheel. The throttle seemed uncomplicated. He gripped it in his right hand and eased it forward. The engine gave a low roar and the boat gathered speed. He turned it around and headed for the shore. If the harbour wasn't dead ahead, he'd be able to find it when he got to the coast.

In less desperate and confusing circumstances, there might have been banter – 'Frank, fancy seeing you out here in the water. Would you like a lift?', 'Are you rescuing me or running me down, Maria?' But now Maria was speaking urgently and intensely from her position at the stern.

'Frank, I swear... I SWEAR... I had no idea about Billy. He was the only one I told about the rape, but I didn't know what he was going to do. I got June to involve me in the case to see if it would help me get closure. I was a fool to tell Billy what we were doing. He must have sent me the text about Mac and Stevie in the pub. And when I asked him to come with me, that was perfect for him. I trusted him. With that. With everything. I'm really sorry.'

Sterling looked round from his skippering.

Maria searched his face with her eyes. 'I had to tip you in the water. It was the only way to save you. He would have shot you. He was asking me to choose, and I pretended to choose him. Then, when we were heading back, he put the gun down to drive the boat and I picked it up and shot him.' She pleaded. 'Why would I have come back if all this wasn't true?'

'Alright,' said Sterling. 'Keep that pad firmly pressed.' He turned forward. It made sense, but that dead-eyed look when he was in the water... He needed to get his composure back and there was a lot to compute.

Fifteen minutes later, with Billy still insensible but with a stable pulse rate, they were guided to the harbour by the blue lights of squad cars and ambulances.

'Maria,' said Sterling, 'the paramedics will take Billy to hospital in an ambulance. I'm guessing he'll need an operation. They'll check us over. I'll at least get a dry blanket. With luck Andy Nolan and Murphy will be there. They'll want statements from us. They'll probably separate us to do that. I doubt we'll be arrested but they won't want to let us go until they know what's what. When you're questioned, tell the truth. I'll be doing the same, and then our stories will match up exactly. And on the boat, when I wasn't there, you grabbed the gun and pulled the trigger out of self-defence. You were scared for yourself and scared for me.' It was funny. There were other cases when he hadn't been so keen on the truth.

'OK, Frank.' Maria was still ashen and was biting her lip, as if the next ordeal was not her highest priority. 'We're good though, Frank, aren't we? You and me, we're good.'

Sterling looked hard and long into her anxious eyes. 'Well, we are if I don't get pneumonia from the soaking you gave me.'

Chapter 38

It turned out, gratifyingly for Sterling when he heard about it from Andy Nolan later, that Billy Jenkins wasn't such a wonder boy after all. Would someone so well-starred, so clever, so competent, have made so many errors? The police search of his garage unearthed Jack Hankinson's original flash drive and even the lanyard to which it was attached at the bottom of a tin of tea. He had used a laptop in his parents' house to access the drive. Forensic analysis revealed dried sediment on his wetsuit from the river Stour where Hankinson had been finished off, and the training shoe that Jimmy Jarvis had spiked in the Greyfriars Garden in Canterbury was still bloody. His fingerprints were still in the phone box on the main road where he'd conducted his business with Charlotte Hankinson (unsullied by anyone else's – after all, who uses a phone box these days?) and records of her phone number. Her £10,000 – the blackmail money – was stuffed in a flipper. A burner phone with Maria's phone number in the Contacts was found in a cutlery tray. There was even some dust from near Barton Mill on the tyres of his bike.

Sterling and Maria had given comprehensive statements, including Jenkins's admission and motive, revealed in the water around Red Sands. Through her

Queen's evidence deal, Hankinson herself would likely be weighing in with an account of the blackmail calls.

Sterling had watched Andy Nolan's press conference the evening after the motorboat escapade. Nolan had had the grace to tip his hat in the direction of Sterling and Maria, and their various helpers, alluding to the bravery and enterprise of a number of ordinary members of the public who'd tackled certain 'law-breaking elements'. Without them, he'd acknowledged, he and his colleagues wouldn't have been able to make an arrest in their murder enquiry, or, related to that, uncover the 'large web of criminality' spread in various strands over the whole of Canterbury. But it was still his show, and he and his team would be the ones getting the accolades – and, like as not, the promotions.

Now Sterling and Maria were sitting in a chichi little café on Whitstable High Street on uncomfortable stiff-backed cane chairs. Their surprisingly indifferent coffee was on an over-embroidered tablecloth. It was the Thursday after Billy's shooting, and a fortnight and a day after Billy had bludgeoned Jack Hankinson on the Canterbury riverside path. They would shortly be on their way to June Selsdon's house to report back and for a final settling of accounts. Sterling had wanted to see Maria by herself first. At the harbour on Monday, they had immediately been whisked away for separate questioning and to make statements. Nolan, Murphy and Mamujee himself had been prominent, and without them, getting released and home would have been far more difficult.

'Don't leave town,' Murphy had said with his customary twinkle as he'd escorted them to the door of Canterbury Police Station.

Sterling popped open a couple of paracetamol caplets and washed them down with a mouthful of coffee. It had been a heavy night in the Cinq Ports, celebrating the conclusion of another successful case, and toasting Angela and Becky for their contribution. The backslapping and excess had been led by Jack Cook, Sandley's gossip king, with plenty of new ammunition with which to shoot his mouth off. He had material to last him weeks.

'So,' said Maria, 'we do the hard yards, the shaking things loose, the fighting, the rescuing, the...' – she gulped – '... shooting, the whole thing, and what do we get? A postscript at a police press conference, while your pal Andy Nolan gets all the credit.'

'Gutting, isn't it? But that's what being a PI is about in the end. That kind of thing, anyway. At least we've got credits in the bank.' He paused. 'All that aside, how are you doing, Maria? You know, personally.'

'Alright. Bruised. Let down. Let down big time. I thought I knew BJ but I ignored the signs. An eco-Marxist – "from each according to his ability, to each according to his needs" – his mantra – pah – I was so gullible. Taken in by a sociopathic risk-taker.'

'Maybe he is those things. But remember, he didn't just fool you. There'll be a lot of red faces around here when it all comes out.'

'It was all a game,' said Maria, looking at nothing out of the window. 'The garage, the Labour Party...'

'Not you, though. He cared enough about you to kill.'

'An idealised version of me, more like. His thinking was utterly warped.'

'You know, you should have told me why you wangled yourself into the investigation. I missed it at the time, but your loathing of Hankinson went far beyond him being a turncoat.'

'I couldn't, Frank. I just couldn't... An assertive, savvy feminist, or so I thought, to get in such a mess. And if you had known, would it have made any difference?'

Sterling looked down at the table and then askance at Maria. 'That's a great motive, right there.'

She smiled. 'I never thought of that. Actually, can we talk about something else? Like, I don't suppose you'll be carrying on your Labour Party membership now the case is over.'

'Oh, I don't know. I might stick around, if only as a wind-up merchant. A lot of the time, when I was growing up with my dad, I didn't really disagree with him. I just took the opposite view to needle him.'

'Typical. Good though, that you're thinking of staying. I've heard from Patrick. That Higher National Diploma qualification he's got – he is managing to convert it to a degree as he planned. He's got a place at Westminster University. The girls will be alright in the Railroad. And Janice is OK – out of hospital and back home. So we did more good than harm then, Frank, didn't we?'

'Sure. Good news about all of them. I liked old Patrick on that brief acquaintance. Are you ready? Let's walk up to June's.'

'And you're certain you want me there.'

'Of course. You're part of the team, so long as you're OK when I get to the bit about Billy's motive.'

'What – he killed Hankinson because Hankinson raped me and ruined Billy's chance of being my boyfriend.'

'So succinct,' said Sterling.

'Well, the police know, and I trust June, and it will all come out at the trial, so yes.'

As they got to the beginning of Clare Road, Sterling's strange feeling came back more strongly than ever, and lingered in June Selsdon's kitchen. He ignored it as he gave his summary and presented his invoice. The older woman shook her head in shock and wonderment as she heard about the rape, the rescuing, the fighting, the shooting and all the other aspects of the case.

'I had no idea that it was going to be so dangerous. I feel guilty about it all now.'

'How could you know? I'm not sure I'd have gone down the road we went down if I'd known myself.'

'But the central thing – Billy is a Labour Party member.'

'Yes, but he was also an employee of Harbour Coastal Water Sports, and from his photo gallery a striker with Atletico Chestfield football club, and a rower in Herne Bay Rowing Club. His Labour Party membership has nothing to do with what he did. The Party is in the clear.'

As the conversation continued – questions from June Selsdon and answers from Sterling, with contributions and interventions from Maria – the older woman became more and more distracted and seemed to be losing interest in the review.

'So dangerous,' she murmured more than once. Her forefinger tapped on the kitchen table, a habit Sterling recognised as one of his own in times of stress.

Wait a minute... Things finally began to add up, a different, even more powerful set from the ones that had sunk Billy Jenkins. There was the odd sensation every time he walked into Clare Road and June Selsdon's house or spoke to her on the phone. There was the concern for his welfare, far more pronounced than case principals normally demonstrated. There was a sudden sense that he'd met this person well before his contract to investigate a fortnight before. And there was the finger-tapping, the exact replica of his own, the clincher. He looked closely at his host, the texture and shade of her hair, the shape of her nose, the tone and colour of the skin on her forearm.

'Jesus Christ and all the saints and angels,' he blurted out. 'You're my…' – he struggled to say the word, barely ever having had any use for it – '… mother.'

June Selsdon's face crumpled, and tears were suddenly pouring in parallel tracks down her face. 'I'm so sorry.'

Maria – the offsider, the foil, the fighter, the shooter – looked more shocked than at any time during the investigation. She sat stock-still and there was silence for a long moment. 'I think I'd better go.'

'No, stay,' said Sterling. 'You're part of the team, remember. After what we've been through, you've a right to be here for all of it.' The truth was, he wasn't sure he wanted to be alone and unmediated with this woman, his mother.

'Frank's right,' said June Selsdon. 'And anyway, there's nothing really awful in the story.'

For ten minutes, Sterling and Maria sat transfixed as his mother talked about her post-natal depression, the subsequent breakdown, the sectioning under the Mental Health Act, and the long road back to health, culminating in a happy and successful second marriage.

'I followed your career, Frank, as best I could. I didn't make contact out of respect for your father. He was a decent man. No blame could be attached to him. It took me half a decade to claw myself back to anything like a normal life, and by that time it was too late. And just as he never deserted you, he never deserted me. I was the one who had to get away. But when, after all this time, my second husband had died and I knew that your father had also gone, I saw the perfect opportunity.'

'It's a lot to take in,' said Sterling. He felt a burning, uncomplicated loyalty to his dead father. 'He *was* decent. He didn't just raise me single-handed. He never said a single negative thing about you.' His feelings about the older woman at the table with him were more complex, but far from negative. 'I don't get it. Why didn't you just make contact in the ordinary way? Why do it through a case?'

'I was scared. I thought you might not welcome it. This way, I could hedge my bets, or I thought I could. I could broach it at an appropriate time. I wasn't expecting you to work it out.'

'He's a detective, June,' smiled Maria. It was the first thing she'd said for some minutes, and perfectly timed to lighten the atmosphere.

During two long drawn-out cups of tea (there being nothing stronger in the house), Sterling and his mother surveyed their respective lives. After that he went off with Maria to catch his bus. Follow-up plans were made, but for the moment Sterling said he needed some time to think everything through.

As they walked towards the town centre along the usual route, Sterling was almost garrulous. 'My marriage. I skated over that back there, and a lot of the other relationship stuff. I might talk about it next time. It's awkward. My wife was a nurse. We were wed when I was twenty-six and divorced five years later. God knows where she is now. I rekindled something with my first girlfriend recently when we'd met up again. That finished not long before this case started. There was a girl in Belgium... One or two others on the way... I'm not telling you this to boast... I push them away... I'm glad June, my moth–, June has made contact and we'll get somewhere together. But her going like that, when I was a baby, it's had an effect...'

Maria was quiet. This was a facet of Frank Sterling she hadn't experienced before – expansive, confessional. The role of confidante had been temporarily added to her job description.

A few wordless minutes later, they were back at the usual bus stop.

'Right, this is me,' said Sterling, restored, it seemed to Maria, to his usual self. 'Thank you for all your help. I'll... I'll be seeing you then.' He offered his hand.

'Soon,' said the girl. 'Soon, when things have settled down a bit and it's all clearer.' She brushed his hand away and thrust her arms around his waist, hugging him fiercely, her head sideways against his chest. He looked down at her blonde head. He couldn't be sure, but he sensed that her eyes were squeezed tightly shut. He responded to her hug with one of his own, feeling her slender, sturdy, MMA-honed shoulders in his arms.

'I won't let you push me away, Frank. Not a chance.' Maria released her clinch and walked briskly away, a knuckle dabbing at an eye. Before long, her slight figure was lost among the locals and down-from-Londons.

The Frank Sterling Series

The Flanders Case – January 2013

Under the Radar – July 2013

Rotten – November 2014

*Fifth Column –
September 2016*

The Golden Spurs –
June 2018

Turncoat – August 2021

Lightning Source UK Ltd.
Milton Keynes UK
UKHW012330270122
397812UK00002B/165

9 781839 756986